shadowspell

Also by Jenna Black

glimmerglass

shadowspell

jenna black

 St. Martin's Griffin ❧ New York

This is a work of fiction. All of the characters, organizations, and events portrayed in this novel are either products of the author's imagination or are used fictitiously.

www.stmartins.com

Library of Congress Cataloging-in-Publication Data

Black, Jenna.
    Shadowspell / Jenna Black.—1st ed.
        p. cm.
    ISBN 978-0-312-57594-6
    I. Title.
    PS3602.L288S53 2011
    813'.6—dc22

                                    2010037871

First Edition: January 2011

10 9 8 7 6 5 4 3 2 1

To my husband, Dan. You are, as always, my inspiration.

acknowledgments

Thanks to all the wonderful people at St. Martin's who helped bring this book into being, including (but not limited to): Jennifer Weis, Anne Bensson, and Hilary Teeman. Thanks to my agent, Miriam Kriss, for her help and guidance, and to the Deadline Dames for their continued support. Lastly, thanks to my fabulous critique partner, Kelly Gay, whose insights and advice never fail to make my books better.

chapter one

Going on a date with a bodyguard hanging over your shoulder sucks.

Okay, technically, it wasn't really a date. At least, that's what I kept telling myself. Ethan was just a friend. A totally hot, sexy friend who made my hormones do a happy dance, but still just a friend. And if I knew what was good for me, I'd keep it that way.

After a couple of nasty betrayals that had hurt me more than I cared to admit, Ethan had risked his life to save mine, and I'd agreed to wipe our slate clean. The problem was, it isn't that easy to rebuild broken trust, especially when I still had so many reasons not to fully trust him.

For three weeks after he saved my life, I tried to keep my distance, but it didn't seem to discourage him. He called, e-mailed, and IM'ed me about a billion times asking me to go out with him, and I finally gave in. He'd wanted dinner and a movie. That seemed way too date-like to me, so I bargained him down to just the movie.

As I sat in the darkened theater beside him, I realized my bargaining skills could use some work. Dinner would have been safer than the movie. I tried to be subtle as I checked over my shoulder to see how closely Finn, my bodyguard, was watching me.

To my relief, I saw that he'd done me the courtesy of sitting three rows back—far enough away to give me the illusion of privacy, but close enough that he could come to my rescue if I needed it.

I wasn't surprised to see I had Finn's full attention, despite the distraction of the movie. He was a Knight of Faerie, and he took his job very, very seriously. Which was a good thing, because both the Queens of Faerie wanted me dead.

I turned to face front again. Ethan held out the bag of popcorn, and I took a handful, getting salt and melted butter all over my fingers.

"Napkin?" I asked, holding out my other hand.

"Sorry," he said, but the corner of his mouth was lifted in his trademark grin. "Forgot to get napkins."

I gave him my best dirty look, not buying the innocent expression he was giving me. Maybe he'd get a kick out of watching me lick my fingers, but I wasn't about to give him the satisfaction. I'd have gone to the lobby to get my own napkins, only I'd have to crawl over three people to get to the aisle. Besides, the movie had already started. Not that I was paying any attention to it. With a grunt of resignation, I grabbed another handful of popcorn and sank a little lower into my seat.

Somehow, Ethan's arm had found its way around my shoulders. I tried to shrug it off—though a part of me would rather have leaned into him.

"This isn't a date, remember?" I hissed at him, trying to sound annoyed instead of breathless. I'd been very clear about that when we'd talked on the phone, and Ethan had agreed to my terms. Of course, just because he'd agreed to them didn't mean he planned to abide by them.

Even in the dark of the theater, Ethan's smile was devastating. "I remember. But you never said I couldn't flirt with you."

"Shh!" said someone from the row behind us before I had a chance to retort.

I fumed a bit as Ethan's arm settled more comfortably around my shoulders. It would be a lot easier to resist him if he weren't so . . . irresistible. He was hot even for a Fae, with long blond hair and gorgeous teal blue eyes. The slight bump on his nose that suggested it had once been broken kept him from looking too perfect—and made him even more sexy.

I reminded myself that there was only so much he could get away with, with Finn back there watching us like a hawk. A bodyguard with a heaping side dish of chaperone. Ethan was incredibly cocky, but he'd always shown a healthy respect for the Knight.

I munched on the popcorn and tried to pay attention to the movie. Ethan didn't help the situation when he started idly stroking my shoulder with his fingers. I felt like I should tell him to quit it, but I liked the way his caress gave me little goose bumps. He leaned closer to me, and I smelled a hint of spicy aftershave blending with the popcorn and butter. Before I knew it, my head was resting against his shoulder.

If I was trying to get across the "not a date" message, I was doing a crappy job of it.

I'd lost my appetite for popcorn entirely, and didn't protest when Ethan set the bag down on the floor. I couldn't quite get myself to wipe my greasy fingers on my jeans, but licking them seemed too . . . tacky. Besides, I'd already decided not to give Ethan the satisfaction.

Ethan solved my dilemma by reaching over, taking my hand, and guiding it to his mouth. I was clueless enough that I had no idea what he was about to do until his mouth closed over my index finger. I made a sound somewhere between a gasp and a squeak.

My brain told my hand to jerk away from Ethan's mouth. My hand didn't listen.

Ethan sucked gently on my finger, his soft, hot tongue licking up the butter and salt. My mouth had gone dry, and I had trouble getting any air into my lungs. I'd have thought having a guy I wasn't even dating put my finger in his mouth would feel gross. Shows how little I knew.

Ethan finished with my index finger and moved on to my third finger. I felt like I was about to spontaneously combust. My face felt flushed, almost feverish, and my heart beat from somewhere around my throat. My conviction that this shouldn't feel good was rapidly disappearing.

The nasty, suspicious part of my brain that said I could never trust Ethan again after he'd tried a roofie-like spell on me once before went on high alert, searching for signs that my reaction was caused by magic rather than my own desires. But though my skin prickled with sensation, it was a toe-curling prickle of pleasure, not the electric-shock prickle of magic.

Ethan let go of my hand, and I found myself turning my head toward him, hoping he would kiss me. His lips were shiny from the butter, and I knew I would practically drown in the taste of them. Lips parted, he leaned in to me.

But before his lips could touch mine, a piece of popcorn bounced off the tip of his nose. We both turned to look behind us.

I hadn't noticed Finn buying popcorn—somehow, that seemed like an odd thing for a Fae Knight to do—but he was holding up another kernel in warning and giving us a stern look. I guess he hadn't been able to see what Ethan was doing before the almost-kiss, or we'd probably be buried in popcorn by now.

My cheeks heated in a blush, but Ethan just laughed softly and leaned back in his seat. I don't suppose the popcorn missiles could have stopped him from kissing me if he really wanted to, but they did kind of spoil the mood.

Just as well, I reminded myself. I'd let Ethan overrule my common sense before, and I'd been burned for it. He claimed he was genuinely into me, but I still had trouble believing it. A guy like him had no trouble attracting girls way prettier—and more willing to put out—than me. It didn't make sense for him to want to date *me* of all people. Unless he had ulterior motives.

Once upon a time, I'd thought of myself as a relatively ordinary girl, though my alcoholic mom had made it impossible for me to be as ordinary as I would have liked. I'd gotten fed up with her drinking and run away from home, coming to Avalon—the only place where Faerie and the mortal world intersect—to meet my Fae father. That was when I'd discovered I was a Faeriewalker—a rare individual who could travel freely between Faerie and the mortal world, with the added "perk" of being able to bring magic into the mortal world and technology into Faerie. The last Faeriewalker before me had died like seventy-five years ago, and I'd found myself the helpless rope in a game of political tug of war. With Ethan and his father on one end of that rope.

So it was a good thing Finn was acting as chaperone as well as bodyguard. The *last* thing I needed was to fall for Ethan, no matter how tempting he was. Not when I couldn't be sure what he really wanted from me.

I spent the rest of the movie fending off Ethan's subtle advances. His eyes sparkled with humor as I glared at him, and I realized it had become a game to him. What could he get away with? What could he do that Finn wouldn't see? I might have been offended by his refusal to take no for an answer, if I weren't so aware of the mixed signals I was sending him. Yeah, I fended him off—but he couldn't help but notice that it always seemed to take me a while to get around to it.

"You're being a jerk," I told him at one point as I grabbed his wrist and moved his hand off my thigh. My *upper* thigh. My voice was a little too breathy to be convincing, and I'd let his hand move way higher than I'd intended to.

His arm—which remained steadfastly around my shoulders— gave me a squeeze. "I'm being a perfect gentleman," he whispered in my ear. "I'm not going to do anything you don't want me to."

Yeah, well, that was sort of the problem. I wanted things I had absolutely no right to want. Or at least that weren't sensible for me to want. And everything I let him get away with gave him that much more reason to take another shot at it every time I shut him down.

By the end of the movie, I was so turned on it was a minor miracle I hadn't started tearing my clothes off in public. If Finn hadn't been back there, I'd have had to rely on my own will-power, and who knows what stupid things I'd have done. I had a feeling I was in way over my head with Ethan, but I didn't know what to do about it.

We walked out of the theater hand-in-hand. I'm sure Ethan would have walked me home if he could, but I was currently living in a secret underground safe house in the heart of the mountain on which the city of Avalon is built. You could count on one hand the number of people who knew where it was, and Ethan wasn't on the list.

He raised my hand to his lips and kissed my knuckles as we stood under the protection of the marquee. A gentle rain was falling, the cobblestone streets shining from the reflected glow of the street lamps.

Ethan let go of my hand, and I immediately missed the warmth of his touch as he helped me into my raincoat. He looked over my head, presumably at Finn, who was hovering behind me.

"Will you flatten me if I kiss her good night?"

"Probably," Finn said drily. He wasn't much of a talker.

I could have called Finn off just then. He wasn't my dad, and "chaperone" wasn't really in his job description. I don't think he much liked Ethan, but I was pretty sure he liked *me*, and a kiss good night was relatively innocent. But I'd let Ethan get away with more than I should already, and it was time to put my foot down.

"This isn't a date," I told him for the millionth time. "You don't get to kiss me good night even if Finn wouldn't flatten you."

Ethan flashed me a rueful, if somewhat skeptical, smile. "Right," he said. "I keep forgetting. Not a date. Got it." He reached out and pulled up the hood of my coat. His finger "accidentally" stroked the side of my face as he pulled away. I couldn't suppress my shiver of pleasure.

"Maybe we can fix that next time," he suggested. "Wanna be my date for Kimber's party?"

Ethan's sister, Kimber, was my best friend. Her birthday party was on Friday night, and I was looking forward to it more than I could say.

"Nice try, Romeo," I said, though I doubted I sounded as sophisticated as I was trying to. "Kimber gets to be the center of attention at her party, not you."

Ethan rolled his eyes. "Obviously, you've never been to a Leigh family party before. But I get the point. Just save me a dance, okay?" He gave me another grin. "Friends are allowed to dance with each other, aren't they?"

Internally, I groaned. I had a feeling dancing with him would entail another battle of wills—angel me vs. devil me.

"Sure," I said. "As long as you keep your hands to yourself."

He raised one eyebrow, and I remembered how badly I'd enforced that rule tonight. I think I blushed again, but I met his challenging gaze as boldly as I could.

Mischief twinkling in his eyes, he winked at me, tweaked my nose like I was a little kid, then headed out into the rain, not seeming to care that he had neither a coat nor an umbrella. I watched, unable to turn away, until he'd rounded the corner at the end of the block.

chapter two

Ethan spelled trouble for me, but if he were the only trouble I had to deal with now that I lived in Avalon, I'm sure I could have dealt with him a lot more smoothly.

I'd come here under the mistaken impression that life with my father would be closer to normal than life with my mother. What a joke! I'd been in Avalon only a handful of weeks, and already I was looking back at the days when I'd been my mother's keeper with something almost like longing. I'd really thought it sucked at the time.

I'd been a total loner at school, not because it was my natural inclination, but because my mom made us move every year or two to keep my father from finding us, and because I couldn't risk letting my classmates/potential friends find out my mom was a drunk. I'd learned that the hard way at one of my least favorite schools, where I'd been ridiculed relentlessly.

I'd also had to act as the adult in our family, because my mom was often too drunk to bother with little things like paying bills or buying groceries. And let's not even talk about how closely I had to watch to make sure she didn't get behind the wheel when she was plastered!

Never in a million years would I have imagined myself looking back on that life with nostalgia. But then, there wasn't a single aspect of my life in Avalon that met the hopes and expectations I'd had when I decided to come.

Instead of living in a nice, normal house in the beautiful city of Avalon, I lived in what was basically a glorified cave, located deep within the mountain. My safe house had all the modern conveniences, such as electricity, running water, and an Internet connection. It was nicely decorated, and if you could get over the total lack of windows, you might even say it was comfortable. But it still felt like a prison to me, complete with a guardroom that was situated between my suite and the front entrance.

I think my dad would have preferred it if I stayed in my safe house twenty-four/seven, but—thank God—he seemed to understand that I would go nuts if he didn't let me out on a regular basis. I never got to go out alone—I always had to have either my dad or Finn at my side—but at least I wasn't a full-time prisoner. I still spent half my time feeling completely stir-crazy, though. I understood Dad's caution, and I didn't want to risk getting myself killed, but I hated living in such isolation. Sometimes it was hard not to hate my father for it, no matter how well I understood.

Mixed feelings or not, when my dad showed up unexpectedly one Sunday at noon to take me and my mom out for brunch, I was so happy at the prospect of going out I could have hugged him. I restrained the impulse, though. He carried himself with the typical icy reserve of the older Fae, which meant a pat on the shoulder was a gushing display of affection in his book. He might not have known what to do with a hug.

My mom was another story. The moment she saw me, she threw her arms around me and hugged me as if she hadn't seen me in years. It had actually only been three days since the last time she'd visited me, but my mom was as much my dad's prisoner as I was, seeing as how he'd bribed or manipulated the courts of Avalon into declaring her legally incompetent. It had been one hell of a dirty trick, but there was a definite upside. As long as my mom was under my dad's thumb, he wouldn't allow her access to alcohol. This was the longest she'd been sober for as long as I could remember, and I found it hard to be mad at my dad for what he'd done.

He took us to one of Avalon's best restaurants, having secured us a table on the balcony. For once, it was a clear, beautiful day in Avalon, and the view from our table was spectacular. At least it would have been if I were willing to look at it. Because I'm a Faeriewalker, when I look out across the borders of Avalon, I see a disorienting, nausea-inducing double image—called the Glimmerglass—of both the English countryside and the forests of Faerie. I therefore kept my gaze strictly within the borders, which was pretty enough as it was.

The picturesque streets and houses of Avalon stretched out below me. The main road that spiraled from the base of the mountain all the way to its peak was a very modern asphalt, but almost all the side streets were cobblestone. The street lamps were made to resemble old-fashioned gas lights, and many of the buildings had existed in more or less their current form for centuries, giving the city an ancient feel despite the occasional chain store.

The mountain was densely populated, the residents of Avalon having crammed as many buildings as possible into the limited space, and yet it still managed to be lush and green. Everyone here seemed to have window boxes overflowing with flowers, and ivy took advantage of every unpaved spot to take root and crawl up the façade of the nearest building. Practically every inch of the city was a postcard waiting to happen.

Because of my unimpeded view, I was able to see clear down to the moat that surrounded Avalon, crossed by the bridge that led to the Western Gate. From up high, the moat looked as picturesque as anything else, despite its muddy brown color. However, a few weeks ago, my Aunt Grace had thrown me into that moat, and I'd discovered it was inhabited by Water Witches— nasty, malevolent monsters. I'd never be able to look at the moat again without remembering the feeling of being grabbed and dragged under. I don't think Aunt Grace was actually trying to kill me when she threw me in. She'd hatched some kind of crazy scheme to use my powers to assassinate Titania, the Queen of the Seelie Court, and when her plans were foiled, she threw me in the water as a diversion while she fled into Faerie.

My dad had great taste in restaurants. The food was fantastic. The conversation . . . not so much. I knew my parents had loved each other once, but that was a long time ago. Although Dad understood why my mom had kept me secret from him, he couldn't seem to forgive her for it. And Mom couldn't forgive Dad for any number of things, not least of which was her enforced sobriety. At this point, they couldn't agree that the sky was blue, much less agree on anything important, like the current topic of debate.

Mom wanted me to go to school like a normal girl in the fall.

Dad decreed that school was too great a security risk, and that I should be homeschooled. Neither one of them seemed to care what I thought—they didn't even bother to ask—but I knew that, in the end, my dad's word would be law. He was my legal guardian, after all. Not that Mom had any intention of conceding the point.

I tuned them both out, trying to enjoy the meal, the weather, and the view. I kept finding my eyes drawn to the moat, and to the bridge that spanned it, despite the unpleasant memories it dredged up. I kept forcing myself to look away, but my gaze always seemed to return.

I was once again staring at the moat when I caught sight of someone running away from the gatehouse at a frantic sprint. It was a Fae man, dressed in a green tunic and tights like an extra in a Robin Hood movie. Even from this distance, I could see the terror on the guy's face, and the blood that streaked his forehead. The sight made me gasp, and others around me must have followed my gaze, because a low murmur started up among the diners on the balcony.

The Fae was about a third of the way across the bridge, still running headlong, knocking slower pedestrians out of his way, when I finally saw just *why* he was running. A tall door in the gatehouse flew open, and a nightmare figure burst through.

He was dressed entirely in black, his face hidden under a grotesque black mask with a leering, fanged mouth and wickedly sharp antlers. His whole body was covered in shiny black armor peppered with vicious spikes. He rode an enormous black horse, also covered with plates of armor. Maybe it was some kind of optical illusion, but I could have sworn I saw the occasional glow of flames bursting from the horse's nostrils.

All around me, chairs were scraping back as people leapt to their feet, and the murmur had risen to a loud buzz of alarm. The horseman drew a gleaming sword from a scabbard draped over his back, and the buzz got even louder.

"Oh no," I thought I heard my father say, although it was hard to hear him over the steadily rising voices of the other diners.

Behind the man in black, several more riders emerged from the door—which I belatedly realized must be the entrance to Faerie—each dressed in a slightly toned-down version of their leader's attire. They fanned out into a V and galloped across the bridge behind him. There were several cars on the bridge, but the Fae riders didn't seem to care, their horses dodging around them at supernatural speed, or just leaping over them as if they were toys, as brakes squealed and horns blared.

"The Wild Hunt!" someone shouted.

"The Erlking . . ." someone else said, voice cold with dread.

I was on my feet, clinging to the balcony rail without remembering having stood up. I was aware of my dad calling to me, but I was too riveted by what I was seeing to answer.

The leader of the horsemen was steadily gaining on the fleeing Fae. Everywhere, people leapt out of his way, and there was no sign that the border patrol was making even a token attempt to stop him or the rest of the riders. The man in black pulled even with the Fae. He rose up high in his stirrups, easily keeping his balance despite his horse's breakneck speed. Someone screamed as the sword flashed in the sun and began to swing down at the Fae man.

I didn't see what happened next, because my mom came at me from behind and slapped her hand over my eyes. But the screams and gasps around me gave me a pretty good idea without having to see with my own two eyes.

Mom turned me around so my back was to the railing. Dad threw a handful of cash on our table, then grabbed both my mom's and my arms and began dragging us away.

"We have to go," he said urgently, and I can't tell you how terrifying it was to see the fear in his eyes. As far as I could tell, my dad wasn't afraid of anything, and if he *was,* he was a master at not letting it show. What did it mean that I could see the fear in him now?

People from inside the dining room were pushing their way out onto the balcony to see what was going on. My dad shoved his way through the gathering crowd, using magic of some sort to knock people out of our path. I might have objected to the rough handling, but remembering that black rider with his sword raised made me want to run and hide.

My dad made about a million phone calls as he frog-marched me back to the safe house. Mom walked at my side, her arm around my shoulders. Her face was deathly pale, and her eyes a little too wide.

"What's going on?" I asked her as my dad continued with his calls. "Who were those guys?" I really hoped they'd turned around and galloped back into Faerie after they'd . . . I tried not to think about what had happened.

My mom shook her head. "That was the Wild Hunt," she said in a breathless whisper, as if saying the words aloud would somehow make them appear out of thin air.

I waited for her to explain, but she didn't. Maybe I was supposed to know off the top of my head what the Wild Hunt was, but there was a lot I didn't know about Faerie. Mom was born and raised in Avalon, and sometimes she forgot that Avalon wasn't like other places.

"What's the Wild Hunt?" I asked.

We'd entered the tunnel system to begin the trek back to my safe house, and I guess Dad must have lost his signal, because he finally put his cell phone away.

"They are the nightmare of Faerie," he said in a tense, clipped tone. "A pack of horsemen who live only to hunt Fae and mortals alike. Their leader—the Erlking—is the only man the Queens of Faerie are said to fear."

"That would be the guy with the sword?" I asked in a small voice.

Dad dipped his chin in a curt nod. "Yes. All the Huntsmen are dangerous, but none more so than he."

I frowned, belatedly hearing the nuances of what my dad had said. "Wait a minute. You said the Queens of Faerie fear him, plural. But he's Unseelie, right?" All of Faerie is divided into two Courts, each with its own Queen. The Seelie Court had the reputation of being the good guys (though since Aunt Grace was Seelie, it's obvious the reputation doesn't always hold true). The Unseelie Court is the Court of monsters and bad guys, but that was a generalization, too. Ethan and Kimber were Unseelie, and they were pretty decent most of the time. The Erlking seemed to fit the Unseelie stereotype to a tee. "If he's Unseelie, surely the Unseelie Queen isn't scared of him."

"He is neither Seelie nor Unseelie," my father said. "He is outside the Courts altogether, a power unto himself. He considers himself a king, although he has no actual kingdom."

"And he's allowed to just ride into Avalon whenever he feels like it and kill people in broad daylight?" I'd seen evidence before that the border between Avalon and Faerie was dangerously porous, but I had at least hoped that it was better defended than *that*.

"No. He is not allowed to hunt in Avalon. It's just that if someone he's hunting in Faerie comes over the border, he's allowed to pursue."

We were moving so fast I was beginning to be a little short of breath, so I decided to hold my questions for the moment. When we passed out of the populated section of the tunnels and into the lightless path that led to my home, Dad cast some kind of spell that created a ball of light, which hovered over our heads and showed us the way. My neck kept prickling, and I kept looking behind me. Not that I really expected to see the Erlking bearing down on me on his fearsome black horse, but I was completely freaked out. I'd never have admitted it, but I was glad my mom had covered my eyes. I'd already seen enough things here in Avalon that would haunt my sleep. I didn't need one more.

When we finally got to the safe house, Dad asked my mom if she would make us all some tea while he and I waited in the guardroom for Finn to arrive. It came out sounding more like an order than a request, but my mom didn't object.

The guardroom wasn't as cozy as the living room in my suite, but there was a reasonably comfortable sitting area. I plopped down heavily on the couch, but my dad was too agitated to sit.

"Okay," I said. "What's the scoop on the Erlking? Why did

we have to head for the hills as soon as you saw him? You said he wasn't allowed to hunt in Avalon."

"It's complicated."

I snorted. "Like anything in this place is simple. Come on, Dad. Tell me what's going on. Don't I have a right to know?"

He let out a frustrated sigh, which seemed to release some of his tension. He stared at the floor as he spoke, and his jaw was tight with strain.

"Once upon a time, the Erlking and his Wild Hunt were the scourge of Faerie. This was a long, long time ago. They would hunt the members of both Courts, slaughtering them at will. Those they didn't kill were forced to join the Hunt, slaves to the Erlking's will. Sometimes, the Hunt would ride out into Avalon and wreak havoc among the mortals living here. Mortals who were forced into the Wild Hunt invariably died, their bodies pushed to the breaking point as they tried to keep up the relentless pace of the Hunt."

My mom entered the guardroom, carrying a tray with the tea. I was more of a coffee girl myself, but the people of Avalon apparently couldn't live without their tea. I was learning to tolerate it in the interest of being polite. Mom put the tray on the coffee table, then poured out three cups as my dad continued.

"Eventually, the Queens of Faerie were able to make a deal with the Erlking, a deal they sealed with magic. The Erlking agreed that he would no longer hunt members of either Court without permission of that Court's Queen. Ever since, he and his Wild Hunt have been the Faerie Queens' assassins and executioners. Still a nightmare, but a *leashed* nightmare."

I frowned as I thought that over. "What did the Erlking get out of this agreement?"

Dad stirred his tea with studied intensity. "He gained the privilege of hunting the Courts' outcasts."

My frown deepened. "But he was hunting them already, right?"

My dad didn't answer.

"I think there was another part of the deal," my mom said, surprising me. "The Erlking lives for the hunt. It's part of his elemental nature, and yet he allowed the Queens to put limits on him. He *must* have gotten some advantage out of it. But it seems that the Fae who are old enough to remember are under a geis not to speak of it."

"What's a geis?"

"It's a restriction that's enforced by magic. The spell was cast by both Queens and binds all the members of their courts. The Fae who are old enough to remember literally *can't* talk about it."

Dad continued stirring his tea, round and round and round. I looked back and forth between him and Mom.

"Are you old enough to remember?" I asked my dad.

He nodded, but said nothing.

"And you're not allowed to talk about it?"

He turned his head and looked at me, but he still didn't speak. He didn't even nod or shake his head.

"It must be a very powerful geis," my mom said. "They can't even tap dance around the truth. They just flat out can't talk about it. They can't even admit that a geis exists, even though everyone knows it must."

"And no one has any idea what they're hiding?"

Mom shook her head. "There are lots and lots of theories, but I don't think any one is more likely than another to be true."

I digested all that for a while, frustrated that I couldn't get the whole story. Obviously, I'd seen more than enough evidence that the Erlking was one scary dude. But I still didn't get why Dad had reacted as if the guy was a direct threat to me.

"If the Erlking can't hunt in Avalon," I asked my dad, "then what are you so worried about?"

Dad finally took a sip of his well-stirred tea. "He can't *hunt* in Avalon. That doesn't mean he can't kill. Or worse. There is a geis on him that prevents him from attacking anyone within the borders of the city—with the exception of people he chases here from Faerie. The geis does not prevent him from defending himself, however, and he's free to do whatever he wishes to anyone foolish enough to attack him or his Huntsmen."

"Still not getting it," I said. "Who'd be stupid enough to attack him when they know that allows him to kill them?" Certainly not *me,* which should mean he was no threat to me whatsoever. "Besides, won't he just go back to Faerie now that his, er, hunt is over?" Once again, I had to fight off the image of that black rider on his black horse raising his sword to kill a helpless, unarmed man.

"The Erlking has a unique ability to provoke people into acting against their own best interests. And no, I very much doubt he'll go back to Faerie. Every time he's pursued someone into Avalon, he's stayed for at least a few weeks. He even maintains a household here."

I shook my head. There were a lot of things about Avalon I liked—if somewhat reluctantly—but the weird-ass details of its treaty with Faerie weren't among them.

"Why even let him into the city in the first place?" I asked. "You won't let Spriggans and other Unseelie monsters cross the border, and he seems way scarier than any of them."

Dad's smile turned wry. "Indeed he is. Which is why the city had to make a deal with him. It was either agree to terms by which he could be allowed to come to Avalon, or go to war against him. Most of the Fae are immortal in that they won't ever die of natural causes. But as far as anyone can tell, the Erlking is *literally* immortal. Back in the days when there was open warfare between him and the Courts, a Seelie Knight actually managed to behead him in battle. The Erlking picked up his head, put it back on his neck, and killed the Knight. It behooves the people of Avalon not to make an enemy of a man who cannot be killed."

I saw the sense in it, but I couldn't say I liked it. It seemed to me that there had to be a better solution. Never mind that I couldn't imagine what it was. I guessed that considering how powerful the Erlking was, we were lucky he'd allowed any limitations to be imposed on him at all.

What the hell had the Faerie Queens given him to persuade him to stop hunting their people? Whatever it was, it had to be huge. And I very much doubted it was anything good.

Dad put his teacup down and turned to face me on the sofa. He didn't have the most expressive face in the world, but I got an immediate "uh-oh" feeling even before he opened his mouth. My hand tightened on my own teacup, and I held my breath.

"It's not impossible that one or both of the Queens may have sent the Erlking here to assassinate you," my father told me, and the bottom of my stomach dropped out.

Okay, I already knew the Queens wanted me dead. I mean, Titania, the Seelie Queen, whose Court I was technically affiliated with—I refused to say I *belonged* to it—would have been satisfied if I'd left Avalon never to return. But because Mab, the Unseelie Queen, would hunt me to the end of my days whether

I stayed or left, my dad had decreed I was better off staying. They worried that my powers as a Faeriewalker—like, say, my ability to carry a working gun into Faerie—made me a danger to their thrones. Considering my aunt Grace had wanted to use me to assassinate Titania and usurp her throne, the Queens weren't just being paranoid.

But even knowing the Queens wanted me dead, it was still a shock to hear that they might have sent that terrifying immortal creature—and his pack of Huntsmen—after me. I was just a kid, for God's sake! It was like using a cannon to kill a fly.

Unfortunately, Dad wasn't finished. "I know this will be an . . . inconvenience, but I think it's best for all concerned if you remain in your safe house for the duration of the Erlking's stay."

"No!" The word was out before I had a chance to think or in any way tone down my reaction. I shot to my feet and put some distance between my dad and myself.

"Seamus," my mom said tentatively, "maybe we should . . ." Her voice trailed off at the cold look he gave her. It was beginning to seem like what backbone she had was fueled by alcohol. Right at that moment, I wished I had the stubborn drunk back.

I shook my head and folded my arms across my chest. "No way are you keeping me trapped down here for however long the Erlking decides to hang around!" I managed to keep myself from shouting, but just barely.

"It's for your own safety," he said, trying the same cold stare on me that he'd just used on my mom.

My will has always been stronger than hers, and it would take more than a look to make me back down. "No way!" I repeated. "You said yourself that he can't attack people unless they attack him first. If you think I'm going to attack that guy, you're nuts. He can't hurt me, and you can't lock me up in this dungeon like a prisoner."

Anger sparked in his eyes, but his voice stayed level. "I can, and I will." He rose to his feet, towering over me. "When you've had some time to calm down, you'll see that it's for the best."

"Like hell I will!" Usually, I did a better job than this at keeping my temper under control around him. Partly because he was always so calm himself, and partly because he had way too much power over me for me to risk antagonizing him. But this was too much.

"You said yourself you won't have any legal power over me when I turn eighteen," I said. "And you want me to stay in Avalon for the rest of my life. If you keep me prisoner down here, I swear I'll be out of Avalon the second I come of age."

I'm not much of a weeper, but I wasn't above a little manipulation. Instead of blinking away the tears that burned my eyes, as I usually would, I let a few spill down my cheeks. Dad had done everything in his considerable power to make my safe house into a homey, comfortable place. But the fact remained, it was a freakin' dungeon, and no amount of pretty decorations could fully hide the fact.

I certainly didn't want to get myself killed. I'm not a total moron. So I didn't complain—much, at least—about having to live down here. And I didn't complain—much—about always having a bodyguard nearby. But I honestly didn't think I could stand it if Dad forced me to stay here until the Erlking decided it was time to go home, and I didn't think the Erlking was a significant threat to me.

My dad isn't exactly the easiest person to negotiate with. He's had centuries—at least—of practice, and he has so much confidence in himself and in his decisions that once he takes a stand, he has no intention of budging. Ever.

He stared at me for a long time, and I could almost see the thoughts flitting back and forth through his head. Maybe he was wondering if there was a perfect argument he could use to change my mind. Or maybe he was wondering if I really meant what I said.

Finally, he let out a loud sigh, and his shoulders slumped. "All right," he said, sounding like the words were being dragged out of him under torture. "I won't insist you stay in the safe house constantly. But I *will* insist you not leave here without at least two powerful guardians, and that you always check with me first before you do."

I was just beginning to relax, thinking I'd won the battle, when my dad dropped a bombshell.

"However, I think under the circumstances, you will have to skip your friend's birthday party. It would be too great a security risk."

I clamped my teeth down on the protest that wanted to erupt from my mouth. I knew Dad had never been thrilled with the idea of me going to Kimber's party. Not only was Kimber a member of the Unseelie Court, while my dad was Seelie, she was also the daughter of Alistair Leigh, my dad's chief political rival. Avalon is ruled by a Council consisting of six humans and six Fae. The thirteenth member of the Council—the Consul—breaks ties and is therefore in many ways the most powerful person in Avalon. The Consulship changes hands from Fae to human every ten years, and both my father and Kimber's father hoped to win the position. My dad thought my attending her party might have political implications, and he'd made it clear he'd rather I skip it. I had made it equally clear that I wouldn't miss it for the world. Now, it looked like the stupid Wild Hunt was giving Dad just the excuse he needed to keep me from going.

He was waiting for my protest. I could see it in his eyes, in the stiff way he held himself. Instinct told me that he'd budged as much as he was going to, that it was in fact practically a miracle that he'd budged at all.

With Dad, I knew I had to pick my battles, and I tried to pick only those I had a hope of winning.

"Maybe the Hunt will be gone by Friday night," I said, trying to sound hopeful, though these days I never expected my life to be that easy. Notice how I failed to explicitly agree to his terms . . .

Dad relaxed, and I guessed he hadn't caught my verbal side step. "We can hope so," he said, in a tone that said there was no hope in hell.

I barely heard him, because I was already beginning to plot how I would get to Kimber's party even without my dad's permission.

chapter three

As soon as Finn arrived to guard me, my dad took off, saying he needed to make additional security arrangements. I expected him to take my mom with him, but he didn't.

"I'll come back for you in a couple of hours," he told her. "I thought you and Dana might want to spend a little time together without me looking over your shoulder."

Mom cocked her head at him suspiciously. "Oh? You're sure you're not leaving me here to keep me out of your hair?"

Dad almost smiled, but the expression was so fleeting I'd have missed it if I'd blinked. "That too." He nodded at each of us—his version of a good-bye—then conjured his little ball of light and headed out into the tunnels.

I stood in the middle of the guardroom, suddenly uncomfortable now that it was just me, my mom, and Finn. On the one hand, it would be nice to have some time alone with my mom. Dad was usually around when I got to visit with her, and even when we were alone, it rarely lasted more than a few minutes.

But I never liked leaving Finn all by himself out here in the guardroom. Yeah, he was my bodyguard, and that was his job, but I couldn't quite master my dad's ability to treat him like a piece of furniture.

Finn was very much the strong, silent type, so we didn't do a whole lot of chatting, but even so, after being around me for a few weeks, I think he was beginning to understand how I think. Without a word to me or my mom, he plopped himself in his favorite chair, turning on the TV. He flipped through the channels until he found a soccer game, then settled in, making it clear that he could keep himself entertained.

Flashing him a smile of gratitude, I gathered up the remains of our tea and led my mom through the short, fortified hallway and into my suite. The layers of protection between me and the outside world were almost ridiculous, if you asked me. If someone wanted to get to me, they'd have to find their way here through the darkness of the tunnel system, then defeat the protections on the front entrance, then fight their way through Finn. And if they managed to do all that, I could still run into my suite and hit a panic button that would lower three separate steel doors to block the hallway. I was safer than the gold at Fort Knox.

"I'm going to make some coffee," I announced to my mom as I carried the tea tray over to my mini kitchen. "Want some?"

"No, but if you'll put the kettle on to reheat, I'll have another cup of tea."

I sloshed the electric kettle around a bit to make sure there was enough water in there, then turned it on before putting on some French roast coffee to brew. Mom waited in my living room while I got the tea and coffee ready and then served it. The coffee smelled heavenly and tasted even better. Thank goodness for Starbucks! Tea was so common it practically fell from the sky around here, but good coffee was hard to come by.

I joined my mom in the living room. As usual, since Dad had forced her to quit drinking, she was fidgety. Her teeth worried at her lower lip so much it was chapped raw, and she plucked at the tiny pills that had formed on her wool sweater. I don't even know if she realized she was doing it.

"So," I said, looking at her over the top of my mug, "how are you doing? Without the booze, I mean. Are you . . . okay?"

"I'm fine," she said, not terribly convincingly. "I don't know why you and your father are making such a big deal out of it." She took a sip of her tea, not looking at me. "Maybe I was drinking a little too much, but it's not like I'm an alcoholic. It's just that I was under a lot of stress."

My hand spasmed on my mug, and I gritted my teeth against the sharp retort that instantly sprang to my tongue. I'd thought she was past pretending she didn't have a problem. Already knowing it was a lost cause, I tried to reason with her anyway.

"Mom, you went through the d.t.'s when you stopped drinking. If that doesn't make you an alcoholic, then what does?"

She waved that away. "I told you I know I was drinking too much, especially after you ran away. But now that I'm here with you, everything is fine. I miss having a drink every now and again, and I don't appreciate being treated like a child."

My throat ached, and I had to swallow hard to try to dislodge the sudden lump that formed there. Dad had told me we couldn't cure my mom's alcoholism by force. He could keep her under lock and key and not let her have alcohol, and that would keep her sober. But it wouldn't cure her.

I really wanted to believe he was wrong. But if she *still* wasn't ready to admit she had a problem, then I had a strong suspicion Dad was right. If she considered drinking constantly from the moment she woke up until the moment she went to bed—or passed out—to be "having a drink every now and then," then she was still in massive denial.

"Let's talk about something else," she said with a tight smile. "Are you looking forward to starting school in the fall?"

I was more than happy to change the subject, though I suspected we were still in denial-land. "I think Dad's made it pretty clear I won't be going to school." My heart sank at the thought. I'd never been that crazy about school, since our constant moving meant I always got to be the new kid, and everyone knows how much fun that is. But after everything I'd already gone through this summer, hanging out with a bunch of other kids and pretending I had nothing more dire to worry about than a pop quiz sounded like paradise on earth.

"If you want to go to school, you'll go to school," she said, and I was pleasantly surprised to find that she did actually care what I wanted. "I can't blame your father for wanting to protect you, but he's going about it the wrong way, and eventually he'll figure that out."

I wished I had her confidence. I still couldn't say I knew my father all that well, but I did know he was very stubborn. And sure of himself. If he'd already decided that school wasn't safe, I honestly didn't see how either my mother or I could talk him into it.

Of course, the fall semester didn't start for another eight

weeks or so. There was always a chance we were both being overly optimistic in thinking I'd be alive when it rolled around.

My back hit the mat with a sound between a squish and a thud. The impact forced the air out of my lungs, so all I could do was lie on my back like a dead bug and try to breathe. Keane came to tower over me, shaking his head and curling his lip in disdain.

"That was pathetic," he told me. So nice to have him heap on the positive reinforcement.

I was struggling too hard to breathe to tell him what I thought of him, but I'm sure he could see it in my eyes. He'd told me once that if I didn't want to bash his face in during our sparring sessions, then he wasn't doing his job. He was doing his job just fine.

"If I were the bad guy, you'd be dead by now," he continued.

Yeah, rub it in, I thought as I finally succeeded in drawing a little air into my lungs. I hated the nasty wheezing sound I was making, but I couldn't seem to make it stop.

Why, oh why had I asked for self-defense lessons? Even my best moves would be useless against the kind of enemy the Faerie Queens would send to kill me. But after Finn had been brutally beaten by a bunch of Knights while I could do nothing to help him, I'd decided I wanted at least the illusion of usefulness. That's why I'd started my lessons with Finn's son, Keane, which I regretted on a regular basis.

Even when my breath finally started to come easier, I stayed lying on the floor, not looking forward to going another round. We were sparring in the living room of my safe house, the furniture pushed up against the walls to make room for the mats.

We'd have had more space if we'd done our sparring out in the guardroom, but we'd also have had an audience—Finn. Keane would have been fine with that, but not me.

It wasn't just that I didn't want Finn to see me making a fool of myself, either. I had a big, whopping favor to ask of Keane, one I didn't dare let anyone else hear. Now, if I could just find the nerve to actually ask . . .

"Are you going to take a nap, or are you going to get off your ass and get back to work?" Keane asked.

I glared up at him. My body ached from being repeatedly slammed into the mats, and my muscles were quivering with exhaustion. Keane was theoretically taking it easy on me, but you couldn't tell it by the way I felt.

"Don't you ever get tired?" I grumbled, pushing myself painfully up into a sitting position.

He snorted. "Not in fifteen minutes I don't."

Was that how long it had been since we'd started? It felt like at least an hour.

"Guess we need to work on your stamina on top of every-thing else."

I knew he was only doing what he'd been hired to do, but I was sick and tired of his attitude. He treated me like I was some kind of idiot because I couldn't fight like a trained warrior. Well, excuse me, but before I'd come to Avalon, brawling hadn't been a big part of my life.

A hint of malice kindled in my chest. Once, just once, I wanted to get the upper hand on my obnoxious jerk of a teacher. And if I had to play dirty, well that was just tough.

I made as if to get up, groaning dramatically. I didn't expect Keane to fall for it—usually, it's like he knows what I'm going to do even before I do—but maybe after a few weeks of these lessons, he was starting to get complacent. I could see in his eyes that his attention had wandered, and I took advantage. Instead of getting up, I propelled myself forward, hitting Keane's legs and knocking them out from under him.

He gave a startled yelp, and I had about half a second to feel a thrill of victory. In retrospect, I should have come at him from the side, so my momentum would have carried me out from under him as he fell. As it was, he landed flat on top of me, smashing my face into the mat as once again my breath whooshed out of my lungs. He was coordinated enough that he could have stopped his fall with his hands, but no, he let his whole weight come down on me, practically crushing me.

"Nice move," he said, and he wasn't even breathing hard. "You've really improved your situation." To emphasize his point, he used his powerful legs to pin my arms to my sides, then held my ankles down.

I wriggled and squirmed—once I could breathe well enough to do even that—but there wasn't much I could do when I was facedown on the mats with my arms and legs pinned. I could move my head, which Keane had taught me to use as a weapon, but I couldn't reach him with it, so I couldn't do any damage. I'd definitely lost this round.

"You can let go now," I grumped. "I got the point."

"Maybe I don't feel like letting go just yet." He sounded really amused. Glad he was having such a great time at my expense.

I let out a little growl of frustration. How could I possibly ask this asshole for help? With *anything*? And yet, there was no one else I could think of who might be able to help me get to Kimber's party without my dad's permission.

It occurred to me that in the position he was in, Keane would be staring directly at my butt. I craned my head around to see if I was right, and sure enough . . .

My face heated with a blush I couldn't help. Granted, I didn't have that much for him to look at—my Fae heritage gave me a figure only slightly more feminine than that of a teenage boy— but it was still embarrassing. Worse, he met my eyes when I looked around, and he was grinning. I didn't like the grin any more than I liked his usual scowls and smirks.

I wanted to say something witty and worldly, something to cut him down to size and make him regret that stupid grin. But everything I could imagine saying would only make things worse. I bit my tongue and closed my eyes, determined to wait him out. I'd take this time to rest up, and when he finally decided he was tired of ogling me, or whatever he was doing, I'd have a little more energy to fight back with.

I guess his mind-reading skills were back online, because the moment I relaxed under him, he let go and rolled off of me. Damn. So much for taking a rest. With a sigh of resignation, I forced myself to my feet once more.

We spent another half hour or so sparring. If you could call me repeatedly getting my butt kicked "sparring." By the end of the session, I was ready to give up for good and leave the fighting to bodyguards. Who was I kidding, anyway? Buffy the Vampire Slayer might have been able to kick butt at the age of sixteen, but not me.

"Don't look so glum," Keane said as he began rolling up the mats. I probably should have helped him, but I was too tired and, well, glum. "You're doing great."

Obviously, he and I had a different definition of "great." I plopped down heavily on the sofa, not minding that I had to climb over the coffee table to get to it. I'd move the furniture back into place later.

"I mean it, Dana," Keane said, shoving the rolled-up mat aside and standing up. He pulled the coffee table out of the way, then sat beside me on the sofa.

It was a little too close for comfort, so I slid over to make more room for him. Being Fae, he was drop-dead gorgeous by birth. I couldn't decide if his pseudo-Goth bad-boy look made him more or less so. I say pseudo-Goth because he didn't quite have the look down. His hair was dyed jet black, his left ear was pierced about a gazillion times, his entire wardrobe appeared to be black, and he sometimes painted his fingernails black. Even so, there was something strangely . . . wholesome about his appearance. If the Jonas Brothers ever decided to go Goth, that's what they'd look like.

I couldn't help liking the packaging, but the personality beneath it grated on my nerves even at the best of times.

"You really get a kick out of humiliating me, don't you?" I asked, then wished I'd kept my mouth shut. I should at least be *pretending* he didn't get under my skin so badly.

I didn't look at him, but I could hear him shrug. "You need to be motivated to fight hard, even when it's only sparring. If you were a guy, I'd motivate you by hitting a lot harder. Would you like that better?"

I turned to glare at him. "Have I ever told you you're a total asshole?"

He laughed. "I think you might have mentioned it a time or two." His smile faded, his emerald green eyes losing their teasing twinkle. "I meant what I said. You're doing great. I've been learning to fight almost from the time I could walk. You can't expect to beat me. And if you *could* beat me, then you'd need a better teacher."

Every time I convinced myself to despise Keane for good, there'd be one of these unexpected flashes of humanity that made me think maybe he wasn't such a bad guy after all. And I had to admit, I liked the fact that he didn't treat me like either a weirdo or a fragile flower because I was the first and only Faeriewalker born in the last hundred years or so. Nor did he want to use me to further some political agenda. That made him comparatively uncomplicated, and that was why I was willing—in theory at least—to ask for his help.

I took a deep breath to steady my nerves, then turned to face him on the couch. "I have a favor to ask you," I blurted before I could chicken out.

He looked startled for a moment, then raised his eyebrows. "You've managed to take me by surprise for once."

I smacked his shoulder with the back of my hand. Luckily, he didn't treat that like an attack and pounce on me. "Quit it. If you keep being a jerk, I'm not going to ask you."

"And I take it this would be a bad thing?"

"Never mind." I let out a grunt of frustration and started to get up. Keane grabbed my arm to stop me.

"I'm just teasing you," he said, and that stupid grin of his was back.

My chin jutted out stubbornly, but I sat back down. "I'm sick and tired of your teasing. It isn't funny."

"I think I'm hilarious. You just don't have much of a sense of humor."

"Having people trying to kill me doesn't really inspire me to yuck it up. What a shocker!"

The expression on Keane's face smoothed out, the glint of amusement fading from his eyes. "The danger isn't going to go away," he said. "You have to learn to live your life in spite of it."

I rolled my eyes. Keane was only two years older than me, which didn't give him the right to go all wise on me. Never mind that he had a point. The moment I'd set foot in Avalon, I'd changed the course of my life forever. I was still trying to absorb the enormity of the consequences.

I swallowed a wise-ass comment, figuring the longer I kept up the bickering, the more chance I'd talk myself out of asking Keane for help. I couldn't help remembering the disappointment in Kimber's voice when I'd called to tell her Dad wouldn't let me go to the party. She'd tried her best to hide it, and I knew she understood, but still . . .

"I guess you could say I need your help living my life in spite of my situation," I said, hoping Keane would see it that way.

"Good for you. Now what is it?"

I clasped my hands in my lap and stared down at them. If Keane decided to tell anyone about this conversation, I would be in big, big trouble. Not the oh-my-God-I'm-gonna-die type of trouble I was trying to learn to live with, but the my-parents-are-gonna-kill-me type of trouble I'd once thought would be a nice dose of normalcy.

"You know I'm friends with Kimber Leigh, right?" I asked. So far, Keane hadn't come into contact with either Kimber or her brother Ethan, at least not while I was around, but I was pretty sure he knew who they were.

"Your Unseelie friend," he said, proving me right.

I nodded. "Her seventeenth birthday party is on Friday," I said.

Keane smiled. "And let me guess: your father won't let you go."

I scowled. "No. He says it's too big a security risk now that the Wild Hunt is in town." I crossed my arms over my chest and sank down lower in my seat. I was still furious with my dad. I couldn't even remember the last time I'd been close enough to anyone for them to invite me to a birthday party. I wanted to go so badly I could taste it.

Keane frowned. "Where's it being held?"

"At this nightclub called The Deep, down in the tunnel system." Kimber said her dad had rented the whole place for the party. That was because he'd made Kimber invite the kids of every potential political supporter in Avalon, which made it even more important that I be there. Kimber deserved to have at least *one* real friend at her party.

Keane shook his head. "I don't see why that would be any riskier than anything else you do when you leave your safe house. He's already making you add a second bodyguard when you leave, right?"

I nodded. Any time I wanted to go out these days, it was this big production. I had a freaking retinue. Just in case there was a person left in Avalon who was under the mistaken impression that I was just a normal girl.

"I think Dad's using it as an excuse," I said. "He thinks me showing up at Kimber's party might be taken as some kind of political statement, like I'm somehow supporting Alistair."

Keane shrugged. "It's Kimber's party, not Alistair's."

"Exactly! But Dad put his foot down."

"So what is this favor you want to ask?" The gleam in his eye told me he knew exactly what the favor was.

"Call me crazy, but you strike me as the kind of guy who's had plenty of experience sneaking out at night . . ."

chapter four

I hadn't been wrong about Keane and his talent for sneaking out at night. Though actually, I'm not sure *sneak* is the right word for what we did.

Finn had to think it was strange that Keane came over for a sparring session on a Friday night. Usually, we practiced in the morning, mainly because Keane wanted me fighting on an empty stomach. The one time I'd managed to snag a little breakfast before we started, I found out exactly why he preferred the empty stomach option. Let me tell you, that doughnut I'd sneaked didn't taste nearly so good on its way back up.

In hopes that Finn wouldn't get too suspicious about Keane's unexpected arrival on my doorstep, we told him we were having a lesson to help me keep my mind off the fact that I was missing Kimber's party. I was sure he wouldn't buy it, but Finn was more trusting than me.

In typical, annoying Keane fashion, he'd refused to tell me what our plan of escape was. All he'd said was to pack my party clothes and be ready to go at a moment's notice.

We practiced in the guardroom this time, right under Finn's nose. Keane said he wanted his father to watch because he might spot any bad habits that Keane couldn't see because he was up close and personal.

Finn was full of helpful pointers, and the more time Keane and I spent sparring, the more I thought that *I* was the dupe in this picture, that he'd never planned to help me but had said he would to keep me from trying anything on my own. I was sore, sweaty, and tired—and at the end of my limited patience—when Keane wrestled me to the mats with a spectacularly disorienting throw, then landed on top of me, his mouth near my ear.

"Be ready to go any second now," he whispered, then jumped nimbly to his feet and gave me one of his condescending smirks.

I had no idea what he meant, and was about to give him a piece of my mind, when I finally realized what he was up to.

My little underground fortress had two bathrooms, one off my bedroom, and one off the guardroom. Even the Fae have to answer the call of nature. In my peripheral vision, I saw Finn heading toward the bathroom, and knew this was the break Keane had been waiting for.

As soon as the door closed behind Finn, I darted into my room and snagged the backpack I'd set right beside the door. My dress for the party was carefully packed inside, and I hoped it wasn't getting all wrinkled. I slipped my arms through the straps and hurried back into the guardroom, where I found Keane quietly wedging a chair under the bathroom doorknob.

I had expected him to use some magical Fae ruse to get us out of here, not the tried-and-true chair-under-the-doorknob trick. I was actually kind of disappointed at the simplicity of it all.

"Hurry," Keane hissed as he jerked open the front door. "That won't hold him long."

With a spike of adrenaline that was half excitement, half fear, I followed Keane out into Avalon's massive tunnel system. We started down the tunnel at a brisk jog, Keane lighting our way with a flashlight. I hoped like hell he knew where he was going. I'd gotten lost in these tunnels once before, and it hadn't been any fun.

We turned a corner at the first intersection we came to. I heard a faint pounding sound in the distance that might have been Finn hammering on the door, and a little shiver ran down my spine. I'd never seen Finn mad before, but I had a feeling that was going to change before the night was out. I wasn't looking forward to it.

We took another couple of turns, and I started to slow down, running out of gas. Keane grabbed my arm and pulled me along.

"Keep moving," he urged me. "If my dad guesses right and stays on our tail, he'll catch up to us in no time."

I didn't have the breath to argue, so I forced my legs to keep moving. Our footsteps sounded frighteningly loud as we ran, but the stone walls of the tunnels bounced the sound around so much I knew it would be hard to judge which direction it came from.

My safe house is pretty deep in the mountain, far off the beaten path—the better to defend it, naturally. I wasn't sure how we managed to get electricity and running water down there—the tunnels themselves weren't lighted this deep in the mountain— but I'd never wondered enough to ask. Well-defended it might be, but it also made it quite a hike to get to the surface.

The Deep is relatively close to the surface, in an underground commercial district that was usually packed on a Friday night. The presence of the Wild Hunt had inspired a lot of people to stay home behind locked doors. You could definitely tell there was a pall on the city, and the news was full of reports about tourists cutting their visits short and fleeing to the relative safety of England.

Keane and I slowed to a casual walk as soon as we stepped into the first lighted tunnel. As usual, he looked fresh and ready to run some wind sprints, while I was gasping for breath and dripping with sweat, my muscles burning with the exertion. I really hoped Kimber would appreciate the effort it took for me to show up tonight.

We stopped briefly at a little tea shop, where I ducked into the restroom to change into my dress and wash the sweat from my face. I'd never heard of a teen's birthday party where you had to wear a dress, but Kimber had been adamant: her party, her rules. (Never mind that her dad had kinda usurped her party by inviting bunches of people she didn't know.)

The dress I wore was one Kimber and I had picked out together. It was a gorgeous deep blue silk that brought out the color of my eyes, and I instantly felt older and more sophisticated when I pulled it on over my head. The neckline was low enough to be sexy on a girl who actually had anything up top. On me, it looked a little more like wishful thinking.

I finished the outfit off with dangly earrings and thick, rhinestone-studded flip-flops. I'd let Kimber talk me into wearing a dress for this thing, but no way was I wearing heels!

I felt surprisingly self-conscious and shy when I stepped out of the bathroom. Keane had never seen me dressed in anything but workout clothes, and though it had never occurred to me that I'd care what he thought, I found myself holding my breath as he turned away from sniffing a cannister of loose tea and caught sight of me.

His eyes widened just a bit, and I watched him give me the once-over. Then he nodded at me. "You clean up nice."

I remembered to breathe and resisted the urge to wipe my sweaty palms on my fancy silk dress. I guessed that was as much of a compliment as I was going to get out of Keane. I was unpleasantly surprised to find I wanted more. Could I be any more pathetically in search of approval?

"That makes one of us," I muttered, and Keane laughed. He hadn't bothered to change out of his sparring clothes, but since he didn't exactly have to work up a sweat to beat me, he was at least presentable.

Okay, he was more than presentable. Those emerald green eyes of his could take the breath right out of my lungs no matter how he was dressed, especially with that one lock of jet-black hair that curled right over his eyebrow. And let's not even talk about his body, which he liked to show off beneath tight jeans and even tighter T-shirts. I doubted very much that Kimber would mind his failure to dress up.

Keane held out his elbow to me. "Ready?"

I raised my eyebrows. What, was he going to escort me in like some matron at a wedding? The gesture seemed quaintly old-fashioned, especially on a self-proclaimed bad boy like Keane.

I found myself snaking my hand through the crook of his elbow without having consciously decided to do so. Blood warmed my cheeks as he led me out of the tea shop toward the stairway that led down into The Deep.

Despite my dad's fear that the party would represent a

"security risk," Keane and I were stopped by a couple of bouncers demanding to see my invitation before we even got to the doorway at the club. I was glad I'd brought it with me, but even when I produced it—for Dana Hathaway "and guest"—the bouncers wouldn't let us through because I wasn't on "the list."

I let out a little groan of frustration. I guess when I'd told Kimber I wouldn't be able to make it, my name had gotten crossed off the list. Luckily, the bouncers weren't total assholes. One of them stayed out in the hall with Keane and me, while the other ducked into the club with my invitation in hand to check with Kimber.

I chewed my lip while we waited. There was no way Finn wouldn't guess where we were headed, which meant it wouldn't be long before he showed up here himself. If we were inside the club, he might have a bit of a hassle getting through the bouncers, and then he'd actually have to *find* us before he could drag us back. But if we were just standing around in the hall like this . . .

"Are you going to get in trouble with your dad because of this?" I asked Keane while I tried not to fidget.

"I'm an adult," he said with a cocky grin. "It's not like he can send me to my room without my supper."

He had a point, at least technically. Though I'd never been there, I knew Keane had his own apartment—or flat, as they called it here—and he actually supported himself as a self-defense instructor. But despite all that, and despite his attempts to make me respect him as a teacher, I often found myself thinking of him as a slightly older kid rather than as an adult.

Just as I was beginning to think there was no chance we

were getting into the party before Finn intercepted us, the door to the club burst open and Kimber practically danced out into the hallway.

"Dana!" she cried, her face lighting up with pleasure. "I'm so glad you could come!"

She shocked me by throwing her arms around me and giving me an exuberant hug. The Fae were known for their quiet reserve, but obviously Kimber didn't care to conform to the stereotype. I wasn't the most touchy-feely person myself, but I hugged her back.

"This is such a nice surprise," she said as she pulled away. "I thought you couldn't come."

I dropped my voice, not sure if the bouncers would kick me out if they heard me. "Yeah, well, we sort of snuck out."

Kimber blinked and seemed to notice Keane for the first time. "Oh!" She had a very expressive face, and I could tell immediately that she liked what she saw. "You must be Keane," she said. "Dana's told me a lot about you."

Her eyes twinkled with mischief as I gave her a dirty look. Most of the times I'd talked to her about Keane, it was to complain about him and his annoying—and often painful—training techniques. I was probably blushing, but the hallway wasn't brightly lit, so I hoped no one could tell.

"Look, can we go inside now?" I said. "Before Finn catches up with us?"

"Of course! Come on, follow me."

I noticed several things at once as Kimber led Keane and me into the club. First was that the music was so loud I felt like my eardrums might explode. Second was that it was absolutely packed with people, not all that many of whom looked like teens. Third was that the place positively reeked of roses.

To the Fae, the red rose indicates an affiliation with the Unseelie Court, and the white rose indicates an affiliation with the Seelie Court. Apparently, this was an integrated party, because red and white roses were arranged *everywhere*. There were huge centerpieces on the tables. There were garlands. There were potted roses lined up against each wall. There were even streamers of them hanging down from the ceiling.

I shot a questioning look at Kimber. She shrugged and looked unhappy.

"Three guesses who chose the decorations," she shouted over the music.

But of course, one guess was plenty. It made me mad that Alistair was ruining Kimber's party by making it into a political statement. It also made me realize that my dad might have been right to believe my appearance here could have political implications.

God, I hated politics! I wanted nothing whatsoever to do with all the crap that went on as the Fae candidates jockeyed for position, but being the daughter of one of those candidates dragged me into the thick of things anyway.

"Come on," Kimber yelled, taking me by the hand and towing me through the crowd. "Let's get you guys something to drink."

I checked over my shoulder to make sure Keane was following. He was, but the look on his face said he already didn't like this party. He wasn't quite sneering, but it was close. Looking around at the partiers, I could see why.

Almost everyone was dressed in their semiformal best, and even in my quick glance around, I could tell this was a high-brow party. There were way more adults than you'd expect at a teen's party, and most of them carried themselves with the snobby arrogance of the filthy rich. The teens in the crowd looked just as snooty, like they'd fit right in at some exclusive British boarding school. I knew Ethan and Kimber were far from poor, but neither of them put out the kind of "I'm too good for you" vibe most of these people did.

It was definitely not Keane's crowd. Although Knights are members of the Sidhe—the aristocracy of Faerie—the rest of the Sidhe treat them like glorified servants, and I presumed that held true for sons of Knights, like Keane. The Sidhe, especially the ones who were born in Faerie, still thought racism and classism were socially acceptable. I wasn't surprised that he wasn't feeling entirely comfortable here.

To tell you the truth, it didn't seem much like my crowd, either. I couldn't help noticing that no one stopped Kimber to talk as she led us to the bar, and I wondered how many of them even knew—or cared—that she was the birthday girl.

I'd found out from my dad that the official drinking age in Avalon was eighteen, but that the law was rarely enforced. The bar at The Deep was ample proof. I spotted a girl sitting at one end of the bar who couldn't have been more than fourteen or fifteen, drinking a bottle of beer right under the bartender's nose.

"It's an open bar," Kimber said, "so order whatever you want."

She ordered a martini—the bartender didn't bat an eyelash— and Keane ordered a beer, but I stuck to Coke. Living with my alcoholic mom took a lot of the appeal out of alcohol for me. Kimber was the only person I'd ever told about what I considered my shameful secret, and I think she understood intuitively why I didn't order alcohol. Keane was another matter.

"Coke?" he asked me incredulously. "Are you serious?"

I was blushing again, but it was way too dark in the club for anyone to notice. On the one hand, I didn't want to seem like a baby. On the other hand, I wasn't much of a conformist. Just because everyone around me was drinking themselves stupid didn't mean *I* had to.

"You have a problem with that?" I asked, glaring up at him. My glare got a lot of practice when Keane was around.

"Leave her alone," Kimber said, startling me by coming to my defense. "She can drink whatever she wants."

The bartender slapped down a glass of ice with a splash of Coke in it. I picked it up and took a sip, pretending to ignore Keane.

"Quite a party you've got here," Keane said, and even at the decibel level he was shouting, I could hear the disdain in his voice. "You sure they don't mind breathing the same air as a lowly commoner like me?"

I smacked his shoulder, thinking I should have snuck out on my own. I could have handled the door-under-the-chair trick myself. Of course, that would have meant making my way to the party alone, which was a bad idea (a) because with my sense of direction, I'd have been lost in five minutes flat, and (b) because, hello, people were trying to kill me. Keane might not be a professional bodyguard like Finn, but I'd seen how good a fighter he was, and I trusted him to protect me. I figured sneaking out with him at my side might be a bit reckless, but wasn't completely moronic like running off by myself would be.

"Could you just *try* not to be a jerk for maybe fifteen minutes in a row?" I asked him as he swigged his beer.

"It's all right, Dana," Kimber said with a smile. "Remember, you've told me all about him. I knew not to expect genteel manners." The smile turned into a smirk very like Keane's second-favorite expression.

"Wow, you really know how to insult a guy," he said. I think he was trying to sound bored, but it's hard to sound bored when you're shouting over music.

Kimber's eyes sparkled. "Actually, I do, but I'm trying to be a gracious hostess."

Keane gave her a patently lewd once-over. She looked absolutely fabulous in a slinky red cocktail dress and strappy heels. Even though he was being deliberately rude about it, I couldn't help noticing the spark of masculine appreciation in Keane's eyes. I felt a quick stab of jealousy. He'd given me an approving look when he'd first caught sight of me in my party dress, but nothing compared to how he was looking at Kimber.

I was being a total dork about this. Keane was certainly hot, and he was occasionally a nice guy, but I wasn't interested in him, not in that way. And Kimber was a full-blooded Fae, so *of course* she was prettier than me. I had no excuse for being jealous.

"Looks like you've got all the graciousness money can buy," Keane said to Kimber. "I bet that outfit cost more than I make in a year."

I opened my mouth to tell him to shut up, hoping Kimber would someday forgive me for bringing this asshole to her birthday party, but she's pretty good at putting on her bitch face when necessary. Apparently, right now she thought it was necessary.

"Are you suggesting that I'm a snob?" she asked with an arch of an eyebrow. He gave her a "well, duh" look, which didn't seem to faze her in the least. "One of us is acting snobbish right now, but it isn't me."

I "accidentally" stepped on Keane's foot before he could lob another verbal grenade. "Why don't you sit here at the bar and be broody and superior," I told him. "Kimber and I are going to the ladies' room." It was the one place I could think of going where Keane and his attitude wouldn't be able to follow. "We'll be right back. Right, Kimber?"

She laughed and finished her martini in one big gulp. "Right-o!" she said. "Lead the way."

Keane looked like he was about to object, but I turned away before he had the chance. Kimber took over the lead after a few feet, since I had no idea where the ladies' room was. The music, the darkness, and the reek of roses combined to make my head throb. Maybe I should have stayed home after all.

The crowd pressed in on us, and I was jostled every other step. Most of the people here were Fae, which meant practically everyone was taller than me and I couldn't see anything but the people directly beside and in front of me. All those bodies radiated a lot of heat—especially the Fae, whose body temperatures run higher than humans—and I was once again dripping with sweat, my hair plastered to the back of my neck. I didn't dare look to see if my fancy silk dress showed sweat stains, because I had a feeling I already knew the answer.

Kimber and I finally broke through the crowd and slipped into the ladies' room. I almost breathed a sigh of relief until I realized the situation had not improved. The ladies' room was almost as crowded as the rest of the club, and though it was festooned with roses just like everywhere else, it wasn't the scent of roses that clogged my nose. The air was so thick with smoke you could cut it with a knife.

Kimber gave a little dismayed whimper and leaned against the wall, closing her eyes. "This is not the kind of party I had in mind," she muttered, and I knew it was true. Entitled rich kids are the same everywhere—even if they are Fae—and though Kimber had the money to fit in with that clique, it just wasn't her style.

Trying not to cough from the smoke—cigarette and other— that filled the air, I slung my backpack off my shoulder and unzipped the front compartment.

"I brought you a present," I told Kimber, hoping to cheer her up.

Her eyes popped open, and her jaw dropped. "You did?"

"Of course I did." The invitation had specifically said we weren't to bring gifts, but I figured that applied to Alistair's cronies and their kids, not Kimber's real friends. I pulled out a small, neatly wrapped package and handed it to her. "I hope you like it."

"I love it already," she assured me. Her eyes were shiny, and her lower lip quivered dangerously.

"Well, open it," I urged.

Kimber bit her lip and picked at the tape, unwrapping the little box so carefully she could probably reuse the wrapping paper if she wanted to. She lifted the lid, and then pulled away the fuzzy cotton padding to reveal the contents.

What do you buy for your Fae best friend who you've only known a handful of weeks and whose father is rich enough she can mostly buy whatever she wants? I'd agonized over the question for days, poking around on eBay hoping to find something that would leap out at me.

What I'd eventually chosen was a handcrafted glass pendant. It was a gorgeous teal blue Chinese dragon hung on a black satin cord. The color had instantly reminded me of Kimber's eyes, and the dragon had reminded me of her fiery temperament and courage.

Kimber lifted the pendant out of the cotton, and her lip was quivering again. This time, she wasn't able to prevent a couple of tears from spilling over. I was so glad I'd decided to ignore the no-gifts thing.

"It's beautiful," she said breathlessly. "Here, hold this." She shoved the box and paper at me so she could undo the clasp and put the pendant on. Then she checked it out in the mirror, her hand caressing its sleek curves. It didn't go with the red dress at all, but she obviously didn't mind.

For the second time that night, I found myself on the receiving end of an exuberant hug.

"Thank you so much!" she said. She let go of me and brushed away the tears. "This party was a total nightmare until you showed. And this is the best present I've ever gotten."

My throat was feeling a little tight, and my eyes were stinging. But that was probably just from all the smoke. "Happy birthday."

Her radiant smile made me glad I'd come.

chapter five

We stayed in the ladies' room for maybe five minutes, tops, before the smoke drove us back out into the club. From where we were standing, I couldn't see the bar, but I assumed Keane was still waiting there for us. I didn't much feel like forging my way through the crowd again, but despite what a jerk Keane was being, I didn't think it was fair to leave him all alone when he didn't know anyone and clearly felt uncomfortable. He had, after all, made it possible for me to get here in the first place. Besides, he was my bodyguard for the evening, and it would probably be smart to keep my body close enough for him to guard it.

Kimber led the way once more, and I followed in her wake. My head still throbbed, and now I felt a little dizzy on top of it, probably from all that smoke. I almost tripped over my own feet, and I stopped a moment to take a couple of breaths of relatively clean air. And that was when my night went to hell.

In the few seconds I'd paused, the crowd had filled in the gap

Kimber had created, and I could no longer see her. I stood on tiptoe to try to find her. A gap opened in the crowd that stood between me and the dance floor. My eyes homed in on someone with blond, shoulder-length hair just like Kimber's. Only it wasn't Kimber.

Ethan was out on the dance floor, swaying to the music, while a gorgeous, red-haired Fae girl did a bump and grind all around him. She wore a skimpy, glittery black cocktail dress that clung to her curvy—for a Fae—figure, and Ethan's tongue was practically hanging out of his mouth as he stared at her. From the way she moved, I'd have guessed she held a side job as a stripper, and she kept finding excuses to brush up against Ethan's body. He gave her what I could only describe as a bedroom smile, then slipped his arms around her waist.

Now to be fair, I'd told Ethan over and over that we weren't dating. If we weren't dating, then it was technically impossible for him to cheat on me. It was therefore totally okay for him to be dirty dancing with someone other than me.

My reasoning couldn't soothe the hurt that stabbed through me when I saw him out on that dance floor with another girl, a Fae girl, as gorgeous as Kimber, and by the looks of her closer to Ethan's age than I was. I guess my naïveté was rearing its ugly head once again. I'd somehow let myself imagine that Ethan was chastely pining away for me, desperately hoping that one day he would win me over. What a moron!

Tears stung my eyes as I turned away from the revolting sight and pushed my way through the crowd in what I hoped was the direction of the bar. I'd known Ethan was a player, even before I'd known exactly how he'd played *me*. He seemed to find me attractive, and he was charming and totally drool-worthy, but although I hardly had boys falling at my feet, I knew better than to get involved with someone like him. At least, I knew better in theory.

I fought the tears fiercely, unwilling to let Ethan have that much power over me. I'd just about gotten my emotions under control—at least enough so I could pretend nothing was wrong—when I reached the bar and got my second helping of bad news.

I had speculated earlier that I would probably see Finn mad before this night was through. Turns out I was right, and it was a sight I could have done without.

He must have seen me coming before I caught sight of him, for he was staring at me with such intensity I could feel it almost like a physical force. His usually bland expression was filled with fury, and he seemed to tower over everyone around him, even Keane, who was about the same height.

Finn had one hand wrapped around Keane's upper arm, and the wince on Keane's face said the grip was tight enough to hurt. Keane hung his head like a penitent child, his gaze fixed on the floor. I'd never seen Keane cowed by anything before, but I supposed this was a night for unpleasant firsts. Beside them, Kimber had shrunk back against the bar, her eyes wide, her teeth worrying away at her lower lip.

I was tempted to turn away and plunge back into the crowd. That's how terrifying the look on Finn's face was. I'd really, really rather he show that face to the bad guys, not me. But I'd known there would be consequences to sneaking out, and it was time to face them. I swallowed hard and crossed the last few feet separating me from my furious bodyguard.

I expected him to yell at me, or at least give me a heated lecture. Instead, he just fixed me with one more glare, then grabbed my upper arm and started dragging both me and Keane toward the front door. He was scary-looking enough that somehow, the crowd magically made a path for him, everyone scrambling to stay out of his way.

I glanced back over my shoulder at Kimber, thinking I should say good-bye or something, but considering how fast Finn was walking, I'd be out the door before I got the words out. She gave me a worried smile, then held up the pendant and mouthed "thank you." I still didn't want to face whatever was going to happen next, but remembering how happy Kimber had been to see me, I couldn't find it in myself to regret having come. Of course, that might change, depending on just what the consequences turned out to be.

None of us said a word as we made our way back to my safe house. It would have topped off a great evening if we'd run into the Wild Hunt, but despite my dad's fear that the Erlking was out to get me, there was no sign of him.

Finn continued hauling Keane and me by our arms while we were in the more populated section of the tunnel system. I tried to ignore the curious looks of passersby. When we were away from other people, Finn gave Keane a shove forward, putting him in the lead. He then sandwiched me between them for the rest of the march. He *still* didn't say anything, every moment of silence stretching my nerves more and more taut.

I expected the explosion to come as soon as we were safely shut in the guardroom, but Finn wasn't meeting my expectations that night.

"You," he said, pinning me with his cold green gaze, "sit down." He pointed to a chair against the wall. He didn't raise his voice, but his words had such sharp edges on them he might as well have.

Shoulders hunched, I slunk over to the chair and sat down on the very edge. I had no idea what would happen next, but I knew it wasn't going to be fun.

Finn turned his gaze to Keane. "You think you're sufficient defense for a girl the Queens of Faerie have marked for death?" Still he didn't raise his voice, though the words held a hint of a snarl.

Something kindled in Keane's eyes. His shoulders straightened, his lip curled, and he met his father's gaze boldly. Here was the Keane I knew and mostly disliked.

"I may not be a Knight," he said, "but I'm perfectly capable of defending Dana if I have to."

My skin prickled with the distinctive sensation of magic being gathered.

"Titania has sent Knights after her before," Finn told his son. "Put up your shields. Show me how well you can defend against a Knight of Faerie."

Keane's confidence visibly wavered.

Finn made a fist and flashed Keane a savage grin. "Put up your shields, or this is going to hurt like hell."

Keane rolled his eyes like he thought this was all ridiculous, but I remembered how he'd looked when Finn first spoke. Arrogant as he was, he wasn't at all sure he could take his father. I suspect that idea made him squirm as much as it did me. I'd told myself I was pretty safe with Keane, but I didn't feel quite as sure of that now.

Keane moved over to the mats that still lay on the floor from our earlier sparring session, and Finn followed. From Finn's words and Keane's attitude, I knew Keane was likely to come out the loser of this fight, but I expected him to at least be able to hold his own for a while. I was wrong.

I thought Keane wiped the floor with me when we sparred, but I didn't know what wiping the floor with someone really was until Finn showed me. Keane hit the mats so many times you'd have thought he was a rug Finn was trying to beat the dust out of. Each time he got up, he was a little slower than the time before. Magic prickled across my skin as the two of them flung spells at each other, but it was obvious Keane ran out of juice long before Finn did.

The longer the fight went on, the redder Keane's face got, and I didn't think it was just from exertion. Every once in a while, he'd glance over at me, and I realized how humiliating this little demonstration in front of me must be. Hell, we usually practiced in the living room because I didn't want anyone watching while Keane repeatedly handed my butt to me, and I'm not a quarter as arrogant as he is. A couple of times, I opened my mouth to beg Finn to stop, but each time I quickly shut it again, knowing that I'd only make it worse.

Eventually, Keane went down hard and didn't get up again. He just lay there on his back, panting heavily, sweat pouring off his face, eyes squinched shut in what had to be pain. His shield spells might stop him from getting injured while sparring, but that didn't mean it didn't hurt. Not to mention that I think even his shield ran out of juice toward the end, because Finn visibly pulled his punches.

Finn came to stand over Keane, folding his arms over his chest and looking like he could go another thirty minutes without being winded. "This is how you fared against your father, who isn't about to hurt you. Imagine if I'd been a hostile Knight out to kill you. And that's not even considering the possibility of going up against the Erlking and the Wild Hunt. Then tell me again that you think you're capable of protecting Dana as well as a professional."

He looked back and forth between the two of us, just to make sure both of us got the message. We did.

Finn turned to me while Keane continued to lie on the mats sucking in air. "I'm not going to tell your father about tonight's escapade, because I believe you have a good head on your shoulders and won't pull a stupid stunt like that again. Am I right?"

I nodded meekly. Finn was doing me a ginormous favor by not telling on me. If my father found out what I'd done, I might not be allowed to leave my safe house for the rest of my life.

"Thank you," I said tentatively. "And I'm sorry."

Finn didn't acknowledge the apology. Guess he was still mad. "You're going to bed now," was all he said.

Keane groaned and propped himself up on his elbows. I had a feeling Finn wasn't through making him pay for my mistake. If I'd thought anything I said would help, I'd have stuck around and tried my best. Instead, feeling totally wretched, I left Keane alone with his father and fled to my room.

chapter six

I woke up on Saturday morning feeling just as bad as I had when I'd climbed into bed and pulled the covers over my head the night before. Keane had basically taken the whole rap for me last night, and that sucked. It wasn't that I thought Finn had hurt him all that much, and considering Keane's choice of profession, he had to have a pretty high tolerance for pain anyway. But I knew his pride had taken a beating, and I knew him well enough to realize how much that must have hurt him.

I can't say I regretted going to the party, though, despite my guilty conscience. If I tried to convince myself to regret it, my mind conjured an image of Kimber's face as she opened the present I'd given her, and I knew it had been worth it. (For me, at least. Keane might disagree.)

Usually, when I got up in the morning, I'd make some coffee for myself and some tea for Finn, who seemed to function just fine on what had to be about three or four hours of sleep a night and was always awake before me. He had his own kitchenette—even smaller than mine—in the guardroom, but he'd always seemed to appreciate the gesture.

A part of me really wanted to forego the ritual this morning. I didn't much want to face Finn after last night. Would he still be mad at me? Would I feel guilty every time I looked at him?

In the end, I decided I'd probably feel worse if I sat around in my suite brooding about it, so I fixed the tea and coffee, then took a deep breath and ventured out into the guardroom.

To my intense relief, Finn acted as if nothing had happened. There was no hint of anger or reproach in his gaze as he looked at me, and he didn't give me any paternal-sounding lectures. Not that he was ever what I would call talkative.

"I need some groceries," I told him when he'd finished his tea and I was preparing to take the dishes back to my kitchen.

Finn nodded. "Give me a list of what you need, and I'll ask your father to stop by the store on his way over for dinner tonight."

I'd totally forgotten Dad was coming tonight, but I wasn't about to let him be my grocery boy. I'd been responsible for buying groceries since I was about ten. Besides, a trip to the grocery store would get me out of the cave for a while. I could see the sun, and breathe some fresh air.

"I'd rather buy my own groceries," I told Finn.

"It would be simpler to let your father do it," he answered.

I grimaced, realizing that an official excursion from my safe house was a pain in the butt these days.

"My deal with my dad was that I could go out as long as I had an extra bodyguard."

Finn looked like he might be about to argue, and I prepared to embarrass the both of us by claiming to need things that a man wouldn't be comfortable shopping for, but he relented before I had to stoop to lying.

"All right," he said. "I'll give Lachlan a call and see if he's available."

Lachlan might be considered by some as an unusual choice of bodyguard. He had been my aunt Grace's boyfriend, before Aunt Grace went completely around the bend. I knew he still loved her, and sometimes when I saw him he'd try to convince me that she wasn't really that bad a person but was just misunderstood. He was never going to convince me of that, but when I saw the pain in his eyes, I couldn't blame him for trying. I also knew that no matter how he felt about Grace, he wouldn't allow anyone to hurt me, and since he was a troll beneath the glamour spell that made him appear human, he was an excellent protector.

My dad was as convinced of Lachlan's reliability as I was. However, Dad had made the location of my safe house into such a deep, dark secret that other than me, only Finn, Keane, and my parents knew where it was. Personally, I thought Lachlan could be trusted with the secret if he was trusted enough to act as my bodyguard, but Dad had been adamant that only those who absolutely had to know the location would be told. Which meant that Finn and I had to meet Lachlan in one of the more populated sections of the tunnel complex.

Finn made me hang back before we turned the final corner, but then I heard him greet Lachlan and beckon to me. I hated that we had to go through all this crap just for me to make a stop at the grocery store. I tried to convince myself this was a temporary inconvenience, that eventually we would find a better way for me to live safely in Avalon. I wasn't entirely successful.

When I joined Finn and Lachlan, the little hairs on my arms prickled with the distinctive sensation of magic in the air. I wondered if my so-far futile attempts to learn magic were actually having more effect than I'd realized. I knew that Finn always had a shield spell up when he went out in public, and Lachlan had his glamour, but I hadn't actually sensed that magic in the past. I really wished I could ask them about it, but my ability to sense magic was another deep, dark secret. When I'd told Ethan about it, he'd told me that Faeriewalkers usually had no other magical abilities. He then warned me that my potential magic skills would paint an even bigger target on my back, and that I should keep it secret from everyone—even my father.

The streets were quieter than usual—a sure sign that the Wild Hunt was still in town. Finn wasn't exactly relaxed, but Lachlan seemed even more tense and watchful. He was usually friendly and talkative, but today he was as talkative as Finn. Which is to say not at all.

They didn't shadow me through the aisles of the tiny neighborhood grocery store where I bought my supplies, probably only because there were only about three people in the place. I took longer than I strictly needed to, but wandering the aisles without my bodyguards felt like such a decadent slice of normalcy that I couldn't help savoring it.

That whole normalcy thing went right out the window as soon as I set foot outside the store, flanked by Finn and Lachlan. The distinctive roar of motorcycles split the air, and both Finn and Lachlan went on red alert. Magic thickened around me, the sensation like a thousand little electric shocks pinging against my skin.

The motorcycles came flying around the corner, and I knew as soon as I caught sight of them just who the bikers were.

The Erlking rode slightly ahead of his Huntsmen, who followed two-by-two behind him. As they had been when I'd first seen them, they were all dressed in black, and the huge motorcycles they rode were as black as their horses.

The Erlking came to a stop directly in front of me, despite Finn's attempts to keep me behind him, and the rest of the Huntsmen quickly surrounded us. They circled us in perfect unison, the Huntsmen effortlessly jumping the curb when necessary. The bikes roared even though they weren't going terribly fast.

Finn put a hand on my arm, and the prickling increased. At a guess, I'd say he'd extended his shield spell over my body. Lachlan stood motionless on my other side. The street and sidewalks around us had emptied as if by magic.

The Erlking twisted the handlebars of his bike, making it growl even more fiercely. Flames shot out from the exhaust pipes, reminding me of how his horse had seemed to breathe fire. I couldn't help cringing at the sound as he revved the engine again. I might have embarrassed myself by covering my ears if Finn hadn't had such a firm grip on my arm. I could hear the Erlking laughing even over the roar of the bikes.

Then suddenly, all the Huntsmen came to a stop at the same moment, the roar of their bikes subsiding to a growling idle.

My heart beating in my throat, I glanced around at these nightmares of Faerie. Each of the Huntsmen was dressed identically in unadorned black riding leathers. Black helmets with reflective visors hid their faces, and black gloves—or maybe I should call them gauntlets—hid their hands so that not a hint of skin or hair was visible. Only the fact that their builds were slightly different from one another stopped them from looking like a bunch of clones.

The Erlking was another story. His black leather was heavily adorned with silver studs and spikes, and he actually had silver spurs attached to his heavy motorcycle boots. The spurs might have made him look silly if he weren't so terrifying.

He, too, wore gauntlets, though his had wicked silver spikes across the knuckles. Yikes! His helmet was oddly shaped, coming to a point in front of his face like it was the helmet from a suit of armor, and silver antlers were painted on each side of his head, reminding me of the grotesque mask he'd been wearing when I first saw him. More frightening still, he wore a familiar scabbard draped over his back, though at least he didn't draw the sword.

When I'd seen him from a distance, I'd known immediately that he was a big guy. Up close and personal like he was now, I saw that he was huge. He had to be at least six foot five, and though his body was well hidden behind all that black leather, I could tell from the way he filled out the outfit that he was solidly muscled. As if he weren't intimidating enough otherwise.

I don't know how long our silent standoff lasted. It felt like forever, but was probably only a few minutes at most. My mouth was dry with fear, even though I knew he couldn't hurt me, and if my heart raced any faster, I'd die of a heart attack.

And then the Erlking reached up and removed his helmet.

I felt like my racing heart had suddenly stopped beating as I watched him shake out his hair and hook his helmet on the handlebars of his bike.

There's no such thing as an ugly Fae. At least not among the Sidhe, the aristocracy of Faerie. Their faces are always perfectly proportioned, their skin always completely devoid of blemishes or wrinkles or freckles. Even so, not all Fae are created equal. Up until this moment, Finn had topped my list of most gorgeous creatures I'd ever laid eyes on. The Erlking set a new standard.

The Fae are usually blond, with a few redheads thrown in for variety, but the Erlking's hair was a deep, glossy black and reached halfway down his back. His eyes were of deepest blue, framed by thick black lashes, and his mouth should be in the dictionary beside the word *sensual.* A striking blue tattoo in the shape of a leaping stag curved around the side of his face from just above his eyebrow down to his cheekbone.

Like all the Fae, the Erlking was ageless, his face belonging to someone in his mid-twenties, but there was something about his eyes that made him look . . . ancient. There were depths of knowledge in those eyes that made me feel like I could drown in them.

I forced myself to remember the sight of him raising his sword to kill an unarmed, fleeing man. The memory didn't make him any less gorgeous, but it did stop me from staring at him in what I suspect was an embarrassing state of awe.

"Dana, daughter of Seamus," the Erlking said in a voice that blended with the rumble of the bikes. "Well met."

He put his hand over his heart, then bowed from the waist. The gesture should have looked awkward while he was straddling his bike, but it didn't.

I figured keeping my mouth shut was the best option when facing malevolent creatures of Faerie. The Erlking's eyes twinkled with humor for a moment before he turned his attention to Finn.

"And Finn, of the Daoine Sidhe." He didn't bow this time, but he did nod his head with what looked almost like respect. "A worthy guardian for Avalon's most precious jewel."

I wasn't surprised that Finn also chose to keep quiet. Like I said, he's the strong, silent type.

I expected the Erlking to greet Lachlan in some way, as he had me and Finn, but he dismissed the troll with no more than a cursory glance and a curl of his lip. As I'd discovered from my father, the Sidhe were notoriously classist, and trolls were considered lesser beings. It pissed me off, but I wasn't going to try to teach the Erlking manners.

The Erlking fixed me with a stare that felt like an icicle piercing my heart. My breath froze in my lungs, and my fight-or-flight instincts urged me to run. My whole body was trembling with the need to flee for my life, sweat breaking out on my forehead and under my arms as my blood turned to pure adrenaline. When I managed to drag in a breath, my lungs wheezed with the effort. I think if Finn hadn't been holding my arm, I might not have been able to resist my body's desperate instinct to get away. Not that I could have gone anywhere with the Huntsmen surrounding me.

"Leave her alone!" Finn barked.

The Erlking smiled and looked away from me. The need to run faded instantly, and I knew that he had used some kind of magic against me to upgrade my general fear to full-out terror. I fought to keep myself from shivering as I tried to calm my frantic heart rate. Whatever magic he'd used, I hadn't sensed it in the air.

The Erlking met my eyes again, but this time he didn't try any tricks. "It is rare for a person with mortal blood to be able to withstand my gaze. Even a full-blooded Fae can be made to feel the effects, though only under the right circumstances. It seems there is more to you than meets the eye."

Nightmare Man then proceeded to wink at me, like he and I were in on some great joke together. I swallowed hard. I don't know how, but I was sure he knew about my affinity with magic. Perhaps it was the magic that had prevented me from surrendering to panic. He was dangerous enough without him knowing my secret.

The Erlking smiled at me. On someone else's face, that smile probably would have looked friendly. But not on his.

"I am not your enemy, Faeriewalker," he said. "I can't in all fairness claim to be your friend, either. However, I will offer you a token of . . ." He tapped his chin and furrowed his brow as if thinking hard, though I got the feeling he was just putting on a show. ". . . good will."

He looked at me expectantly. I still thought keeping my mouth shut around this guy was the smartest move. However, I didn't want to leave him with the impression that I was a frightened little rabbit, quivering with terror and hoping the big bad wolf wouldn't eat me.

"Thanks," I said, and I managed to get some sarcasm in my tone, though I sounded scared even to my own ears. "But no thanks. Somehow, I don't think accepting tokens from you would be such a hot idea."

The Erlking laughed, and his Huntsmen echoed him in eerie unison. The Erlking was terrifying, but his Huntsmen were just plain creepy.

I had no clue why what I'd said was so funny, but despite my resolve to appear unaffected, I knew blood was rising to my cheeks. Mockery is something I've never taken well.

The laughter stopped as abruptly as it had started. The Erlking picked up his helmet. I hoped that meant he and his buddies were about to leave.

"I'll give you the token whether you wish it or not," he said. For the first time, he turned his full attention to Lachlan, who had been so still and quiet I'd almost forgotten he was there.

"Things aren't always what they seem, now, are they?" the Erlking asked Lachlan with a grin.

To my surprise, Lachlan paled and took a step backward, as if he was thinking of running. The Erlking had suggested that his power of terror didn't work so well on Fae unless they had some mortal blood in them, which I was sure Lachlan did not. I didn't even know if trolls were *capable* of breeding with humans.

Finn was giving Lachlan a funny look, too. "Lachlan?" he asked. "What's wrong?"

I practically jumped out of my skin when the Erlking suddenly revved his bike again. The Huntsmen broke their circle, freeing us as they lined up in formation behind their leader.

"Remove his glamour, Finn of the Daoine Sidhe," the Erlking said. "Then you will understand why my gaze affected him as it did."

With another laugh, he put his helmet back on. The roar of the Wild Hunt's bikes was deafening as they rode away.

I didn't exactly feel safe now that the Hunt had left, but I did at least feel capable of turning my attention elsewhere. I looked at

Lachlan, who was holding his hands up in front of him in what looked like a defensive gesture as he backed away from Finn.

Magic built in the air, pouring off Finn in waves, and the look on his face was not promising. I had a good guess what was going to happen when Finn cast whatever spell he was about to cast, and it made my stomach do a flip-flop.

Finn released his magic, and it hit Lachlan like a physical blow, knocking him back—and blowing away his glamour. Without his glamour, he should have looked like a monster: a massive, ugly troll with clawed fingers and a mouth full of fangs. Instead, there was a muscular man of middling height with the uptilted eyes of a Fae, but sporting a scraggly beard that said he had a good dose of human blood in him.

One thing was for sure: it was not Lachlan.

Finn reached for me—no doubt to shove me behind him—and the moment he took his eyes off the imposter, the bastard turned tail and ran.

"Stop him!" I yelled at Finn, but I knew before the words had left my mouth that he wouldn't. His job was to protect me, so he couldn't chase the imposter. But if the imposter got away, then we might never know who had sent him—and what he'd done with the real Lachlan.

In retrospect, what I did next was flat-out dumb. Keane might have been training me in self-defense, but I was still a beginner, at best. Usually, I'm a pretty cautious person, into the look-before-you-leap philosophy. But being in Avalon, learning to fight, and constantly being in danger was changing me in more ways than one.

Fake-Lachlan was going to get away because Finn had to

babysit me, and I didn't want Fake-Lachlan getting away. So I dropped my bag of groceries and ran after him.

My reckless charge took Finn completely by surprise, so he was a beat too slow when he tried to reach out and grab me. I heard him yell my name as I dodged out of reach, but I ignored him and kept running. The arrival of the Wild Hunt had effectively cleared the streets, so both the imposter and I were able to run full speed. I heard the sound of Finn's feet pounding the pavement behind me, and I allowed myself a little smile of satisfaction. *I* might not be much of a match for the imposter, but the guy wouldn't be running like his life depended on it if he thought he could handle Finn.

The smile disappeared when the imposter suddenly stopped in his tracks, whirling around to face me. I tried to put on the brakes, but I'd been running headlong and couldn't stop in time.

I crashed into the imposter's body, my momentum pushing him back a few steps as his breath whooshed out. But apparently, he'd been ready for me, because he recovered his balance much faster than I did, and he wrapped his arms around me, turning me around so my back was to his chest. One of his arms pinned mine to my sides, while his other arm came around my neck.

"Stay back!" he yelled at Finn. "Come any closer, and I'll break her neck."

Finn stopped much more gracefully than I had and glared daggers at my attacker.

But I hadn't been taking all those self-defense lessons from Keane for no reason, and we'd practiced any number of different escapes from this particular hold, which was apparently an old standby for bad guys. Without a moment of hesitation, I did three things in quick succession. I stomped down as hard as I could on his instep. Then I lowered my head and sank my teeth into his forearm. He screamed and started to let go, and that was when I snapped my head back as hard as I could.

Whoever he was, the guy wasn't particularly tall, and the back of my head made satisfying contact with his nose. The crunching sound made me wince, as did his howl of pain. But he let go of me in a hurry.

I was wondering if I should turn around and give him a good kick in the knee to make sure he couldn't run away, but before I could decide, Finn yanked me away and planted his fist in the imposter's face. Every muscle in his body went limp at once, and he collapsed to the pavement in a heap.

chapter seven

Despite my frequent complaints about how visitors from Faerie can practically get away with murder in Avalon, the city does have a justice system and a police force. By the time the Lachlan impersonator went down for the count, the Wild Hunt had been gone long enough that people were starting to poke their heads out to see if the coast was clear. Someone must have seen what happened, because before Finn had a chance to round on me and congratulate me on my brilliant performance—hey, it could happen!—we heard the sound of sirens approaching.

The look on Finn's face said he was considering grabbing me and making a run for it, but by now there were enough witnesses that the cops would have tracked us down if we tried it, and that couldn't be a good thing.

Finn shook his finger in my face. "You are not to speak to the police, Dana," he said. "You're a minor, and they can't question you without your legal guardian's permission, so just keep your mouth shut."

I frowned up at him. "Why? It's not like we did anything wrong." At least, not as far as I knew.

Finn gave me a long-suffering look. "Will you just this once do as you're told without the thousand and one questions?"

"Well, *excuse me* for wanting to understand why I'm not supposed to talk to the police."

Finn didn't have time to respond before the police descended on us.

From the way Finn had been talking, I half expected the cops to arrest us or something, but when Finn told them what happened, they accepted his word without question and slapped handcuffs on Fake-Lachlan. When the cops asked me if I'd be willing to answer a few questions, I bit my tongue and told them I wanted to wait for my dad. I didn't like it, but Finn wouldn't have told me to keep quiet without a good reason. I thought maybe the cops would get mad about that, but it didn't seem to bother them much.

They were just asking us to come to the police station to give formal statements—or at least for Finn to give a formal statement while they tried to contact my dad—when my dad made a surprise appearance. I knew Finn hadn't called him, and the police hadn't had time to yet, so I wondered how he knew where to find me—and that I *needed* him to find me. He worked as a Council Liaison, whatever that was. All I knew was that it was some kind of government position, and that it gave him some degree of power.

I can't say for sure what happened next, but my suspicion is that some money changed hands, or my dad pulled some strings. Whatever the reason, the police decided Finn and I didn't have to make a formal statement after all.

"Take her home immediately," my dad told Finn as the cops stuffed Fake-Lachlan into the back of one of their cars. "I'll be there as soon as I can, and I'll expect a full report."

Finn acknowledged his orders with a formal nod.

"What about Lachlan?" I asked. "He might be in trouble."

Dad made one of his nose-in-the-air faces that said a troll was beneath his concern. "We won't be able to do anything for Lachlan until we've had time to question the imposter. For all we know, he's a willing accomplice."

I opened my mouth to say something indignant, but Dad cut me off before I could.

"We'll get to the bottom of this," he promised. "And if Lachlan is in trouble, I'll do everything I can to help him. Now hurry home. You've had an eventful enough day already."

I might have argued some more, except he turned away from me. I didn't like being dismissed like a pesky child, but I figured if Finn was going to give a thorough recounting of the day's events to my dad, it would be best to put that off as long as possible. Call me crazy, but I didn't think my dad would be happy to hear that I'd chased the imposter.

As Finn led me away from the scene of the crime, I looked back over my shoulder and saw my dad getting into the front seat of one of the police cars. Somehow, I didn't think it was business as usual to let a civilian do that. However, no one seemed to object, and both cars drove away.

Miraculously, my bag of groceries was still sitting right on the sidewalk where I'd dropped it. Even better, nothing had spilled or broken, though I suspected the bananas I'd bought for my cereal were going to be covered in nasty, mushy bruises. Because of what I'd done, no matter how dumb it might have been, the imposter was in police custody, and I couldn't help feeling proud. I'd spent a lot of time in Avalon feeling like a damsel in distress, so it felt good to have scored this minor victory. No matter how fiercely Finn frowned as he escorted me back to the safe house.

"If that man had had a weapon," Finn said quietly once we were in the privacy of the darkened tunnels, "you could well be dead by now."

I fought down a superstitious shiver. "Good thing for me he didn't, then," I responded with as much bravado as I could muster. If I thought too hard about what *might* have happened, I could totally freak myself out.

Out of the corner of my eye, I saw Finn shake his head. "That isn't the point, and you know it. You can't keep taking risks like that. I'm good at my job, but I'm not invincible. And right now, you're making my job a lot harder than it has to be."

I hunched my shoulders a bit at the rebuke. If he'd yelled at me, or started barking orders at me, I'd have dug in my heels and fought back. His calm, quiet reasoning was a lot harder to fight against.

"I'm sorry," I mumbled. "I didn't really think about it at the time. I just saw that he was getting away, and I reacted."

He sighed. "And what about last night? Did you think about it before you went gallivanting about at night without a bodyguard?"

So much for my hope that last night was water under the bridge. The fact was, at the time I'd decided to sneak out with Keane, I'd felt pretty safe with him. Yes, I'd known I was taking a risk, but it hadn't seemed like a particularly big one. After seeing how badly outmatched Keane was against Finn, I knew I'd taken a much bigger risk than I'd realized. I couldn't come up with anything to say in my defense, so I kept my mouth shut.

When we got back to my safe house, Finn wouldn't let me head back into my suite, but insisted I sit on the couch in the guardroom. He sat in an armchair and leaned forward, his elbows resting on his knees as he fixed me with that green gaze of his.

"Your father is going to be very angry with you," he warned.

Well, duh! If Dad had his way, I'd be holed up in this stupid cave twenty-four/seven, so I could hardly expect him to be happy that I'd taken the risk of chasing the imposter. He probably wasn't going to be too happy to hear I'd gotten to meet the Erlking, either, though that wasn't my fault.

"He has been a person of power all his long life," Finn continued. "Working as a bodyguard, I'm intimately familiar with how hard it is for someone who's not used to being in danger to adjust. Protecting himself is second nature to your father, and he has trouble understanding that it isn't to you."

I blinked at Finn in confusion, not sure where he was going with this. I'd been expecting a lecture, but that didn't seem to be what I was getting.

"What are you trying to tell me?" I asked.

"I guess I'm trying to prepare you for his reaction and make sure you see his point of view. *I* understand that you're going to make mistakes. I've guarded too many people over too many years not to expect it. But *he's* not going to understand that, at least not right away. That's why I'm not going to tell your father about last night's adventure. Just remember that he's trying to keep you safe, even if he goes about it in ways you don't like."

I don't think I'd ever heard Finn string that many words together all at once. It almost made me want to do as he said and cut Dad some slack. But if Dad came down here and started shouting at me, I knew I wouldn't be able to help getting mad right back.

It was several hours before I had to face my dad and his anger. He apparently had some kind of an in with the police, and he'd hung around while they'd questioned the imposter.

It turned out the imposter was an underworld mercenary who was officially a citizen of Avalon but had enough Fae blood in him that he spent much of his time in Faerie. He'd been hired by my aunt Grace to kidnap me.

Grace had given him some kind of spelled amulet that would have allowed him to knock Finn out, and he'd been waiting for the perfect opportunity to use it. Then he would have grabbed me and dragged me into Faerie, where he'd turn me over to Grace. That would have sucked big-time, since Grace wanted to use me as a weapon to kill Titania and snatch the Seelie throne. Also, she hates my guts—and the feeling is mutual.

Lucky for me, the mercenary was intimidated by Finn and had trouble working up the nerve to attack. Also lucky for me that the Erlking had happened along and had revealed him as an imposter. Why the Erlking had done that was a mystery, especially if he'd been sent here to kill me. I hoped I never got a chance to hear him explain.

Lachlan was fine, thank goodness. The imposter had used

another of Grace's spells to bind the troll, leaving him paralyzed and helpless in his apartment. The police were able to cast a counterspell that freed him.

I tried to convince Dad it was a case of "all's well that ends well," but he didn't buy it. He grounded me for a week. I'd never been grounded before in my life, and this was now the second time since I'd come to Avalon.

There was a part of me that wanted to push, to once again threaten to leave Avalon as soon as I turned eighteen if my dad insisted on doing this to me. I managed to shout that part of me down. For one thing, if I kept using the threat, it would lose its power. For another, I had to reluctantly admit that I kinda sorta deserved it.

Knowing I had it coming didn't make the week that followed any easier to endure. Dad had me under such a severe lockdown that I couldn't even have my sparring sessions with Keane. Never in a million years would I have guessed that I'd miss them, but I did. If for no other reason than because they helped pass the time.

Well, okay, there was another reason, too. Most of the time, Keane got on my nerves in a big way, but it was nice to hang out with someone my own age. Yes, technically he was two years older, but he was a lot closer to my age than, say, Finn, who was my only company during my captivity. Even Dad stayed away, which I thought was rubbing it in.

I managed to talk to Kimber every day, and I think that was the only thing that kept me sane. We made plans to go to a spa for manicures as soon as I was free to leave my safe house. I'd never had a manicure in my life. When I was living with Mom, we were always strapped for money, and I couldn't afford luxuries like that. Not to mention that I hadn't had girlfriends to go with. It was a small thing, but the prospect helped me tolerate my punishment.

Not quite so pleasant were the phone calls from Ethan. After seeing him at Kimber's party with that redhead, I really wasn't interested in talking to him, so when his name popped up on caller ID, I didn't answer. The first couple of times, he hung up without leaving a message. But then he started asking me to call him back. I even picked up the phone to do it once or twice, but never got so far as to dial his number. What did I have to say to him? I worried that I'd come off sounding like a jealous girlfriend, even though we weren't dating. And I would probably die of humiliation if I actually started to cry.

But Ethan isn't the kind of guy who takes no for an answer. When the phone rang on Wednesday and the caller ID said it was Kimber, I picked up without a moment's hesitation. But just because the call was coming from Kimber's phone didn't mean she was the one making it.

"You haven't called me back," Ethan said as soon as I answered.

I bit my tongue to keep myself from groaning. If I had any sense, I'd hang up on him and then unplug my phone. Of course, we'd already established that I was a little short on sense.

"News flash," I said. "If I don't call you back, it means I don't want to talk to you." *Hang up, Dana,* I told myself. But I didn't listen.

I could almost hear his puzzled frown. "Why don't you want to talk to me?"

Anger spiked. He *had* to know by now that I'd been at Kimber's party. Surely he could figure out for himself why I might not want to talk to him. That he would play innocent just made me more pissed.

"Gee, I don't know, Ethan," I said through gritted teeth. "Maybe it would be because I saw you with that redhead at Kimber's party. Yeah, I'm pretty sure that's it." I found myself holding my breath, hoping that Ethan would have some perfectly innocent explanation for why the redhead had been draped all over him. Hell if I know what that explanation could have been, but that didn't stop me from hoping.

Ethan's momentary silence shattered that admittedly fragile hope.

"Asshole," I muttered under my breath, and once again ordered myself to hang up. Too bad I wasn't any good at taking orders, even from myself.

Ethan finally found his voice. "It didn't mean anything. We were just . . . having a good time at the party. Besides, you've made it perfectly clear we aren't dating, so I figured there was no harm in it."

On the one hand, he had a point. I had been really clear with my words that we weren't dating. On the other hand, he'd made it just as clear that he hoped to change my mind, which should have meant he wasn't hooking up with other girls at the same time.

"You're right," I said flatly. "We're *not* dating."

I finally found the willpower to hang up on him, and barely resisted the urge to hurl the phone across the room. Angry tears burned my eyes, but I refused to let them fall.

I took a deep breath, trying to calm down. Every logical

bone in my body told me Ethan was bad news for me. He was older than me, he was a player, and he was a liar. He was exactly the kind of boy I *didn't* want to get involved with. And yet, stupid me, I wanted him pursuing me, making me feel like a grown woman, rather than a kid. The idea of having a hottie like Ethan choose me over all the other more beautiful, more worldly girls he knew made my heart skip a beat.

But hello, reality here, he *wasn't* choosing me over all those other girls. In fact, if he was up to his usual tricks, he wasn't bothering to choose at all.

Seeing him with that girl at the party had hurt like a slap in the face, but it was probably good for me. Maybe it would help me get my head out of the clouds, help me see Ethan as he really was, rather than how I wanted him to be.

The phone rang again, but I let the answering machine pick up.

"Come on, Dana," Ethan said after the beep. "Talk to me."

I folded my arms and resisted the urge to pick up the phone. Ethan sighed dramatically.

"You're making something out of nothing," he said. "I was just dancing with her. What's the big deal?"

If I were a less guarded sort, those words might have made me feel like a melodramatic idiot. Surely Ethan had a right to dance with other girls at a party, especially when he was under the impression I wasn't going to be there myself. I might even have been able to talk myself into thinking I'd misinterpreted the level of flirting I'd seen.

But I *am* a guarded sort, and I couldn't help remembering Ethan's initial hesitation when I'd asked him about the girl. If he really thought what he was doing with her was so innocent, he wouldn't have reacted like that.

Reminding myself once again of some of Ethan's less noble moments—like when he'd tried to seduce me with magic, and when he'd engineered for me to be attacked so he could play the knight in shining armor—I found the willpower to ignore his voice on my answering machine.

Eventually he gave up. Or so I thought.

chapter eight

I ended up in a nasty, broody mood after talking to Ethan. I tried to get my mind off him by tooling around on the Internet. Then I tried watching TV, but I've never been a daytime TV fan. Then I tried reading a book.

Nothing seemed able to distract me from my gloomy thoughts. Now more than ever, I wished I were still having my lessons with Keane. When I was sparring with him, there was no room in my brain for anything other than survival.

Realizing I needed something that would absorb more of my mental energy than anything I'd yet tried, I decided to take one more shot at teaching myself to use magic. I had to shout down the little voice in my head that told me it was a futile effort. I'd been trying ever since the first time Dad had grounded me, and although I could now call the magic to me with relative ease, I didn't know how to make it do anything.

I'd really have liked to ask for help with it, but I believed Ethan was right and I was better off keeping my affinity with magic secret. According to Kimber, who'd explained the basics of magic to me before I'd had any idea I could use it myself, magic is an almost sentient force—an idea which still creeps me out—that's native to Faerie. As far as anyone knew, the magic had always treated Faeriewalkers as human in the past, meaning Faeriewalkers couldn't even *sense* the magic, much less use it. But for some reason, the magic seemed to have taken a liking to me. Something about my distinctive singing voice, with its Fae purity and its human vibrato, seemed to draw the magic in.

A lot of people were already scared of me. Well, not of *me* exactly, but of what I was capable of doing. Not only could I travel freely between Faerie and the mortal world, but I—and those within my field of influence—could also carry magic into the mortal world and technology into Faerie. Grace wanted to use me to kill the Seelie Queen because with me at her side, Grace could carry a gun into Faerie and shoot the Queen.

If everyone knew that I could call on the magic myself, some of the people who just wanted to use me might decide I was too dangerous and side with those who wanted to kill me. Which meant I couldn't admit to anyone—not even my father—that I could sense when magic was in the air. It made my insides quiver to know that Ethan knew my secret, because I couldn't completely trust him. And the idea that the Erlking might have guessed . . .

I shook off these thoughts as best I could, then shut myself in my bedroom as far away from Finn as I could get. I didn't know how close he'd have to be to sense the magic building, but he hadn't come running the previous times I'd tried to gather magic, so I hoped that meant my bedroom was far enough away.

I took a deep breath to calm myself—the idea of calling on

the magic automatically kicked my pulse into overdrive—then started on the series of vocalises I used to warm up my voice before I practiced singing. (Don't ask me why I still practiced when I didn't have a voice teacher here in Avalon.)

The first few times I'd tried to call the magic, it had taken me a while to manage it. I'd gone through the vocalises, then had to sing a few songs before I'd start to feel the prickle of magic on my skin. Today, it went much faster. By the time I'd finished my first set of scales, I already felt a sense of something . . . foreign in the room.

I wasn't sure at first what it was, wasn't sure it wasn't my imagination. But when I moved on from scales to arpeggios, the feeling intensified, and the hairs at the back of my neck stood at attention. My voice faltered, and I was a bit flat at the top of the arpeggio, but the prickling presence remained. Apparently it didn't mind a sour note here and there.

Hoping to build on my early success, I skipped the rest of my warm-ups and went straight on to "Brahms' Lullaby," one of the very first songs I'd learned when I started taking voice lessons. It was a lot simpler than the songs and arias I'd been working on when I'd run away from home, but the simplicity and familiarity made it easier for me to stay on key as the presence of magic made my concentration waver.

The air felt thick around me, harder to breathe, and it was all I could do not to rub my arms to try to dispel the prickling sensation. It felt like little clawed mouse feet were racing back and forth across my skin, the feeling more intense than ever. Despite my usually perfect pitch, I was floundering now, my voice sometimes sharp, sometimes flat as I fought to keep myself under control.

This was progress, I knew. The magic that surrounded me was stronger than ever before, and had come more quickly to my call. Now if only I could figure out how to make it *do* something. Other than make me feel like a hallucinating mental patient, that is.

My breath came shorter in the heavy air, and I wasn't able to sustain the long notes. My head spun, and I realized if I didn't do something fast, I was going to hyperventilate and pass out.

I focused my attention on the door to my bedroom. Kimber had told me that there were certain simple spells that almost all the Fae could do. One of them was locking or unlocking doors. I had nothing more than a little button lock on my bedroom door, and I concentrated on the image of that button being pressed by an invisible hand.

The lullaby was nearing its end, and I was having to sneak a breath every few notes. I don't even want to know what I sounded like. I'm sure it wasn't pretty, between the sour notes and the gasps for air. It was bad enough now that even the magic seemed to be losing interest. I could feel it receding, the air becoming easier to breathe, the prickling starting to subside.

Still, I kept staring at my door, willing it to lock itself with the power that was left in the room. But nothing happened, and moments later, when the lullaby came to an end, I was alone in my room once more.

I tried two more times to call the magic during the remaining days of my captivity, and the result was the same. Lots of magic in the air, and nothing to show for it. I was so frustrated I could scream.

When Monday finally rolled around, I was so ready to escape my cave that I wished Kimber and I had scheduled our spa visit for first thing in the morning. Unfortunately, our appointment wasn't until one o'clock, which made for what felt like the longest morning in the history of the universe.

The Erlking was still hanging around Avalon, so I still had to take two guards with me whenever I left the safe house. I'd assumed that my second guard for this outing would be Lachlan—and that Finn would do some kind of hocus-pocus to confirm it was really him before letting me near him—but it turned out I was wrong.

My dad showed up promptly at noon, carrying a to-go bag that smelled heavenly. He smiled at my surprise.

"I'm sure Lachlan is a perfectly capable second guard," he told me, "but I have the luxury of having some free time for once, so I thought I'd fill in for him. You don't mind, do you?"

He made the question sound casual, but there was something almost . . . tentative to his manner. Was he worried I'd hold a grudge over him grounding me? It was true that living with my mom had meant I'd had practically zero experience with true parental authority, but though I hadn't exactly enjoyed being grounded, there was something so normal and ordinary about it that I found it hard to resent him. At least not for that.

I shrugged, wondering if my gesture looked any more genuinely casual than his. "Fine with me. What have you brought?"

Dad held up the takeout bag for display. "Lunch from Lachlan's bakery. I wasn't sure what you liked, so I brought a selection."

We were in the guardroom, and Finn was stationed across the room from us—as far away as he could get, so we could have an illusion of privacy. Dad didn't spare the Knight a glance as he gestured for me to precede him into my suite.

I was doing my best to accept the fact that my dad was a snob. The Fae are extremely class-conscious, and even though Knights were the sword arm of Faerie, they were treated almost like servants. I doubted I'd have any luck bringing my dad's attitude into the twenty-first century—the Fae take being set in their ways to a new level—but I couldn't help trying.

"Did you bring anything for Finn?" I asked my dad, standing my ground.

Dad arched one eyebrow at me, then turned his attention to Finn. "Have you had lunch yet?"

Finn blinked in surprise. To tell you the truth, I was kinda surprised myself. I'd been sure Dad would stick his nose in the air at my suggestion. Maybe I could bring him into the twenty-first century after all.

"I have already eaten," Finn said, shifting uncomfortably from foot to foot. The color that rose to his cheeks screamed that he was lying.

"No, you haven't!" I said. "I'm sure Dad's got enough food in there for three people." I slanted a look at my dad, whose face was completely impassive. "Maybe even four, based on the size of that bag."

The color in Finn's cheeks darkened, and he bowed his head slightly. "Go on and eat your lunch, Dana. I'm not hungry."

I shook my head, so not getting what was the matter. I looked up at my dad with narrowed eyes.

He lifted one shoulder in a hint of a shrug. "It's not just me." Once again, he gestured toward the door to my suite.

I didn't get it right away. "*What* isn't just you?" I asked as I headed toward the door.

Dad didn't answer, and as we walked down the fortified hallway to my suite, I started to understand. "You mean this whole classism thing you Fae have going on goes both ways."

Dad nodded. "Finn is a Knight, and while he may accept assignments in Avalon—and often does—he was born and raised in Faerie. He has enough experience to understand that humans have a much more egalitarian attitude than the Fae, but he himself is still Fae. He would never be comfortable sitting down to eat with me like an equal."

Dad made himself at home in my kitchen, putting down the bag and rummaging through my cabinets for plates. I understood what he was saying, but that didn't mean I had to like it.

"I still think it's a crappy way to treat someone who's willing to take a bullet for me."

Dad turned to look at me. "Perhaps it is. But that doesn't change the reality." He smiled. "And just because protocol insists Finn and I not socialize doesn't mean the same applies to you."

I refrained from pointing out that I didn't care what his stupid protocol said. I wasn't treating Finn like a piece of furniture like my dad did, and I never would.

Dad halted his efforts to serve lunch and gave me another of those almost vulnerable looks of his.

"I can't help being who I am," he said. "I know I seem terribly set in my ways, but it's just part of being a native of Faerie. We have deeply ingrained expectations of one another. I'm truly sorry it makes you uncomfortable."

My dad was still pretty close to a stranger to me, but I believed he was sincere. He'd never told me how old he was, but I knew it was *old* old. It wasn't fair of me to expect him to change, especially not overnight. When I'd come to Avalon to meet him, I'd had no idea what to expect. Half the time, my mom had made him out to be the devil incarnate; the other half, she'd made him sound like a candidate for sainthood. The reality was that he was somewhere in between.

"I know, Dad," I said. "And I'm trying my best to understand. Honest."

He smiled at me, and it was impossible to miss the paternal affection in his eyes. Maybe as an old Fae, he couldn't be as demonstrative as I might like, but I knew he loved me, even having known me only a short time. All in all, he was a pretty good dad, even if there were things about him I'd have liked to change.

I met Kimber in the lobby of the spa. I felt weird and conspicuous walking around with both my dad and Finn acting as bodyguards. I felt even weirder walking into the spa with them.

The lobby was every bit as girlie as I could possibly have imagined. The walls, furniture, and carpet were all in gently muted pastels, and a wall-mounted fountain filled the room with the sound of trickling water. Candles flickered from sconces on the walls, and little bowls of potpourri scented the air.

My dad and Finn looked completely out of place, and the woman at the reception desk looked at them with wide, startled eyes. I'm sure they weren't the only men ever to have set foot in the spa, but at the moment, it kinda felt like it.

Kimber had gotten there before me, and she leapt to her feet as soon as I walked in, dropping the fashion magazine she'd been looking at.

"Right on time!" she declared, looking as excited as a five-year-old at Christmas.

Although Kimber had only just turned seventeen, she'd be starting her sophomore year of college in the fall. We hadn't really talked about it in any detail, but I was pretty sure she had about as much experience making friends her own age as I did. Which is to say practically none at all. No wonder the two of us got along so well.

I smiled at her enthusiasm and did my best to ignore my dad and Finn. I was more relieved than I could say that they agreed to wait for me in the lobby instead of insisting they had to loom over me while I got my nails done.

A beautiful Fae woman (I know, redundant) escorted Kimber and me into the depths of the spa and into a private room set up with two manicure tables.

"Go ahead and pick your colors," the Fae woman said. "Sharon and Emily will be right with you."

I looked at the enormous set of shelves stacked with nail polish and was at a complete loss. Too many choices!

I'd never had a manicure before, but I did sometimes paint my nails. However, I chose my colors mostly based on what was on sale. That wasn't much help here. I shook my head.

"You're going to have to help me," I told Kimber, hoping I didn't sound as awkward as I suddenly felt. Maybe *I* didn't belong in a classy spa any more than Finn or my dad did.

She grinned at me, and there was a mischievous twinkle in her eye. "It'll be a real hardship, but somehow I'll manage."

I laughed and let some of the tension ease out of my shoulders. "Yeah, I've noticed how telling other people what to do is not your thing."

Kimber gave me a mock dirty look. "Here's the perfect color for you," she said, snatching a bottle off the topmost shelf and sticking it in my face.

It was the most hideous shade of puke green I'd ever seen. Why they even *made* nail polish in that color was anyone's guess.

"Ha ha," I told her, then reached for a bottle of neon orange. "How about this one for you?"

We went back and forth for a bit, each choosing the ugliest colors available—and let me tell you, there were plenty of ugly ones to choose from—before we settled on shell pink for Kimber and a shimmery copper for me. Then the manicurists descended on us with clippers and files and cuticle-pushers, and other . . . stuff.

I'd expected to have my nails filed and then painted. The rest of the ritual came as a complete surprise. I wasn't too fond of having my cuticles pushed and nipped, so I turned to Kimber to distract myself.

"Why did you let Ethan use your phone to call me?" I blurted, then wished my hand were free so I could smack myself in the forehead with it. I honestly hadn't meant to sound like I was accusing her of something, but the truth is I was a bit annoyed with her for helping Ethan ambush me. However, I really wished I'd brought it up on the phone, instead of here in front of a couple of strangers.

Kimber didn't seem to think my timing was inappropriate,

however. She wrinkled her nose and gave me an apologetic look. "Sorry about that. He used the phone while I was in the kitchen making tea. I heard him talking to you, but by then it was too late."

Kimber had tried to warn me away from Ethan from the very beginning. I should have known she hadn't willingly helped Ethan trick me into answering the phone.

"He wouldn't tell me what he did to make you so mad at him," Kimber continued.

No, of course he wouldn't. I looked at the two women who were busily fussing with our nails, wishing that if I'd had to bring this up, I'd done it while Kimber and I were still alone.

"Come on," Kimber said impatiently. "Spill."

Reluctantly, I told her about seeing Ethan at the party with the redhead. My cheeks heated with a blush as I spoke. I felt like such a dork for getting upset about this when Ethan and I weren't dating.

Kimber let out an exasperated sigh and shook her head. "I love my brother—most of the time—but he can be a total ass-hat."

I choked back a laugh. The woman working on Kimber's nails smiled faintly before she got her expression under control. I reminded myself that spa staff probably got to hear a lot of girlie secrets on a regular basis. That still didn't make me comfortable talking about it.

"Yeah, well, that's why I don't want to talk to him," I said.

Kimber looked a little grim. "He also doesn't give up easy."

I groaned. "Yeah, I kind of figured that." He'd been lying low lately, but I didn't expect that to last forever. I tried not to think about how he might be keeping himself entertained while I was giving him the cold shoulder, since it shouldn't matter to me.

"For what it's worth," Kimber said, dropping her voice, although it wasn't like the manicurists couldn't hear her, "I think he really cares about you."

I rolled my eyes. "Yeah, I can tell by the way he was practically making out with that girl on the dance floor."

"I doubt he'll ever stop being a flirt, but I also doubt he'd put this much effort into talking to you if you didn't mean something to him."

I bit my tongue to keep from saying anything stupid. From what Kimber had told me about him before, I knew that Ethan planned to follow in his father's footsteps. Hell, he was head of the Avalon Student Underground, which was supposedly a group of subversive political activists who wanted to promote change in Avalon. I say "supposedly" because the only time I'd ever met anyone from this Underground, their meeting had been nothing more than a glorified keg party.

Whatever his Underground was really up to, I knew for certain that Ethan had . . . ambitions. And that having a Faeriewalker on his side couldn't hurt those ambitions. Which made his motives in chasing me suspect, at best.

"I think I liked it better when you were telling me Ethan was just using me and I should stay away from him," I said, sounding a little sour.

One corner of Kimber's mouth rose in a wry smile. "In other words, you wish I would butt out?"

"Nah," I told her, returning her smile. "It's nice to have

someone to talk to about it. Even if you do give conflicting advice."

Kimber examined the perfectly polished hand the manicurist had just released. "I'd whap you upside the head, only I don't want to ruin my nails."

"Ditto," I said.

chapter nine

Kimber wanted to visit a little tea shop just down the road from the spa, and I wasn't anxious to return to my safe house. I had to ask my dad for permission, since I needed him to come with me to act as a bodyguard. I don't think I'd asked my mom permission for anything since I was about eight. She'd generally been too drunk to care what I did, and though I was glad her brain was no longer pickling in a sea of alcohol, there was a part of me that really missed the freedom I had once taken for granted.

Luckily, Dad said he had the whole afternoon free, so there was no reason he couldn't keep watch over me for a while longer.

The tea shop was kind of like a Starbucks or Caribou Coffee would be in the United States, with a ton of varieties of tea available for sale by the pound, and a counter where you could order something on the spot. There was a patio-like area to the right of the shop, which featured a number of round outdoor tables with umbrellas. In the States, those umbrellas would be to shade the customers from the sun. In Avalon, I think they were more likely meant to keep off the rain.

Kimber, who had been on a crusade to convert me to the Church of Tea, insisted I try a variety called "Faerie Rose."

"It's called that because the roses used for it come from Faerie," she told me.

"Eww," I said, wrinkling up my nose. "Who wants to drink roses?"

She gave me a patronizing look. "Trust me, it won't taste like roses."

If the place had offered coffee, I would have stood firm, but they didn't, so I let Kimber browbeat me. The tea was the color of a blush wine, and when I sniffed it, I practically sneezed at the strength of the rose smell.

"Trust me," Kimber said again as we headed out to one of the sheltered tables. It wasn't raining at the moment, but the sky was a bleak, solid gray, and the air felt damp. If a day went by without at least a sprinkling of rain in Avalon, that was probably a sign of the Apocalypse.

Neither my dad nor Finn had ordered tea—I think it was against the bodyguard code—and when they followed us outside, they each stood just far enough away that Kimber and I could talk in private, as long as we kept our voices down.

As I blew on my tea—more to stall having to drink it than to cool it down—Kimber glanced over at Finn, then turned to me with a smile. Finn was in his Secret Service Man mode today, wearing a bland dark suit and dark glasses that hid his striking eyes. But Kimber had seen his less formal look, and had made no secret of how much she appreciated the view.

She leaned forward, the smile turning into a grin. "If I

hadn't seen Finn without those glasses, I'd wonder if Keane was adopted."

I stifled a laugh. It was true that Keane and Finn were polar opposites in the looks department. Especially when Finn was on duty, when his look was extra-ultra-conservative. I couldn't help thinking Keane had created his bad-boy look as a way of rebelling against his father, though Finn showed no sign of minding.

"There's more of a resemblance than you might think," I said, then finally took a sip of my tea, bracing myself for it to taste disgusting.

Weirdly, although the smell of rose was as strong as ever, the taste of the tea was all spice and honey. No spice I could recognize, mind you, but it didn't taste like roses at all. I took another sip and rolled it around my tongue.

"Well?" Kimber asked with a smug smile.

I shrugged and swallowed my sip. "You were right: it doesn't taste like roses." I still wasn't sure I *liked* it, but I could drink it without gagging.

"Of course I was right. Being right is my specialty." She took a sip of her own tea, then stole another glance at Finn. "So you were saying there's more of a resemblance than I'm seeing . . . ?"

I nodded. "If you see them right next to each other and you ignore Keane's dye job, you can definitely tell they're related."

She looked unconvinced. "I saw them next to each other at the party," she reminded me.

I couldn't help making a face at the memory. I hadn't seen Keane since. I hoped his wounded pride was all healed up. "You saw them in a dark nightclub, and Finn was so pissed off he was scary. I don't think you were comparing their looks. Oh, and by the way, I'm sorry Keane was such an asshole to you. If I'd known he would behave like that . . ." I let my voice trail off because I didn't know what I would have done if I'd known. My choices at the time had been go with Keane, or skip the party. I couldn't help noticing that Kimber was wearing the pendant I'd given her, which reminded me why I'd taken the risk of going in the first place.

Kimber licked her lips, and a hint of pink colored her pale cheeks. "You don't have to apologize. I actually, um, kind of liked him."

My eyes widened, and my jaw dropped. I reached up and wiggled my ear. "Excuse me, but I think there's something wrong with my hearing. Did I just hear you say you *liked* him?"

The color in her cheeks deepened. "Boys are often intimidated by me," she confided. "Either because of who my father is, or because I'm smart. I liked that he wasn't intimidated."

There went that annoying little stab of jealousy again. I fought it down ruthlessly. "What about that guy I saw you with the first night I met you?"

It had been my one and only meeting with the Student Underground, and Kimber had been hanging out with a Fae boy who I thought at the time might be her boyfriend. Though come to think of it, if he'd been her boyfriend, she'd have talked to me about him by now. And it wasn't like they'd been all over each other or anything.

Kimber leaned over the table and lowered her voice even more. "I assume you mean Owain. He's a friend, but . . ." She stared at her tea as she swirled the cup around. "The members of the Underground all know I'm younger than them and treat me like a kid. Owain flirts a little, but I know he doesn't really mean it."

"Do you want him to mean it?"

She frowned in thought. "No," she said at last with a resigned sigh. "He's a nice guy, but he doesn't really . . . do it for me, if you know what I mean."

That I did. "But Keane does?" I prompted, hoping I was keeping my highly annoying and inappropriate jealousy deeply hidden.

Her smile turned mischievous. "I'm not sure yet, but I think it's a possibility."

"You're nuts," I replied with authority. "Or a glutton for punishment."

"If I only liked to hang out with people who were agreeable, what would I be doing here with you?"

I threw my little wooden stirrer at her. She laughed and ducked. She needn't have bothered, not with my lousy aim and the poor aerodynamics of wooden stirrers. I tried to imitate Keane's fierce scowl, but that was hard to do when fighting laughter.

Kimber sat up straight, still giggling. But then her eyes focused on someone or something behind me, and the laughter died.

"Shite," she said.

I looked over my shoulder to see what had bothered her. And that's when I saw Ethan threading his way between the tables toward us.

My heart made a strange, fluttery feeling in my chest, and my breath caught in my throat at the sight of him. When I'd first met him, his looks had struck me speechless, but I'd been in Avalon long enough now that I was getting used to the other-worldly beauty of the Fae. So it wasn't his looks that made my insides start doing backflips.

I licked the taste of Faerie Rose tea off my lips and put my cup down. I'd been prepared to have to face Ethan eventually, because I knew he wasn't through with me, but I certainly wasn't prepared to face him *now*. Then again, there's a distinct possibility I was lying to myself and I'd never have been prepared.

Out of the corner of my eye, I checked on Finn and my dad. My dad tolerated Kimber, despite her being Unseelie and Alistair's daughter. He was less fond of Ethan, whether for political reasons or just because Ethan was a guy. I half expected Dad to chase Ethan away—or have Finn do it for him—but they both held their positions.

Great. No rescue from that quarter. I turned to Kimber, hoping she'd help me shoo her brother, but the traitor smiled sadly at me, then pushed her chair back and headed into the shop, claiming she wanted a different kind of tea. I glared holes in her back as she retreated.

I heard the scrape of metal on stone as Ethan pulled out a chair and sat, but I refused to look at him. I picked up my tea and sipped it just to have something to do.

Ethan sighed heavily. "Tiffany—the girl you saw me with at the party—is an ex. *Very* ex."

I snorted. "Yeah, I could tell by the way she was hanging all over you." I stared into my pretty pink tea, but couldn't bring myself to take another sip. I'd have to unclench my jaw to do that, and I wasn't about to.

Ethan sighed again. "She'd been drinking. She hung all over the next three guys she danced with, too."

I finally found the courage to look at him. His teal blue eyes had a haunted look to them, and for half a second, I almost felt sorry for him. Maybe I hadn't really seen enough to justify being so jealous. Then I remembered the way Ethan had looked at the redhead—Tiffany—and I knew I wasn't making something out of nothing.

He must have seen my opinion of him in my eyes, because he squirmed and dropped his own gaze.

"I'd probably had a little too much to drink myself," he admitted. "I don't claim to be a saint, but trust me when I say that two months dating Tiffany was about one month too long."

I rolled my eyes at him. "Yeah, it looked like you were hating every minute of being on the dance floor with her. If this is the best you've got, you might as well leave."

To my surprise, Ethan actually blushed a little. "I can't make myself not notice when a girl is sexy. When I first started going out with her, that was *all* I noticed. But I was with her long enough to know what she's like underneath the pretty trappings, and it isn't pretty at all. I can't help liking the way she looks, but I have no interest in *her.* If I'd known you were going to be there . . ."

His voice trailed off, probably because my glare was ferocious enough to be scary. If Ethan thought it was okay to flirt with other girls just because I wasn't there, it was one more piece of evidence that I was better off without him. Now, if only I could convince *myself* of that fact . . .

Ethan sat back in his chair and folded his arms across his chest. He dropped the hangdog look, raising his chin and meeting my eyes with something that looked like a challenge.

"What about Keane?" he asked.

I blinked at him, startled by the change in subject. "What *about* him?" I asked. He gave me a knowing look, but I remained clueless.

Ethan shook his head, and a muscle in his jaw twitched. "I guess you never once noticed his looks, huh?"

"What?" I cried, my jaw dropping.

Ethan looked exasperated. "Don't act so shocked. He's a nice Seelie boy who comes with an automatic seal of approval from your father. And I know girls go for that whole bad-boy thing he's got going on. You mean to tell me there's nothing going on between the two of you?"

I honestly couldn't think what to say. It had never occurred to me that *Ethan* might be jealous. I was too focused on my own jealousy to consider the possibility. And let's face it, before coming to Avalon, I'd been such a loner that I wasn't really used to boys being interested in me. This was uncharted territory.

"He's just teaching me self-defense," I said, but it sounded lame even to me.

"Uh-huh. Now compare how many hours a week you spend with him and how many hours a week you spend with me."

My cheeks were heating with a blush. It was true that I spent a lot more time with Keane, but that was hardly my fault. Unfortunately, it was also true that I'd noticed more than once that Keane was a hottie. Maybe I wasn't in a position to throw stones after all. That didn't mean I was going to admit it.

"I spend even more time with Finn," I retorted. "Are you going to get jealous of him, too?" The spike of guilt his words had caused started to recede. "Are you trying to tell me you started flirting with that Tiffany girl because you were jealous of Keane? So what, you did it to try to make *me* jealous? Even though you didn't think I'd be at the party?"

I didn't get a chance to hear his answer, because all of a sudden, the air filled with the deafening roar of motorcycles.

chapter ten

The Erlking must have been doing some kind of magic to muffle the roar of the bikes, because by the time I heard them, they were practically on top of us. Cries of alarm filled the air as the Wild Hunt effortlessly wove through the pedestrians and onto the patio as people scattered and scrambled out of the way. Ethan and I both knocked over our chairs leaping to our feet.

"Dana!" my dad shouted, and I saw both him and Finn sprinting across the short distance that separated us.

They were Fae, and therefore fast, but not as fast as the bikes. Before they could reach me, the Wild Hunt pulled its little circle trick again, the bikes barely an inch apart, surrounding my table, forming a wall between me and my bodyguards. Dad was shouting something, but I couldn't hear it over the roar of the bikes.

Magic prickled over my skin, and I was pretty sure it came from Ethan. He was a magical prodigy, capable of spells no one his age should be able to cast, but I seriously doubted he was a match for the Wild Hunt.

A slight gap opened up between a pair of the circling bikes, and the Erlking strode through it. He was wearing the same frightening leathers he'd worn the last time I'd seen him, but he'd ditched the helmet. He smiled at me, but there was no hint of warmth in it.

My mouth had gone completely dry, and I think I was even shaking a bit. Without thinking about it, I reached for Ethan's hand. His palm was sweaty, but I didn't mind. The Erlking noticed the gesture and raised an eyebrow, but didn't comment.

I reminded myself that as scary as the Erlking was, he couldn't hurt me. Somehow, that wasn't very comforting when his Hunt had me trapped and he was looming over me. I clung to Ethan's hand a little harder.

The Erlking bowed from the waist without ever taking his eyes off me. "We meet again, Faeriewalker," he said.

"Am I supposed to curtsy when you do that?" I asked. The quaver in my voice undermined my attempt at sarcasm.

Ethan poked me in the ribs with his elbow, but the Erlking laughed like I'd said something absolutely hilarious. The laugh even reached his cold blue eyes, though his first smile had not.

"You may curtsy if you like," he said, his lips still twitching in amusement. "However, it is not required."

I looked longingly past the riders and caught the occasional glimpse of Finn and my dad, standing helplessly outside the circle. They couldn't get to me without knocking the riders out of the way, and I suspected that would release the geis that kept them from attacking.

"What do you want?" I asked the Erlking.

"Don't talk to him, Dana," Ethan warned.

I didn't exactly *want* to talk to him, but if it would make him go away faster, I was all for it.

"What do you want?" I repeated, ignoring Ethan's dismayed groan.

The Erlking licked his lips like a dog about to chomp down on a bone. "I want the freedom to hunt like I did in the days of old," he said. "The Fae are adequate game, but the Queens dole them out far too rarely. I am lucky if I am allowed a handful of hunts a year. And, too, I long for more variety." The smile that stretched his lips now was pure evil. "Before Avalon seceded from Faerie, I could hunt the mortals here whenever I grew tired of hunting only the Fae the Queens allow me. I have not hunted a mortal for a century."

Oh, crap. I did *not* like where he was going with this.

"So what you're saying is you want me to use my Faeriewalker mojo to take you out into the mortal world so you can kill a bunch of people?"

He cocked his head to one side, looking puzzled. "If by 'mojo' you mean 'magic,' then yes."

"Um, let me think about that a minute," I said, tapping my chin. I didn't know where I was finding the nerve to be such a smartass with him, especially not when my knees were so wobbly it was a miracle I managed to stay standing.

I shook my head. "Nope. Don't think I can do that. Sorry."

I thought being denied might piss him off, but he surprised me by smiling again. When he let that smile reach his eyes, he was a thing of beauty. Terrifying beauty, but beauty nonetheless. "Ah, well. There was no harm in asking."

Somehow I didn't think he was planning to give up that easily.

"I guess we have nothing more to talk about, then," I said, trying to sound confident.

The Erlking's smile broadened, and he looked me up and down slowly. A shiver crawled up my spine. His eyes said he was mentally undressing me, and I had to glance down to convince myself his magic hadn't stripped my clothes away. My face burned with embarrassment as if I really *were* standing there naked in front of him.

"Stop it," Ethan said, letting go of my hand and stepping between me and the Erlking.

Once again, I felt the prickle of Ethan's magic. I didn't like having the Erlking leer at me like that, but I didn't want Ethan getting all protective and getting himself into trouble. Fae boys suffer from testosterone poisoning as badly as human ones do.

I reached out and put my hand on Ethan's arm, giving it a little pull so he was standing beside me instead of in front of me. He gave me a startled look, but didn't argue.

"Are you certain you can't be persuaded to ride with me?" the Erlking asked, and his voice was strangely different now, lower and huskier. Sexy, even, though in a way that gave me the shivers. "You might find the ride more enjoyable than you expect." He raised one eyebrow suggestively.

Beside me, Ethan stiffened, and his muscles went taut under my hand. It occurred to me exactly what the Erlking was doing, and it was almost a relief to see through it.

"Don't take the bait, Ethan," I said while keeping my eyes on the Erlking. "He's hoping you'll do something stupid so he can hurt you."

The Erlking shook his head, making a face of exaggerated

regret. "Alas, you see right through me, Faeriewalker. My wiles are wasted on you."

He finished by heaving a big sigh. Then the expression on his face changed, turning cold and menacing once again.

"'Tis a pity we cannot reach an agreement," he said. To my horror, he reached over his shoulder and grasped the pommel of the sword. "Faeriewalkers are born so seldom it's a shame to waste one."

The sword made an ominous hissing sound as it slid free of the scabbard. The metal shone as if there were a light inside it, and the blade was as long as my legs. It looked like it weighed a ton, but the Erlking held it in one hand like it weighed no more than a butter knife.

I shook my head, trying to hold on to my courage. "You can't hurt me," I said, hoping I sounded surer than I felt. "The geis won't let you."

He gave me another one of those cold smiles of his, the kind that didn't reach his eyes. "Is that so?" he asked. Then he swung the blade toward my neck.

I screamed and ducked. Beside me, Ethan bellowed in what sounded more like rage than fear. Instead of ducking or dodging the blade as any sensible person would do, he was surging forward. I screamed again when I saw the silver knife in his hand. He and Kimber always carried hidden knives. Kimber said it was because their affiliation with the Student Underground put them in danger. I tried to grab Ethan's arm to stop him, but my first instinct to duck made me too slow.

One corner of the Erlking's mouth rose in a triumphant smile as his blade passed harmlessly over my head. It wasn't because I'd ducked, either—he'd missed on purpose, had never had any intention of hurting me. But Ethan didn't know that.

The Erlking winked at me, then raised his arm to stave off Ethan's attack. He didn't even wince when Ethan's silver blade sliced through his leather jacket and drew a line of blood on his forearm.

I think at the last second, Ethan realized he'd been tricked, but it was too late and he couldn't stop in time.

"Too easy," the Erlking said, but he didn't sound a bit unhappy about it. Putting the sword back in its scabbard with one hand, he casually backhanded Ethan with the other.

Blood flew from Ethan's cheek as the blow knocked him back. He swayed for one moment, then his legs crumpled. I ran to his side as the Erlking examined the bloodied spikes on the back of his gauntlet.

I dropped to my knees beside Ethan, relieved to see that his chest still rose and fell with his breaths. How long that was going to last, I didn't know. My mind churned frantically, trying to figure out how I could save Ethan without doing anything that would allow the Erlking to attack me. I came up blank.

But when the Erlking squatted down on Ethan's other side, he made no hostile move. The smugness was gone, and when he met my eyes over Ethan's body, I thought I caught a hint of something sad in them. His voice when he spoke was surprisingly gentle, and so soft that only I could hear it.

"He is mine now, Faeriewalker." He reached down and plucked a strand of Ethan's long blond hair out of the blood that marred the side of his face. "His wound will heal within the hour, but he will not be the same man you once knew."

Tears spilled down my cheeks as he scooped Ethan's limp

body up and rose to his feet. I reached out, wanting to stop him, but not sure how.

He made a gesture with his chin, and the Wild Hunt quit circling us. They even left enough space between them for my father to slip through. I wanted to throw myself into my dad's arms and sob, but I was afraid if I moved or took my eyes off the Erlking, he'd disappear with Ethan.

The Erlking just stood there, Ethan's body completely limp in his arms, as my dad came to stand beside me. In one of his extra-demonstrative moments, Dad put his arm around my shoulders and gave them a squeeze. For a moment, I wondered if Dad was glad that the Erlking was removing Ethan from the field of play. Like I said, he'd never liked him. But that moment was fleeting.

There was a slight tremor in the arm that draped my shoulders, and I was able to tear my eyes from the Erlking to look up at my father's face.

His jaw was clenched so tight you could see the outlines of his bones, and I'd never before seen such fury in his eyes. His cheeks were flushed with it, and I was half convinced there really was such a thing as a look that could kill.

My dad's face isn't what I'd call expressive, but he was so shaken by what had just happened that he was completely unguarded. Under that murderous anger, there was such a weight of pain and sorrow that my own chest ached with it. I didn't know what that was all about, but I knew it couldn't be just because of Ethan.

The Erlking gave my dad one of those chilly smiles that didn't reach his eyes. "Will you fight me for this one, Seamus?" he asked. "Truly my Hunt would be honored to have one such as you in our midst."

Dad's arm slid off my shoulders, and both his hands clenched into fists beside him. "Leave my daughter alone, Arawn," my dad replied through clenched teeth.

The Erlking—Arawn, apparently—frowned in feigned puzzlement. "I have done your daughter no harm. And this one"—he raised and lowered Ethan's body briefly—"is no kin of yours."

Dad swallowed hard, and to my horror, there was what I could swear was a sheen of tears in his eyes.

The Erlking made no visible gesture, but one of the Huntsmen lowered the kickstand on his bike and dismounted. He kept his back turned to my dad and me while he unbuckled his helmet, then took it off and laid in on the seat of his bike. Long blond hair cascaded down his back. Then he turned around.

My dad made a horrible choking sound, and I reached out and grabbed his arm, afraid he was about to collapse.

The Huntsman's boots made metallic clicking sounds against the pavement as he came to stand by the Erlking's side. The Huntsman stared at my dad, his attention so focused you'd have thought there was no one else around.

My heart thudded against my breastbone, and for a moment I forgot to breathe as I stared at the unmasked Huntsman. He was a little shorter than my dad, and his chest was a lot broader. But his eyes were a dead match, and the shape of his face was just similar enough to make the resemblance unmistakable. A smaller version of the Erlking's tattoo curved around his brow and under his eye.

The Erlking handed Ethan to the Huntsman, who took him without looking away from my dad. There wasn't much of an expression on the Huntsman's face, but the look in his eyes was haunted.

"Connor," my dad said, his voice raw with pain.

The Erlking smiled wide, then patted Connor on the head like he was a pet dog. "I'm sure your son would greet you," he said, "but as I'm sure you know, my Huntsmen do not speak."

Even though I'd already begun to guess exactly what was happening, I couldn't help gasping.

I had a brother.

At least, a half brother. There was no way Connor had any mortal blood in him. He looked far too Fae for that.

The Erlking turned to look at Connor. Connor bowed his head at the Erlking, then cast one last longing look at my dad before he carried Ethan back to his bike. Ethan still hadn't regained consciousness. I didn't know how Connor was going to drive his bike with an unconscious man on it, but I had no doubt he would manage.

The Erlking focused his attention on me once more. "You might want to remind your father he still has a daughter to protect, Faeriewalker," he said. "While I would rejoice to have him join my Hunt, it would hardly be sporting of me to take him now."

I grabbed on to my dad's arm just as he started to take a step forward. He was shaking with rage, and the look in his eyes was so inhuman a part of me wanted to let go and run away.

"Don't, Dad," I said. "Please. I need you." I felt the tears streaming down my cheeks, and I didn't even know who I was crying for—Ethan, Connor, my dad, myself. Maybe all of the above.

Dad hesitated, but I could feel his urge to pull away in the tightness of his muscles. He looked at me briefly, then focused on the Erlking once more. I knew with every cell in my body that he was about one second short of throwing everything away in a futile attack. So I did the only thing I could think of that might stop him.

I threw my arms around my dad's waist, then buried my face against his chest and let my sobs loose.

For a long, agonizing moment, he just stood there stiffly, though at least he didn't push me away. Then slowly, tentatively, his arms closed around me.

I didn't look up as the sudden gunning of engines told me the Erlking and his Hunt were leaving.

chapter eleven

There was a lot of fuss and commotion after the Wild Hunt left, but I was in something of a state of shock and don't remember much about it. I remember Kimber having hysterics—she and Ethan fought constantly, but he *was* her brother, after all. I was in no shape to comfort her, and I doubted she'd have wanted my comfort anyway. It was because of me that the Erlking had taken Ethan, and a crushing sense of guilt almost over-whelmed my grief.

Dad and I ended up going to his house while Finn escorted Kimber home. Dad deposited me on the living room sofa, then headed upstairs to release my mom from her guest room/prison cell and tell her what happened.

I was out of tears by then, and a kind of numbness had settled over me. Unfortunately, the numbness didn't stop the guilt from gnawing away at me. The Erlking had used me to provoke Ethan into attacking him, and that made the whole thing my fault. Worse, I couldn't help thinking that the Erlking's interest in Ethan was entirely because of me in the first place.

I heard my mom and dad come downstairs, but I was too miserable to bother looking at them. Dad came to join me in the living room, and I could hear my mom clattering around in the kitchen, which meant she was making tea. Ugh. If I never saw another cup of tea again, it would be too soon.

No one said anything for a long time. I pried off my shoes, then put my feet on the sofa and hugged my knees to my chest. Dad sat on the love seat, staring at his hands. My mom brought in the tea tray and poured three cups in silence. I ignored mine.

"Tell me about Connor," I said to my dad when the silence became too much to bear. The fact that I had a brother I'd never even known about hadn't sunk in yet, which was maybe just as well.

Dad sighed heavily and shook his head. At first, I thought that meant he wasn't going to talk about it, but he surprised me.

"My firstborn," he said, his eyes fixed on the steam that rose from his tea. His voice was scratchy. He cleared his throat and took a sip of tea, but he didn't sound any better when he continued.

"Long ago, when the Erlking hunted unchecked through Faerie, I was Titania's consort."

I gasped. My dad had been described to me, before I'd met him, as "one of the great Seelie lords." I knew that meant he was an important figure in the Seelie Court—though technically, as a citizen of Avalon, he wasn't supposed to owe allegiance to the Court—but it had never occurred to me that he had once been the Queen's consort.

"She rarely keeps a consort more than a century or so, but those who have provided her with offspring tend to last longer.

I know she was tiring of me near the end, was already looking for my replacement. But then she had Connor, and I rose in her esteem once more.

"My son won me another century by Titania's side. But then she decided it was time to put a stop to the Erlking's marauding. She sent a contingent of Knights, led by Connor, to hunt him down and kill him. Only, as I've told you, the Erlking cannot be killed. He and his Huntsmen killed all the Knights in Connor's army, but he decided to send a more . . . powerful message to Titania by binding Connor to the Wild Hunt. It was Connor's abduction that finally convinced both the Queens that they had to make a deal with the Erlking."

"A deal that didn't include letting Connor go?" I asked, my voice rising despite the numbness. I would have thought freeing her son would have been Titania's primary motivation in making a deal with the Erlking. Then again, the Fae are not human, and the ones who live in Faerie don't even make a pretense at it.

Dad closed his eyes in obvious pain. "I know she tried to get him back," he said. "But the Erlking wouldn't give him up." He opened his eyes and looked at me, and although I could still see the pain in his expression, there was sympathy as well. "It is a point of pride with him never to release anyone he has captured."

My throat tightened, and my eyes stung, hinting that maybe I wasn't all cried out after all. "There has to be a way . . ." I started to say before the tightness of my throat stopped my voice.

"Titania herself couldn't find a way to make him release Connor," my dad said, shaking his head. "Ethan is gone, too, and there will be no saving him."

I swallowed the protest that wanted to rise to my lips. Maybe the Seelie Queen hadn't had the kind of leverage I had with the Erlking. After all, *she* wasn't a Faeriewalker. *She* couldn't give him access to the mortal world.

My thoughts came to a screeching halt. Yeah, I might have something the Erlking wanted. But I'd already determined it was something I could never give him. I'd seen how easily and remorselessly the Erlking killed. I couldn't unleash him on the defenseless humans of the mortal world. Not even to save Ethan.

"I know what he wants from you, Dana," my dad said, and I supposed it wasn't hard for anyone who knew I was a Faeriewalker to figure that out. "You mustn't give it to him."

Anger welled in my chest, and I'd probably have said something I'd later wish to take back if my mom hadn't startled me by putting her arms around me and pulling me into a hug.

"Give our daughter more credit than that, Seamus," she said, and she sounded about as angry as I felt. "I can't even believe you would *consider* the possibility that she would help the Wild Hunt enter the mortal world."

I felt my dad's hand briefly touching the top of my head, though I hadn't heard him move from the love seat to the sofa.

"The Erlking is an ancient evil," he said, and I think he meant the words for both of us. "He is a master at getting what he wants, and a sixteen-year-old girl—no matter how sensible she might be—is no match for him."

I pulled away from my mother's arms and glared at him. "Just stop it, okay? I don't *want* to be sensible right now! Can't you at least wait until tomorrow to try to convince me you're always right about everything?"

I knew that wasn't what he was trying to do, but right that moment, I didn't care. I didn't want logic or reality or morality. I just wanted to be comforted, to be told everything was going to be okay, even though it wasn't.

The Fae are reserved by nature, and seeing Connor had shaken my dad enough that he'd actually let me see how he was feeling for a while. But it wasn't enough. I wanted the father I'd always daydreamed about having, the one who would protect me and nurture me and love me. Not the one who would try to explain to me after the worst day of my life that it would be wrong for me to let a homicidal maniac loose in the mortal world.

Suddenly, I couldn't stand to be in his presence anymore. I sprang up from the couch, shaking off my father's arm when he tried to reach for me. The bedroom upstairs was no longer mine, but my mother's; however, it was the only place I could think of to go to get away from my dad.

With a fresh round of tears already on their way, I slammed open the door to the stairwell and charged up the stairs two at a time.

It took a while to get control of myself again. Every time I thought the tears were going to slack off, I'd come up with a new round of reasons why everything that had gone wrong was my fault. If only I'd found the strength to just deal with my mom and her problem, I'd never have come to Avalon, and Ethan would never have been captured by the Erlking.

The only thing that finally allowed me to stop the pity party was my absolute determination not to give up on Ethan. My dad might think it was impossible to save him from the Wild Hunt, but damn it, I was going to find a way. *Without* letting the Erlking go on a killing spree.

I went into the bathroom to splash some cold water on my face, then made the mistake of looking at myself in the mirror. I was not a pretty sight. My eyes were all red and puffy, and my hair was stuck to the tear tracks on my cheeks. I took a couple deep breaths, then cleaned myself up as best I could. My eyes still looked like crap when I was done, but at least I'd managed to brush out the tangles in my hair and get it pulled back into a neat ponytail.

My plan was to go downstairs and apologize to my dad for blowing up at him. I still thought he should have known I wouldn't lead the Wild Hunt out into the mortal world for their version of fun and games, but I knew I'd overreacted. After all, it was obvious that seeing Connor had hurt him. Much as losing Ethan hurt me, I doubted it could compare to the pain of losing a son.

My mom intercepted me before I could go talk to my dad. She was waiting for me when I stepped out of the bathroom.

"I know you haven't grown to love tea," she said, holding up a mug, "so I made you some coffee."

Damn if my throat didn't start tightening again. I swallowed hard and managed to hold it together. "Thanks," I said, taking the mug from her and wrapping my hands around it. The only coffee my dad kept in the house was instant, but it was better than nothing. I took a sip and managed not to grimace. At least it was warm and soothing.

Mom sat on the edge of the bed, then patted the mattress beside her to indicate I should sit down. Despite my intention to apologize to my dad, I can't say I was in any hurry, so I was perfectly happy to obey. She put her hand on my back and rubbed up and down while I sipped my coffee. I usually would have shaken her off, but right now, I was too desperate for comfort.

"You really like this boy, don't you?" she asked softly.

I squirmed a bit. Mom and I didn't exactly have a warm and cuddly relationship. I'd never talked boys with her, and I certainly hadn't told her much about Ethan. I didn't exactly feel like talking now, but Mom was reaching out to me in a way she never had when she was drinking. If I shrugged her off, she might never try it again.

"I guess," I told her. "It's kind of complicated, though."

I didn't look at her, but I could hear her smile in her voice. "It always is."

I made a little sound that was almost a laugh, then took another sip of terrible coffee as I gathered my thoughts. "I don't think it would make a difference if I hated his guts," I said. "I'd still feel awful that he was hurt because of me."

"It's not your fault, honey."

I shook my head. "Yes, it is. The only reason the Erlking targeted Ethan was because of me. If I'd just listened to you when you'd tried to warn me about Avalon . . ." It showed a bit about my state of mind that I would actually make that argument. My mom had told me so many conflicting stories about my dad and about Avalon that I'd had no idea what to believe. I'd finally decided I would have to see for myself, and that's what had started this whole nightmare.

Out of the corner of my eye, I saw my mother wince. "That's hardly your fault," she said, looking unhappy. "I know I didn't make it easy for you to know what to believe. Maybe if I hadn't tried to embellish the story to make you not want to come . . ."

Maybe she hoped I would let her off the hook for that, but I wasn't about to. We were having a warm, mother/daughter moment here, but that certainly didn't mean I was ready to forgive her for the wreck she'd made of her life and mine.

She shook her head and continued as if she hadn't been expecting me to say anything. "Then again, if you hadn't come, you'd never have met your father. I know he's not perfect, and I hate that you've had to go through so much, but I am glad you got to meet him. And that he got to meet you. I always felt so terrible about hiding you from him . . ."

"Did you know about Connor?" I asked, watching her face carefully in search of a lie. I don't know whether knowing I had a half-brother would have had any effect on me, either growing up or since I came to Avalon, but it would be yet another strike against her if she'd known and hadn't told me. And seeing as she hadn't told my dad he had a daughter, I couldn't help suspecting her.

"No," she answered, and something about the pained look in her eyes convinced me she was telling the truth. "He never talked about it. I knew he'd lost someone who mattered to him to the Wild Hunt, but I didn't know who it was, and I didn't know whether 'lost' meant dead, or captured."

"Would you have told me if you'd known?"

Back when she was drinking, Mom didn't hesitate to lie to me. It didn't matter how blatant the lie was, or how obviously I didn't believe her—if it was a choice between telling the distasteful truth or making something up, she'd make something up. I suspect this particular question would have warranted a lie in her mind back then; now she told me the truth with a grimace.

"Probably not, honey," she admitted. "What purpose could it possibly have served?"

On the one hand, I was glad she was being honest with me. On the other hand, she was honestly telling me that she wouldn't have told me the truth.

I shook my head at her. "Why would it have had to serve a purpose? Wouldn't I have the right to know I had a brother? I'm not a little kid anymore, Mom. You don't need to protect my delicate sensibilities, or whatever the hell you think you need to do."

I couldn't miss the hurt in my mom's eyes. Great. First I'd picked a fight with Dad, now I was going for round two with Mom. I could hardly expect myself to be Little Miss Sunshine under the circumstances, but I knew better than to lash out like that.

"Sorry," I mumbled, looking away from the hurt in her eyes.

She reached over and patted my back. "It's all right, honey. I know you're angry with me. You have every right to be."

I bit my tongue. Hard. She still didn't have a clue *why* I was angry with her. After all, we'd already established that she wouldn't admit she had a drinking problem. If she didn't have a drinking problem, then I couldn't be angry with her about it, right?

Someday, I was going to totally lose it and we were going to have a screaming argument about her drinking. But I didn't have the energy for it today. I just wanted to go home, crawl into bed, and pull the covers over my head. So I kept my mouth shut and stuffed my anger back down into its hiding place, where it could fester some more.

chapter twelve

My parents wanted me to spend the night at Dad's house. I guess they thought I was in need of their nurturing comfort or something. If I stayed, they'd probably expect me to talk to them and let them coddle me, and I was afraid I'd lose control of my fragile temper and make the evening even uglier than it already was. Besides, though my dad obviously had money, his house wasn't exactly huge, and my mom was in the only spare bedroom. Mom offered to sleep on the couch so I could have her room, but I refused.

Dad could have made me stay, of course. But I think he's the kind of guy who'd rather be left alone when he's miserable, so he understood where I was coming from.

Whatever the reason, he agreed to take me back to my safe house. Finn met us there, and when Dad left, I retreated to my suite to be alone with my thoughts.

I knew I should call Kimber to check and see how she was doing. But I *knew* how she was doing, and it was lousy. Calling her would be the right thing to do, but that night, I just didn't have it in me to do the right thing. I didn't want to face the guilt her grief would stir up. And I didn't want to cry anymore, which I knew I'd do the moment I heard her voice. Even looking at my freshly manicured nails practically set me off, and if I'd had any nail polish remover, I'd probably have put it to use. I thought about trying to call the magic again as a way to distract myself, but I wasn't sure I could sing even "Row, Row, Row Your Boat" right now. So instead, I went to bed way early, then lay there wide awake wondering if there was anything I could have done to save Ethan.

I must have fallen asleep eventually, because I woke up to the sound of someone pounding on my bedroom door. I groaned and tried to settle back down into the covers. Sleep was the greatest invention in the history of mankind. When I was sleeping, I wasn't feeling guilty, or miserable, or sad.

The pounding on the door continued until I realized that sleep was not among my options. I have one of those alarm clocks that gradually brightens in the morning so I didn't have to wake up to the pitch-black of the cave. When I finally forced my eyes open, I saw that the clock's light was at its brightest, so even though it took me a moment to focus my bleary eyes, I knew immediately that it was morning.

The pounding on my door was relentless. And annoying.

"All right!" I yelled. "I'm up." Why couldn't Finn just let me sleep? It wasn't like I had somewhere I had to be.

"Sorry to wake you," Finn called through the door. He didn't sound very sorry. "Keane's been waiting over an hour, and I figured that was enough."

It took like five minutes for me to process what Finn said. Then I remembered this was Tuesday morning, which is one of my regularly scheduled lesson days with Keane. A glance at the clock told me it was well after ten, and my lessons usually started at the ungodly hour of nine.

I pushed my sleep-matted hair out of my eyes and stifled a curse. I hadn't expected Keane to show up today. I know life goes on and everything, but still . . .

I'd have tried to crap out on the lesson, but I knew Keane too well. He'd come into my room and drag me out of bed if he had to, then carry me over his shoulder to the practice mats.

"Tell him I'll be out in a few minutes," I said with resignation.

Usually, I shower before our sparring sessions, even though I know I'll land right back in the shower as soon as the lesson's over. Today, I just didn't feel like it. I was pretty sure I didn't stink, although one glance in the bathroom mirror was almost enough to make me flee in terror. Yeah, I looked that bad.

I brushed my teeth, washed my face, then combed out the tangles in my hair and arranged it in a messy knot at the back of my head. Then, still yawning, I dressed in yoga pants and a form-fitting tank top. When I'd first started training, I'd worn loose, comfortable T-shirts. I'd quickly discovered that loose, comfortable T-shirts don't do such a great job of keeping you covered when you spend half of your time upside down or being dragged across mats. It still made me blush to think of the up-close-and-personal look Keane had gotten of my bra. (Thank God I'd been wearing one! I'm flat-chested enough that I could go without.)

Keane was waiting for me in the sitting room. The furniture

had already been moved aside, and he'd laid out the mats. It was the usual routine, and yet when I got a look at his face, I saw that at least part of the usual routine was missing.

Keane is all about arrogance and attitude, and his catalog of facial expressions usually runs to smirks, smugness, and glowers. Today, he looked different. Whatever he was feeling, I wouldn't call it a happy emotion. Was it because he knew what had happened with Ethan yesterday? Or was he still sulking about how his dad had kicked his butt in front of me?

Whatever it was, I didn't want to deal with it. Hell, I didn't want to deal with *anything*.

I gave myself a mental slap upside the head. Ethan hadn't wanted to be captured by the Wild Hunt, either. What we want out of life and what we get are two entirely different stories.

I wondered what was happening to Ethan right now. Was his wound all healed? What had the Erlking done to him? Ethan was apparently destined to become a member of the Wild Hunt, but what did that entail? I remembered the Erlking saying that his Huntsmen don't talk, and I shuddered as my mind tried to send me pictures of just what he might have done to them to keep them mute.

Damn it, tears were burning my eyes again. I blinked fiercely, determined to keep them back. Crying wasn't going to save Ethan, and it wasn't going to make me feel any better.

Keane proved to me once again that he was all heart. While I stood there in the doorway trying to get control of myself, he crossed the distance between us in a couple of long strides. Was he coming over to give me a hug, or commiserate with me, or tell me everything was going to be all right?

Not exactly.

Before I had a chance to react, he'd grabbed me and yanked me forward, pulling me off balance and then sweeping my legs out from under me. I was completely unprepared for the attack, and I found myself heading face-first toward the stone floor, since we hadn't even gotten to the mats yet. Instinctively, I put my hands out to stop my fall, but Keane grabbed me under the arms and hauled me to my feet before I hit the floor. He then shoved me, hard, onto the mats.

Graceful as a wounded rhinoceros, I tripped over the edge of the mats and went sprawling. I'd had enough lessons with Keane by now to know that I didn't dare lie there and catch my breath, so I rolled quickly to the right, avoiding Keane's pounce. I hadn't secured my hair well enough, and a strand came loose to dangle in my face.

I pushed to my feet, my body going on autopilot now that the lesson had started—whether I was ready for it or not. Keane was frowning at me and shaking his head.

"How many times have I warned you not to put your hands out like that?" he barked, doing his best drill-sergeant impersonation. "You could have broken your damn wrists!"

I tried not to flinch. I'd thought I'd gotten used to the way he yelled at me when we sparred, but I guess I was in a particularly fragile state of mind. It was true, though, that Keane had spent a lot of time teaching me how to fall, and taking the full impact on my outstretched hands wasn't in the lesson plan.

Usually, I'd have had some kind of snappy comeback. Well, at least a lame comeback that I could pretend was snappy. Today, I kept quiet and wished I'd stayed in bed. Keane wouldn't have been able to come drag me out if I'd hit the panic button and lowered the security doors in the hallway.

Keane must have been in as foul a mood as I was. Instead of waiting for me to say something or to brace myself, he swung his fist at my head. Once again, my body went on autopilot, and without thinking about it, I stepped into the punch, taking away his momentum, while sweeping my arm up to block it. I was too slow to block it completely, and ended up taking the blow on my shoulder.

I know Keane holds back during our sparring sessions, but that doesn't mean it doesn't hurt when he hits me. When we'd first started, the pain had often shocked me into immobility, at least for a moment. Today, it just made me mad. I countered with a kick to his knee that would almost certainly have broken something if it weren't for his shield spell.

We were fighting in earnest now, my entire being concentrating on blocking his blows and evading his holds, while still looking—unsuccessfully—for a way to get through his defenses. There was no actual teaching going on, not right now anyway. If my brain weren't so busy trying to keep me in one piece, I might have wondered what had gotten into Keane this morning.

I was doing a pretty good job of defending myself, but each blocked punch or kick hurt, and the pain made me madder and madder, until finally I threw a punch of my own.

My lessons with Keane were all about self-defense, not offense. Yeah, I'd learned to kick and punch and grab, but always with the goal of learning to momentarily disable my attacker so I could get away. I was only supposed to attack the most vulnerable parts of his body with the least vulnerable parts of my own. Which was why I took us both by surprise when my fist made contact with his jaw.

If he'd been a real bad guy, it would have been a terrible decision. I'm not strong enough to do a lot of damage with a punch, unless it's to something really sensitive. Plus there's the little-advertised fact that, duh, when you smash your fist against something hard, it hurts, and jaw bones tend to be pretty damn hard. So do the shield spells Fae fighters use to protect themselves.

I felt the impact all the way up my arm to my shoulder, and for a moment my fingers went completely numb. I had half a second to register the surprise on Keane's face—and to feel a malicious thrill of triumph—before the numbness went away and my hand screamed with pain.

I half-expected Keane to take advantage of my distraction—he wasn't exactly taking it easy on me today—but I couldn't help cradling my hand against my body, gritting my teeth against the pain. It left me completely undefended, but at that moment I didn't care.

Keane heaved a dramatic sigh and reached for me. "Let me see it," he said in a long-suffering tone.

I jerked out of his reach, anger still simmering in my veins. "Don't touch me!" My knuckles throbbed to the beat of my heart. I saw no evidence that my punch had actually hurt him. Surprising him seemed to be the best I could do. Somehow, that wasn't quite as satisfying.

Keane rolled his eyes. "Don't be a drama queen. Let me see the hand. If it's just bruised, I can heal it. If you broke something, we need to get you to the emergency room."

"I didn't break anything." At least, I hoped I hadn't.

"Then let me heal it."

Even the least powerful of the Fae have enough power to

heal minor injuries like bruises. Keane, with his Knight heritage, could heal more serious ones than the average Fae, but fixing broken bones was beyond his capabilities. It was a sign of Ethan's magical genius that he could heal broken bones even though he was neither a healer nor a fighter.

Thinking of Ethan took the last of the fight out of me, and I meekly held out my hand for Keane to examine. The knuckles still throbbed, and my middle finger was starting to swell. I tensed in anticipation as Keane ran his fingers lightly over the back of my hand, examining the damage.

Considering what a hardass he was as a teacher, he was surprisingly gentle with me now as he prodded and poked and forced my fingers to move. Gentle or not, it still hurt, and it took all my willpower not to yank my hand out of his grasp.

"Not broken," he finally declared with a nod.

I let out a sigh of relief. I needed a trip to the emergency room like I needed another enemy out to kill me. I expected to feel the tingle of Keane's magic gathering, but instead he let go of my hand and went to pull the coffee table away from the couch.

"You'll want to sit down for this," he said in reply to my questioning look. "Unless you want to go to the hospital after all. A real healer can make your hand go numb before fixing the damage, but I can't."

I shrugged and walked to the couch. "You've healed bruises for me before, and I haven't swooned." I put my wrist to my forehead in the classic damsel-in-distress swooning pose.

Keane's lip twitched like he almost smiled—imagine that! But he didn't change his mind. He sat on the couch and patted the seat beside him.

"This is different. There's more damage, and fingers are super sensitive. It won't last long, but it'll hurt like a bitch."

Fantastic. Just the thing to cheer me out of my doldrums. But if I let Keane take care of it, it would all be over in a couple of minutes. If I insisted on seeing a real healer, I might not be able to get an appointment—and assemble an entourage my dad would approve of—for hours.

I plopped down heavily on the sofa, grabbing a throw pillow and clutching it to my chest with my left arm as I once again let Keane take my right. Gripping my wrist firmly with one hand, he laid my hand on his lap. The touch might have been embarrassingly intimate if I hadn't been hurting so much.

The pain didn't improve when Keane used his other hand to coax my swelling finger as straight as it would go. I probably should have closed my eyes, or at least looked the other way, because seeing the redness and swelling made me a bit queasy. Still, I couldn't help watching in sickening fascination as his fingers lightly stroked mine.

"Dana."

I almost jumped at the sound of his voice. I tore my gaze away from my wounded hand and met Keane's stunning emerald eyes.

"Sorry," he whispered, his eyes narrowing in a wince even as he held my gaze. I belatedly realized he'd distracted me on purpose, but the pain hit before I had a chance to tense up in anticipation.

I'd thought the pain when I'd first hit him was bad. The healing was far, far worse. The electric tingle of Keane's magic prickled, and then it felt like a car had just run over my hand, breaking every bone into tiny fragments. I couldn't fight my instinctive urge to pull away, but Keane held my hand trapped against his thigh as his magic sank into my flesh.

If it had lasted even a millisecond longer, I wouldn't have been able to hold back a scream. As it was, I managed to limit myself to a pained whimper.

The pain stopped as suddenly as it had begun, although Keane didn't release my hand. I let out a shuddering sigh as he ran his fingertips across my skin. The touch was almost like a caress, and now that the pain had stopped, I couldn't help noticing that my hand was almost within touching distance of something I had no desire to touch. Funny how I failed to pull away, even when I noticed that.

I glanced at Keane's face but was unable to tell what he was thinking. Was he stroking my hand like that because he was searching for signs of more injuries? His touch felt too much like a caress for that. But I was like a bratty kid sister to him, so why would it be a caress?

No way he was coming on to me, I told myself firmly as he let go of my hand and I fought the urge to leave it right where it was. Keane didn't even like me, much less *like* me. And what kind of a slut did it make me that I was even *thinking* about this when Ethan had just been kidnapped? Maybe Ethan's jealousy hadn't been as misplaced as I'd thought . . .

I held my hand up in front of my face and examined my now-healed fingers, wiggling them experimentally. They all moved on command, and there was no residual pain.

"Good as new," I said, a little breathlessly. But I was just breathless because the healing had hurt so much, not because I was reacting to Keane's touch. That's my story, and I'm sticking to it.

"Good," Keane said, then folded his arms over his chest and gave me one of his disapproving-teacher looks. "Now, want to tell me what that was all about?"

My eyes widened. "You're asking me? I'm not the one who went on the attack without even saying hello."

He gave me one of his smug looks, the kind I hated. "You think the bad guys are going to warn you before they attack?" He unfolded his arms and did a manly-man pose, making his voice comically deep. "Excuse me, miss, but I thought I should warn you I'm about to try to kill you. Please prepare to defend yourself."

"Hardee-har-har," I growled. "You're so funny I'm about to die laughing." I remembered the strange look on his face when I'd first entered the room, and I had a hard time believing he was telling me the truth, the whole truth, and nothing but the truth. Something had prompted him to be especially aggressive today, and it wasn't just part of his lesson plan.

"So," he continued, "what was with the Muhammad Ali impersonation?" He rubbed his jaw approximately where I'd hit him, but I doubted it was because I'd hurt him.

Much as he'd annoyed me, I had to admit, it was my fault I'd gotten hurt. I knew better than to punch him in the face. We'd fought for maybe five minutes—probably less—and I'd made two major mistakes, both of which could easily have been fatal in a real fight. I'm not what you'd call a pro at this self-defense stuff, but that was bad even for me.

"I can't do this today," I said, shaking my head. "I can't act normal. And anything you try to teach me is going to go in one ear and out the other."

There was a long, uncomfortable silence, and I glanced over

at him again. His eyes were closed, and a muscle ticked in the side of his jaw. Why he would get so bent out of shape about me not wanting my lesson was a mystery. When he spoke, it sounded like he was forcing the words out through clenched teeth.

"The bad guys aren't going to wait until you're in the mood for a fight."

I made a sound between a huff of exasperation and a growl. "I'm sick to death of that argument. I don't care what you think. I need a day off after seeing my . . ." My voice trailed off, because I'd been about to call Ethan my boyfriend, and I'd made it clear to both him and me that he was no such thing. I swallowed hard. ". . . my friend captured by the Wild Hunt because he was trying to defend me."

If I'd hoped talking about my trauma would make Keane take pity on me, I was sadly mistaken.

"I'm sorry about what happened," he said. "I wouldn't wish that on anyone. But if you think Ethan Leigh is your friend, you're deluded."

I gaped at him. Where was all *this* coming from?

"Tell me you weren't falling for his song and dance," Keane continued, giving me an intense stare that made me squirm.

"Oh for God's sake! Don't tell me you're jealous." It wasn't like Keane had any cause to be jealous. He and I weren't even friends, much less dating. And I couldn't imagine Keane being jealous of Ethan's success with girls. I suspected girls fell at Keane's feet on a regular basis.

"All right: I'm not jealous," Keane said, and he sounded like he meant it, despite the way his eyes flashed dangerously.

"You don't even know him!" I said, ignoring his claim. I knew jealousy when I saw it, and I was looking right in its face.

Keane gave me an incredulous look. "Says who?"

I stammered, because, of course, I had no idea if the two of them knew each other. I'd just assumed they didn't.

"There are exactly two secondary schools in Avalon," he said, his voice tight with repressed anger. "I had the bad luck of going to the same one as your 'friend' Ethan. There may have been a couple of girls in our class he failed to hit on, but only because they were ugly. As soon as he got what he wanted from one, he'd move on to the next. Even if his next target already had a boyfriend. That just made it more of a challenge for him. His ego was far more important to him than anyone's feelings. You're fooling yourself if you think you're the one who's going to make an honest man out of him. That's what he wants *all* of his conquests to believe."

I didn't know what to say. I knew Ethan had a reputation as a player. And I'd seen for myself how easily he turned on the charm—and how determined he was to get his way once he'd set his sights on someone. But there was more to him than that, I was sure of that. *Much* more.

"He saved my life," I said in a hoarse whisper. "He jumped into the moat when Grace threw me over. He knew all about the Water Witches, and he jumped in anyway."

Keane made a sound of frustration and leapt to his feet, quickly turning his back on me. I remembered how he'd failed to visit me while I was in the hospital recuperating from the Water Witch's attack. I'd been puzzled by it at the time, but now I wondered if maybe he'd been pissed off because I'd run off with Ethan. Not that there'd been anything romantic about it, though I supposed Keane couldn't know that.

"Would you rather he'd let the Water Witch get me?" I asked Keane's back.

He turned to look at me again. "Of course not. I'm glad he was there, and I'm glad he saved you. I despise him, but I won't claim he has no redeeming features. I just . . ." He shook his head, then bent to start rolling up the mats.

"You just what?" I asked.

He continued rolling. "Let it go, Dana."

"No. You're the one who came into my home and started saying hateful things about a guy who got captured by the Wild Hunt because he was trying to defend me. If you're going to start something, you're sure as hell going to finish it."

He shoved the rolled-up mat out of the way so hard it bounced off the wall. He was still kneeling on the floor as he turned to glare at me. It was a weird expression, because as pissed off as he looked, there was also a world of pain in his eyes, pain I didn't understand.

Something clicked in my brain, and I winced in sudden sympathy. "One of those girls Ethan went after in school was your girlfriend, right?" That would certainly explain the level of rivalry I'd seen between the two of them.

Keane neither confirmed nor denied my guess, but I knew I was right. Eventually, the intensity of his eyes was too much, and I let my gaze slide away. When I looked up again, it was to see Keane's back as he left without another word.

chapter thirteen

After Keane left, I wished I'd kept my mouth shut and had my lesson, even if it meant getting my butt kicked and making embarrassingly stupid mistakes. While we'd been sparring, there hadn't been enough time for me to brood about Ethan. Plus, even though it hurt, I had to admit that in my current state of mind it felt kinda good to hit things.

Once Keane was gone, I couldn't get my brain to shut up. Wave after wave of guilt beat at me, especially because I still couldn't get myself to pick up the phone and call Kimber. We were best friends, and she had to be hurting. Her father had made no secret of the fact that he loved Ethan more, because Ethan was the magical prodigy. I doubted she was getting a whole lot of paternal comfort right now. She needed me, but I was too much of a coward to face her.

In an attempt to keep my mind occupied with anything other than Ethan, I tried once more to learn how to use magic. My voice was weak and quavery, but I felt the magic come to me before I'd even finished the first scale. I tried to feel excited at the improvement, but it was too hard to be impressed when I couldn't cast even the simplest spell.

Eventually, I gave up in disgust. Maybe my affinity with magic went no further than being able to sense it and call it. Maybe all the practice in the world was futile. I wished I'd decided to trust Ethan and asked him to teach me magic. Now I'd never get the chance . . .

I shook my head to try to erase that thought from my mind. Ethan was *not* going to be a permanent member of the Wild Hunt. His father was a powerful man. Maybe he'd be able to find a way to reason with the Erlking where my father had not. There had to be *something* someone could do.

Having grown up as the only responsible member of my household, one lesson I'd learned at an early age was that I couldn't really count on anyone other than myself. If I wanted to make sure we had electricity, I had to pay the bill myself. If my mom hurt herself and had to go to the emergency room, I had to get her there myself.

I remember one time when I was maybe six or seven, and my mom got a horrible case of food poisoning. She was so sick, I thought she was going to die. I wanted to call 911, but Mom said she wasn't that sick. Back then, I was still young enough to think I had to do as I was told.

I'd tried to get one of our relatively friendly neighbors to drive us to the hospital, but she wouldn't. I don't remember what the excuse was, but even then, I suspected the true reason she'd refused was because she didn't want my mom puking in her car. I'd eventually had to call a cab, and then practically drag my mom down the stairs to get her in. She was too out of it—I think she was drunk as well as sick—to pay the driver, and when I'd dug through her purse for money, I'd found only a couple of dollars. I still remember the sound of that driver's voice as he yelled at us, cursing and furious at being "cheated" of his fare.

When I'd come to Avalon, I'd been hoping that I would find in my father someone I could finally count on, someone who would take charge and fix problems for me. But I realized, in one of those peculiar moments of clarity I'd been having lately, that if anyone was going to save Ethan from the Wild Hunt, it would have to be me. I'd be pleasantly surprised if Ethan's father managed to do it himself, but it was time for me to stop hoping someone else would step up to the plate.

It was time to start planning Operation Rescue Ethan.

That sounded real good. Now, if only I had some clue how to go about it . . . How was I, a sixteen-year-old girl, supposed to defeat the ancient leader of the Wild Hunt? A leader even the Queens of Faerie were afraid of? I fought not to let myself drown in the apparent hopelessness of the task.

I spent several hours mulling over the problem, not coming to any helpful conclusions. My mind kept insisting that the only way to convince the Erlking to release Ethan was to offer to take the Wild Hunt out into the mortal world. I can't say there weren't times I was tempted to give in, but I knew I could never live with myself if I did. The Erlking, with all his magic intact because of my presence, would make Jack the Ripper's reign of terror seem small scale.

The phone rang late in the afternoon. I checked caller ID, but there was no name displayed and I didn't recognize the number. I figured it had to be a wrong number, but I couldn't help hoping it was Ethan, escaped from the Erlking's clutches, maybe calling from a pay phone or a borrowed cell.

"Hello?" I said, knowing my hope was wishful thinking, but unable to suppress it. I held my breath as I waited for the caller to speak.

"Hello, Faeriewalker," said the Erlking, and I gasped in shock.

"How did you get this number?" I demanded, although that was hardly important.

"My Huntsmen keep no secrets from me," he answered, sounding amused.

My heart lurched in my chest. I didn't know exactly what happened to people who were captured by the Hunt, what the Erlking did to them to keep them bound, but I should have guessed that anything Ethan knew about me, the Erlking would now know. Like my phone number.

Thank God Ethan didn't know the location of my safe house!

I wished I could think of something clever to say, something that would cut him down to size and show him I wasn't afraid of him. Instead, I just stood there like an idiot, holding the phone to my ear, my tongue glued to the roof of my mouth.

"He is quite the catch, your Ethan," the Erlking said. "Not as exalted as your brother, but his bloodline is more than respectable, and his powers are formidable."

My hand clenched around the phone. "Did you call just to gloat, or do you have something important to say?" My voice came out hoarse and raspy.

"A little of both," he replied. "But then, I suspect you know exactly why I've called, don't you, Faeriewalker?"

"My name is Dana!" I snapped, not sure why I cared what he called me.

"Dana. Of course. Do you know why I've called, Dana?"

There was only one reason I could think of. "Now that you've got Ethan as a hostage, you want to set up a trade." A trade my conscience wouldn't allow me to make, no matter how much I wanted to save Ethan.

"Very good. In the old days, before Avalon seceded from Faerie, I could have taken you by force. Of course, in the old days, I was free to hunt in Avalon to my heart's content, so I wouldn't have needed to. In these modern times, neither I nor my Huntsmen can hurt you even slightly, so I cannot use you to enter the mortal world without your consent. Give me that consent, and Ethan will be free to go. He would be the first person ever to be released from the Wild Hunt by anything but death."

I took a deep breath to steady my nerves. If I had any sense, I'd end this call immediately. I don't know if I ever would have been in any shape to negotiate with the Erlking, but I certainly wasn't at that moment. The grief and shock of losing Ethan were still too raw.

"You know I can't do that," I forced myself to say.

"I know no such thing. Perhaps you would not be able to stomach granting me unlimited access, but I would be happy to negotiate. I am not an unreasonable man."

No, because he wasn't really a *man* at all.

"Make me an offer," he said.

"Unless your plan is to go into the mortal world for sightseeing, I can't do it. I saw you kill that man when you first rode into Avalon. There's no way—" My voice choked off as I tried to block out the image of the Erlking bearing down on the fleeing Fae, sword raised and ready to strike.

"I am a hunter, Faerie— Dana," the Erlking said, his voice gentling. "That is the essential core of my being. I've no interest in visiting the mortal world for sightseeing. If we strike a bargain to go there together, I will hunt, and I will kill. Let there be no illusions between us."

A little sound, almost like a whimper, rose in my throat.

"I'm sorry that distresses you," he continued. "I bear you no ill will. But I don't think sugarcoating the truth will make it any more palatable. I am willing to consider making certain concessions in order to convince you to ride with me, but a hunt is not a hunt if the quarry does not die in the end."

"Then we have nothing to talk about," I said, though it was practically killing me. Bad enough that I already felt so guilty about what had happened to Ethan. Now the Erlking was rubbing my face in the fact that I could save him—if only I didn't mind sacrificing who knew how many strangers for the privilege.

"Perhaps you need some time to think it over. I'm not demanding that you make a decision this instant. You have my phone number now. If you decide you might like to negotiate after all, don't hesitate to call me."

Once again, I found myself at a loss for words. I expected the Erlking to hang up, or maybe give an evil laugh or something. But I obviously hadn't come close to figuring him out yet, because he did no such thing.

"Remember what I told you when we first met," he said. "I am not your enemy, even if we do at times find ourselves at cross-purposes."

I remembered him saying that, though he'd also pointed out that he wasn't my friend, either.

Thinking about our first meeting, I remembered the Erlking

warning Finn and me that we had an imposter in our midst. A "token of goodwill," he'd called it.

"It's been a pleasure speaking with you," he said, and I realized he was about to hang up.

"Wait!" I said, surprising myself.

I thought I was too late, but a moment later the Erlking said, "Go on."

"Why did you warn me about the imposter the other day?"

"I suspect you're clever enough to figure it out on your own. But then I've put you into a stressful situation, and I suppose that isn't conducive to clear thinking." He managed to say that without sounding particularly condescending, though I don't know how he managed it.

"I want something from you, Dana," he continued. "I want it very badly. If your enemies should kill you, they will ruin my chances of getting it. I am highly motivated to keep you alive." He laughed a little. "You may not feel it, but you are safer now than you have been from the moment you first set foot in Avalon. I will not let any harm come to you."

What the hell was I supposed to say to that? Thank you? Uh, no.

It didn't occur to me until after he hung up that the Erlking was suggesting my life had been in danger when I'd been out with Fake-Lachlan. But the imposter had been meaning to kidnap me and take me to Aunt Grace. Aunt Grace wanted me alive, so she could use my powers to usurp the Seelie throne.

Either the Erlking was lying to me, or Aunt Grace's plans had changed.

chapter fourteen

Over the course of the next few days, I tried to act as normal as possible under the circumstances. On Thursday morning, I had my regularly scheduled lesson with Keane. I still sensed a bit of strain between us, but on the whole it wasn't too bad. I manufactured reasons to leave my safe house at least once a day, craving the sunlight and fresh air. Well, this was Avalon, so I got rain, fog, and fresh air instead.

I still hadn't nerved myself up to calling Kimber, and every day that passed without me calling just dug the hole deeper. In my gloomiest moments, I wondered if I'd been wrong when I'd blamed my mom and her embarrassing addiction for my inability to make friends in the past. Maybe I just wasn't good friendship material.

On Friday, I started my morning with a trip to Starbucks to replenish my coffee supply. Even though the Erlking had already done his worst, my dad still insisted I not leave the safe house without two guards, so I had Finn and Lachlan with me. I wondered resentfully if it had ever occurred to Dad that I'd had two guards with me when the Erlking had taken Ethan, and that those guards had proved useless.

My mood had sunk to an all-time low. I'd spent hours trying to figure out how I could help Ethan, and I didn't have a single workable idea to show for it. My mind kept circling back to the same territory, the same useless ideas playing endlessly in my brain. I didn't know who I thought I was kidding, how I thought I could defeat the Erlking when no one else could. It all seemed so hopeless . . .

While I was waiting for the nice lady at Starbucks to ring up my purchase, I heard the rumble of motorcycles approaching, and my day went from bad to worse. My stomach clenched with dread.

How did the Erlking keep finding me? Avalon is small, but it's not *that* small. It couldn't be a coincidence that of the hand-ful of times I'd left my cave since he'd arrived, I'd run into him three times.

The other customers all fell silent, as did the baristas. Every-one turned to stare out the large picture windows that looked out onto Avalon's main road. Finn's magic prickled over my skin as he and Lachlan closed ranks around me.

"Don't worry, Dana," Finn said. "Neither Lachlan nor I will fall for any tricks he might pull."

That wasn't what I was worried about, but I didn't bother to correct him. My instincts told me that the Erlking wasn't going to attack anyone today. He'd already made his move when he'd captured Ethan. And I knew he was going to rub my face in it, remind me just what my refusal to make a deal with him was costing Ethan.

I should have closed my eyes, turned away, ducked into the

ladies room. Anything to avoid letting the Erlking's strategy work. Instead, I stood motionless by the window and watched as the Wild Hunt came into view.

The Erlking was at the head of their pack, as usual, though he wasn't wearing his helmet. His hair blew free in the wind, and even though he was the enemy—no matter what he claimed—I couldn't help noticing for just one moment the wild, masculine, dangerous beauty of him.

Then my eyes were drawn to his Huntsmen. Unlike their leader, they were all wearing their helmets, faces obscured behind the darkened visors. My eyes roved frantically from one to another, wondering if one of those nameless, faceless Huntsmen could possibly be Ethan. At first, they all looked the same to me, the differences in height and build not enough of an identifier. But then my eyes caught on the rider bringing up the rear. The height and the build were right for Ethan, but that wasn't what drew my eyes to him. What drew my eyes were the wisps of blond hair that trailed from under his helmet.

There was not a hint of skin or hair showing on any of the other riders. Their bodies were completely encased in their leathers, and if any of them had long hair, it was kept under their helmets. Except for that one rider. It was not a coincidence.

The Hunt drove slowly by. The Erlking gave me a jaunty wave as he passed, but he didn't stop, and the rest of his Huntsmen looked straight ahead. Except for the last one, who turned his head toward the window as he rode by.

My throat ached. Was that really Ethan? Unless he raised the visor on his helmet, I couldn't be sure. I felt the pressure of his eyes on me, though I couldn't see them. He made no gesture, and he didn't slow down, his bike maintaining a perfect, uniform distance from the one in front of him.

Who was I kidding? Of course it was Ethan! The Erlking had gone out of his way to make sure that one Huntsman let his hair stray from underneath the helmet, giving me the clue I needed to differentiate Ethan from the rest.

Ethan turned to face front again. Even without seeing his face, I knew that look had been a cry for help. Maybe a cry the Erlking had forced him to make, but one I couldn't refuse.

Everyone in the shop kind of held their breath for a minute or so after the Hunt had passed us by, wondering if they were going to come back and make trouble, but they didn't. Finn and Lachlan were both visibly relieved that the Erlking and his Hunt were gone. I don't know if either of them had realized the point of the Erlking's display, or if they'd even realized that one of those faceless riders was Ethan. They might feel like the Erlking had left without attacking, but I knew better.

Seeing Ethan bound to the Hunt like that was a shock to my system; a shock that woke me up, shook me out of my despair.

I was having no luck trying to figure out how to defeat the Erlking. All well and good to label myself the only reliable person in my life, but clearly I couldn't do this on my own, no matter how much I wanted to.

As Finn and I returned to my safe house, I thought long and hard about who I could approach for help. My parents were, of course, out of the question. Dad had already written the cause off as hopeless, and neither he nor Mom would let me take even the slightest risk to help Ethan. Finn and Lachlan were out for the same reasons. After Keane had told me exactly how he felt about Ethan, I could hardly expect him to want to help me launch or even plan a rescue. That left me with only one option.

Once back at the safe house, I retreated to my suite and closed the door behind me. Then I retreated even further, to my bedroom. I grabbed the phone, then sat cross-legged on my bed and willed myself to make the call I so dreaded.

It took me forever to scrape up the nerve, but eventually I turned on the phone and dialed Kimber's number. It would have served me right if she hadn't been home and I'd had to spend hours upon hours working myself into even more of a nervous wreck, but fate—for once—took pity on me.

Kimber picked up on the third ring, although she didn't say anything. She had caller ID, too, so she had to know it was me. Her accusatory silence made me cringe, and at first I couldn't force myself to speak.

"Hey," I finally said, then cursed myself for being so lame. Unfortunately, my brain had gone on strike, and I couldn't think of what else to say.

"Hey yourself," she answered, sounding cool and distant. When I'd first met her, she'd acted like the stereotypical Fae ice princess—just like this.

Words finally formed in my mind, though they weren't any less lame. "I'm sorry I didn't call earlier. I . . ." My voice died. Anything I said to explain my silence would just be an excuse, and a sorry one at that.

Kimber sighed. "I could have picked up the phone, too," she said, and she sounded slightly more like herself.

I shook my head, though she couldn't see me. "It was up to

me to make the first move, and I blew it." Please don't let me have ruined this friendship, I prayed silently.

"No, *I* blew it. You've been going through hell ever since you set foot in Avalon, and I'm supposed to be your friend. I just . . . I didn't know if I could stand it if you blamed me for what happened."

Blamed *her*? Surely she was joking. "I think we've got a bad connection," I said. "I thought you just said you were worried *I'd* blame *you* for what happened. But that's about the stupidest thing I've ever heard, so I must have gotten it wrong."

"You mean you don't?" she asked, her voice so tentative it made my heart ache.

"Of course I don't blame you! Why on earth would I blame you when it was all because of me that the Erlking took Ethan?"

"Because neither of you would have been there if it weren't for me. The spa trip was all my idea, and so was visiting the tea shop. And then I left the two of you alone." Her words were coming out in an almost frantic rush. "If I'd been there with you, I could have stopped Ethan from trying to play hero. You didn't want me to leave you alone with Ethan, but I thought I knew better. I—"

A laugh burst out of me, completely unexpected. "All this time," I started, then the laughter took me again. I was bordering on hysterical, and I knew it. That didn't mean I could stop. "I've been afraid to call you." Hiccups joined the laughter. "I was afraid you'd hate me because it was all my fault Ethan got taken."

Kimber caught a bit of my hysteria, and she started to giggle. "No way," she said. "It's not your fault at all!"

The laughter died as fast as it had started, which was just as well since it was hard to laugh and talk coherently at the same time. "Of course it's my fault. The Erlking wouldn't have had any interest in Ethan if it weren't for me."

Kimber sobered at the same time. "That doesn't make it your fault," she told me quietly. "Are you going to blame your mom, too? Because if she hadn't given birth to you, you wouldn't be here, and the Erlking wouldn't have been interested in Ethan, and Ethan wouldn't have been captured. So that makes it all her fault, right?"

"When you put it that way . . ."

"Besides," she continued, "if you think it's your fault just because you exist, then it has to be at least partly my fault for being Ethan's enabler. By ducking out on you, I put him in harm's way."

"It's not like you meant to."

"Exactly."

"Oh." Hearing her lay it all out like that made me feel just a little bit stupid for having wallowed as much as I had.

Kimber blew out a deep breath. "Ethan isn't blameless, either," she said. "He knew the Erlking couldn't hurt anyone in Avalon unless that person attacked him first. Why did he have to give the Erlking the chance?"

"I'm sure he didn't have time to really think about what he was doing."

She snorted softly. "It wouldn't have mattered. Ethan is so full of himself he's biologically incapable of resisting an opportunity to save the day."

Her words were scathing, but I heard the pain under them. Ethan drove her nuts, but he was still her brother, and she did love him.

"I'm not giving up on him," I told her.

"Everyone else has," she said bitterly.

"I know. But not me. And, I hope, not you. That's actually why I was calling. I was wondering if you could help me brainstorm a bit, see if we can come up with a way to help Ethan."

She hesitated a moment. "What can the two of us possibly hope to do against the Erlking? We're a little outclassed."

"Maybe," I admitted. Paranoia said that discussing possible rescue plans over the phone wasn't such a hot idea. "Can I come over so we can talk about it in person?"

"I don't know," she said with a laugh in her voice. "*Can* you?"

I managed a feeble laugh in response. She could never resist teasing me about my misuse of the word *can,* and it had now become something of an inside joke.

"Sorry," I said. "I forgot I was talking to the Grammar Nazi. *May* I come over?"

"Of course."

"You know I'll have my bodyguards with me," I warned.

"I'll make tea. They can stand guard in the living room, and we can talk in my bedroom. They'll give you that much space, won't they?"

"Yeah," I said, though I figured it might take some persuading. "It might be a little while before I get there. I have to get hold of Lachlan and let my dad know where I'm going first. I'll call as soon as I know my ETA."

"I'll be waiting."

Conveniently—if completely by accident—I arrived at Kimber's apartment right at tea time. Playing the gracious hostess, she served Finn and Lachlan a selection of finger sandwiches with their tea. I could tell Finn wasn't comfortable with being treated as a guest, but Kimber pretended to ignore that, practically shoving the tea into his face until he was forced to take it. She then led me back to her bedroom, where she'd laid out a very different tea spread for the two of us.

I couldn't help smiling the moment I stepped into the room and sniffed the air.

"Hot posset?" I asked hopefully. I'd never even heard of a hot posset before coming to Avalon, but Kimber now had me addicted to the hot milk-and-honey drink.

"Of course," she said. "If there ever was a situation that called for hot posset, this would be it."

Kimber had described it as a cure-all, and it certainly was comforting to drink. Too bad it couldn't cure what currently ailed us.

We both sat on Kimber's bed and picked up a mug. Having learned from painful experience in the past, I took a small, cautious sip before diving in. I wasn't completely surprised to find that sip burning all the way down my throat and into my stomach. I blinked and shook my head.

"How much whiskey is in this?" I asked her. When she made posset for me, she used only a touch of whiskey for flavor, but I knew she liked it strong enough to make an elephant drunk.

She grinned at me over her steaming mug. "You don't want to know. Now drink up."

I eyed my mug doubtfully. "I don't want Finn and Lachlan to have to carry me home." I hated to admit it, but because of my mom, I was just a little afraid of alcohol. I never, ever wanted to become the sloppy, stupid drunk I'd seen my mom become. No buzz in the world was worth that to me.

"Trust me, it's not *that* much whiskey. I know better, re-member?"

I relaxed and took another sip. Kimber did indeed know bet-ter. I wasn't all that good at trusting people, and Kimber hadn't always played things straight with me in the past, but I believed I could trust her now. I'd just try not to gulp the posset down too fast, and I'd be fine.

"The Erlking called me," I told her, and she practically choked on her swallow of hot posset. "Sorry," I said, wincing as she coughed and put the mug down.

"He *called* you?" she asked, appalled.

I nodded. Here came the hard part. I really hoped Kimber would agree with me that I couldn't make a devil's bargain with the Erlking, because otherwise, this could get real awkward, real fast. "He wants to set up a trade. I take him and his Hunts-men out on a killing spree in the mortal world, and he'll free Ethan."

Kimber was naturally pale, but she became even more so as what little color she had faded from her cheeks. "You aren't thinking of actually *doing* it, are you?"

I stared into my mug, afraid to meet her gaze. "What if it's the only way to free Ethan?"

"Then he'll just have to live with being part of the Wild Hunt," she said. There was a faint quaver in her voice, although she still managed to sound firm and decisive.

I risked a glance at her face, and there was no missing the determination in her expression. "Are you sure?" I asked.

She nodded. "I'm sure. Ethan wouldn't want to be freed if it cost other people their lives. He can be a selfish, egotistical bastard, but he's a good guy at heart. And if you ever tell him I said that, I'll never speak to you again."

"Your secret is safe with me," I vowed, relieved that she and I were in agreement. "So, giving the Erlking what he asked for is out of the question. But there must be *something* else he wants, something that only a Faeriewalker can give him. I just can't for the life of me think of what that might be."

"And that's where I come in, eh?"

I gave her an apologetic smile. "Well, you are the brains of this outfit, you know."

chapter fifteen

Kimber and I talked for more than an hour, and by the time we were done, we'd hammered out something that vaguely resembled a plan. A crappy, stupid, probably futile plan, but it was better than what I'd come up with on my own—which was nothing.

I felt better than I had for days, and I wished I'd called Kimber sooner. I hadn't realized how much I'd come to count on her, or how much I craved the human—well, Fae, really—contact.

The trip back to my safe house was uneventful, though I was tense the whole time, thinking the Erlking might want to rub my nose in Ethan's captivity some more. My ears strained for the sound of motorcycles, but the Erlking had apparently made his point, and he left me alone.

The smart thing for me to do once I got home was to give myself at least one night to sleep on my plan. Anything Kimber and I had hashed out in an hour's time couldn't exactly be the most bulletproof idea in the world. The problem was, I was afraid if I slept on it, I'd chicken out, and then I'd hate myself forever.

That night after dinner, I once more retreated to my bedroom to make a phone call. Only it wasn't Kimber I was calling.

Hands damp with sweat, I scrolled through the caller ID log until I found the Erlking's number. My stomach felt all tight and twitchy, and my mouth was so dry it would be a miracle if I could talk.

He answered on the first ring, like he'd been sitting by the phone anticipating my call. Maybe he really had been. It wasn't like I knew all that much about his powers, beyond the fact that if you cut off his head he could pick it up and put it back on.

"So, you've changed your mind about negotiating," he said. There was a hint of triumph in his voice. He must have figured parading Ethan in front of me this afternoon had broken me and made me see things his way. There was no point in arguing that assumption.

I swallowed the lump of dread in my throat. "Yes."

"I'm happy to hear that," he said. "I'm sure Ethan will be, too. Becoming part of my Hunt can be quite the adjustment for anyone, much less for someone as accustomed to power as he."

"If you hurt him . . ." I wanted to slap myself for the pathetic, empty threat. If the Erlking wanted to hurt Ethan, he would, and there was nothing I could do about it.

Luckily, the Erlking passed up the opportunity I'd given him to mock me mercilessly. However, what he said instead wasn't much better.

"I am ready to meet and discuss terms at your convenience," he said.

Meet? Oh, hell, no! "I'm ready, too," I said. "And we can talk just fine on the phone."

"I prefer my negotiations to be face-to-face."

"Well *I* prefer them on the phone."

"If we reach an accord and I release Ethan from my Hunt, he will need your help. He will be weak. So weak he may not be able to walk, or even stand, without assistance."

I closed my eyes and tried not to imagine what the Erlking had done to him to put him in that condition. Surely the Erlking or one of his Huntsmen could take Ethan home once he was freed. Or hell, just call him a cab. My gut instinct told me the Erlking wasn't going to budge on this point, so I raised an objection I thought was more likely to succeed.

"In case you haven't noticed, I'm under twenty-four-hour guard here. Somehow I don't think my dad or my guards are going to be okay with me meeting up with you."

He chuckled. "No, I imagine not. However, I must insist that we meet in person. I will send you a charm that will allow you to walk unnoticed past your guard. It will also lead you to my house."

"You've got to be kidding me. People are trying to kill me, you know."

"Yes, yes, I know. It isn't just your guard my charm will lead you past. No one will see you, neither friend nor foe."

I couldn't count high enough to list all the ways this idea sucked. "This is so not happening," I said, trying to sound strong and firm instead of scared and out of my league.

"If you want to free Ethan, you must come to me," he said, and he had sounding firm down pat. "I will not harm you, nor will I allow anyone else to harm you."

"What is it you have against the phone?" There was a noticeable hint of desperation in my voice.

"I'm not doing this to be cruel," he responded, his tone turning gentle. "The telephone is an inadequate medium for negotiations. It is too . . . impersonal. I promise that you will be safe with me, and that I will use no coercion, magical or otherwise, to bend you to my will."

And what, exactly, was the Erlking's promise worth? I had no clue. Lots of the old legends of Faerie claim that the Fae are incapable of lying, but I'd seen more than enough evidence that that wasn't true.

"How can I believe you will offer me anything of worth if you are not willing to come face-to-face with me to talk?" he asked.

Damn it! I hated to admit it, but he was right. Any deal I made would require me to face him one way or another. Shivering in superstitious dread, I said, "All right. You win this round. I'll come meet you." Oh, God. How big a mistake was I making? "You said you would send me a charm. How exactly are you planning to do that? It's not like the postal service delivers down here." My mail theoretically went through my dad's address, though it wasn't like I had any mail to speak of. I rather doubted my dad was going to give me anything that came from the Erlking.

"You will see," he said, and I could hear the smile in his voice. "I will see you soon, Dana Faeriewalker."

He hung up without saying good-bye.

I had a hard time falling asleep that night. Go figure.

I kept replaying my conversation with the Erlking over and

over, wondering if there would have been some way I could have reached a different outcome. I doubted it. He held all the cards.

Of course, I also wondered just how crazy I had to be to even consider sneaking out of my safe house to go meet the very enemy I was supposed to be hiding from. Well, one of them, anyway. But the alternative was to turn my back on Ethan, and I couldn't do it. I might not want Ethan for a boyfriend—the jury was still out on that—but I couldn't deny I cared about him. Not to mention that little detail of how he'd risked his life to save mine. If I had to put myself in danger to save him, then I was just going to have to suck it up and do it.

I tossed and turned for hours, not getting to sleep until after three. I figured that meant I would sleep in—I wasn't expecting Keane this morning—but despite my exhaustion, I woke up at a little after six. I groaned.

My alarm clock glowed at about half strength, which meant we were somewhere in the vicinity of dawn. Not an hour I'm very fond of even at my most well-rested. I flopped over and closed my eyes, hoping to sink right back into sleep. But the moment I settled down, I heard it: a soft tap, tap, tap. It was that sound that had woken me up.

I was still tempted to go back to sleep, but the sound made a chill go down my spine. I had no idea what it could be, but it was way too close to me for comfort.

Telling myself it had to be something completely innocuous, I turned toward the sound and opened my eyes.

At first, I didn't see anything out of the ordinary. I'm not the neatest person in the world, so my nightstand was covered with crap, only the little space in front of the clock uncluttered so I could see the time.

Tap, tap, tap.

I blinked. The sound was coming from my nightstand, I was sure of it. I sat up, my eyes scanning the piled books, papers, hair bands, and other junk that lay discarded on the table. And that's when I saw something among the clutter that definitely wasn't mine.

It was a small silver statue of a stag, maybe about three inches high. Its body was sleek and curved, almost like a greyhound, and its antlers, almost as big as its body, were sharp enough to draw blood.

My heart went ka-thump, and another chill traveled down my spine. I remembered the antlers on the Erlking's mask and his helmet, and I remembered the tattoo he and his Huntsmen wore. No chance in hell this stag didn't belong to him. But how on earth had it gotten here?

Tap, tap, tap.

I blinked, wondering if maybe I was having a bad dream. But no, the stag did it again, lifted one delicate leg and tapped its hoof against the wooden table. It then tilted its head up as if to look at me, then looked over its shoulder at the door to my bedroom.

"Holy crap," I said in a choked whisper.

The stag repeated the gesture, tapping on the table, looking at me, then looking at the door. Call me crazy, but I think it wanted me to get moving. My heart hammering, my palms clammy, I slid my feet out of bed. The stag nodded, then leapt from my nightstand to the floor, its hooves making an almost crystalline ringing sound when it landed. It trotted a few steps toward the door, then once again looked over its shoulder at me.

I sucked in a deep breath and tried to get a grip on myself. The Erlking had said he'd send a charm. I guessed I was looking at it. He'd said the charm would lead me to him while keeping anyone from seeing me. If I was really planning to go through with our meeting, I would have to follow the creepy little statue.

"Hold on a minute," I said, feeling ridiculous talking to what should be an inanimate object. "I'm not going out in my jammies."

It cocked its head to the side, then nodded as if it understood. Maybe it did, but I wasn't sure how long it would wait. As soon as I got out of bed and headed for my closet, it started the little tap-tap-tap routine again.

I was scared and creeped out, but I was still tired enough that I couldn't stop myself from yawning hugely. I wondered if the Erlking had decided to lead me to him at this ungodly hour because he thought it would give him the edge in his negotiations. I also wondered if he might be right.

It shows how groggy I was that I didn't fully realize what the stag's presence in my room meant until I was pulling a heavy wool sweater over my head.

"Oh, shit!" I said as I yanked on the sweater, making my hair stand on end in static ecstasy.

I stared at the little silver stag as it continued to tap its hoof impatiently. My knees felt wobbly, and I grabbed hold of my dresser to steady myself.

"He knows where I live," I whispered, not sure if I was talking to the stag or to myself.

Not only did the Erlking obviously know where I lived, he'd also been able to get his little charm past all the defenses and into my room without ever raising an alarm. So much for my "safe" house.

I took a couple of deep breaths to steady myself. I wasn't even remotely happy that the Erlking knew where I lived and could get to me here, but there was nothing I could do about it. If he could find me here, odds were he could find me anywhere. He hadn't hurt me so far, and I tried to convince myself that his knowing my location didn't matter.

I stuffed my feet into my favorite pair of sneakers, then looked all around my room, wondering if there was anything I should take to this meeting other than myself. Nothing jumped out at me except for an umbrella. I had no idea how far I'd have to walk to get to the Erlking's house, and in Avalon, there was always about a fifty percent chance of rain. I grabbed it, wondering if I was going to end up needing it as a weapon before the day was through. Then I nodded at the stag.

"I'm ready," I said.

chapter sixteen

I held my breath as I followed the stag through my suite then into the guardroom. I could hear Finn rattling around in his kitchen, and figured he was making breakfast. I hoped the Erlking's charm worked the way he said it did, because I was going to hate it if I ended up having to explain myself to Finn.

The stag continued into the guardroom with no hesitation, and I forced myself to follow. Finn was frying something on his hot plate—he didn't have a stove—and he looked as awake and alert as if it were the middle of the afternoon. I kept expecting him to look up and see me, but he didn't. The stag walked right past him to the front door, then passed through the door as if it weren't there. I suppressed a shiver.

Keeping an eye on Finn, I eased the door open. He paid no attention, and I wondered what the chances were that this was all a dream.

I belatedly realized I should have grabbed a flashlight. The tunnels were pitch-black, and even if the stag could lead me through the dark, I'd probably die of terror before we reached the surface. I turned to duck back into the guardroom to get a flashlight.

Tap, tap, tap.

I looked at the stag, wondering if it would have the patience to wait for me—and if Finn would see me if I went back in without it. But when I took a closer look, I saw that the stag was glowing faintly, a blue-white light like a little star. It started trotting down the tunnel, its light brightening as it moved farther away from the light that poured out of the guardroom.

"This has got to be the world's worst idea," I muttered to myself as I eased the door closed and plunged into the darkness after the Erlking's charm.

The stag's glow was barely enough to guide the way. I'd seen night lights brighter than that. I walked as close to it as I could, my eyes straining in the oppressive darkness. The tunnel floor was mostly smooth, but the dark messed with my depth perception and I tripped about a million times.

When we'd been in my safe house, the stag had waited for me, however impatiently, but once we'd turned a couple corners in the tunnels, it picked up the pace. I think it knew I was fully committed to following it now, since my alternative was to try to find my way back to the safe house through the pitch-black tunnels. Even when I tripped so bad I almost did a face-plant, the stag kept going. I climbed to my feet in a hurry, desperate to stay close to my only source of light.

Eventually, we ventured out into the more commonly used tunnels with their electric lighting. I breathed a sigh of relief, even as the stag picked up its pace a little more. I didn't need its light anymore, but I wasn't finding the Erlking's house on my own, so I hurried to keep up.

Avalon is a pretty weird place, but even here a tiny animated statue trotting along would attract notice, so when the stag managed to walk past people without them paying any attention, I knew its magic was working. Trying not to feel like there were neon signs pointing to me saying "fresh meat," I continued to follow.

There weren't a whole lot of people out at this hour, although the streets weren't completely deserted, either. But even after we left the tunnel system, no one seemed to notice us. It was wet and drizzly out, although not enough to make me use the umbrella, which I kept shifting from hand to hand as I warmed the free hand in my pocket.

The dampness added bite to the early morning chill, and by the time the stag bounded up a flight of four stone stairs to a covered stoop, my teeth were chattering, and I suspected my lips were tinged blue. I was not looking forward to seeing what Avalon was like in the winter. But, I reminded myself cheerfully, I might not live that long anyway.

I would have liked to have taken a moment to collect myself before ringing the doorbell, but I didn't have that chance. Before I'd even reached the top step, the door swung open. I came to a screeching halt and was lucky I didn't fall back down the stairs and break my neck.

The Erlking was dressed a little less outlandishly than usual today, in a pair of tight-fitting black leather pants and an untucked black button-down shirt that shimmered faintly in the light. His hair was loose around his shoulders, except for two thin braids that framed his face. If he weren't the stuff of nightmares, I'd think he was seriously hot.

He smiled at me, then crouched and reached out his hand to

the stag. It leapt onto his palm, and he stood up, closing his hand around the little statue. I remembered the sharpness of the antlers and wondered how the Erlking managed to hold it without drawing blood.

When he was fully upright again, the Erlking opened his hand; there was no longer a statue in it. Instead, there was a delicate silver brooch in the shape of a leaping stag. It didn't exactly match the Erlking's mark, but it was close.

"My gift to you," he said, raising his hand and indicating I should take the brooch.

Of course, I hesitated. I had no desire to take *anything* from him, much less something that was basically his emblem.

One corner of his mouth tipped up in a half smile. "You do not have to wear it. But there may be times you will find it useful." He turned the brooch over, showing me the pin. "If you need to make yourself unseen, prick your finger on this." He touched the point, and a spot of blood beaded on his fingertip. "The spell will wear off in thirty minutes, but while it's active, no one will see, hear, or feel you, even if they bump into you." He put his finger into his mouth, sucking off the little drop of blood, and held the brooch out to me again.

I still didn't want to take it, but I didn't think he'd take it kindly if I refused. I picked it up gingerly, as if afraid it would bite, then stuffed it into the pocket of my jeans. If he thought I was going to thank him for his nice gift, he was sorely mistaken.

He opened the door wider. "Come in, come in," he said. "You must be cold."

The power of suggestion had my teeth chattering again, and I stepped into the Erlking's house. I had to stop myself from gawking as soon as I did. *House* wasn't the right word for the building I'd stepped into. *Palace* probably fit it better, though it was like no palace I'd ever seen.

The floor of the entryway was black marble, shiny as glass, not a scuff mark in sight. The walls were covered in black and silver–striped wallpaper that had the texture of raw silk. From the ceiling hung faceted crystals in varying shapes and sizes, so dense it was impossible to see the source of the light that shone from behind them. The Erlking reached up and brushed his fingers over the crystals, showing off that he was tall enough to reach the ceiling. The crystals clinked together like wind chimes, the sound echoing off the marble.

Past the foyer, the ceiling rose up into a dome, painted night-black and dotted with tiny white lights like stars. A grand stair-case like you might see in *Gone with the Wind* led to a second-floor balcony, almost completely hidden in shadow. The inside of this building seemed a lot larger than the outside had indicated, and the shadowed hallways upstairs made it seem positively vast.

"Cozy," I muttered under my breath, and the Erlking smiled.

"This is home to myself and all of my Huntsmen whenever we are in Avalon. Cozy would not suit us."

My heart leapt at the realization that Ethan must be here, hidden in the depths of this house. I wondered if he was in-stalled in a comfortable room somewhere, or if he and the rest of the Huntsmen resided in some old-fashioned, cramped ser-vants' quarters up in the rafters. It then occurred to me that for all I knew, the Erlking kept them chained in a dungeon, and I decided to abandon that line of thought.

The Erlking led me down a long marble hallway and into a room that I suspected he called a "parlor." Like everything I had seen so far, it was decorated entirely in black and silver, and if it weren't for the color of the Erlking's skin and eyes, I might have wondered if I had suddenly been struck color blind.

I shivered again, the chill having sunk all the way down to my bones. The Erlking frowned, then gestured to the fireplace, which suddenly burst into flame. I jumped, then blushed at my reaction. Duh, magical, mythical creature can do magic! What a surprise.

"Come sit by the fire and warm up," he said, gesturing me toward an armchair covered in black silk with silver embroidery. "I will have some coffee brought in." He grinned at me, his eyes glittering in the firelight. "You are not overly fond of tea, I hear."

I stiffened, knowing exactly where he'd gotten that little bit of knowledge. "Thanks," I said through gritted teeth. I hated to show that he'd wounded me, but my emotions were too raw to hide. I turned my back to him so he couldn't see my face, and I headed toward the chair as I tried to compose myself.

When I sat down, the Erlking took the other seat in front of the fire, pulling a small ebony table over so that it sat between us. Footsteps echoed in the hall behind me, and I turned to see who was coming. But the predatory look in the Erlking's eyes told me everything I needed to know, even before Ethan turned the corner and stepped into the room.

He was dressed like a Huntsman now, wearing nothing but black, head to toe. The Erlking's mark stood out starkly against his pale skin. In his hands, he carried a silver tray on which sat a tea set. He met my eyes briefly, and the despair in his expression sent a sharp pain knifing through my heart—just as the Erlking no doubt planned.

Ethan broke eye contact, then braced the tray with one arm and began unloading the tea service onto the table. I could feel the Erlking watching me, soaking in my pain. I tried my best to keep my expression neutral, but I doubt I managed it.

Ethan took one last item off the tray and held it out to me. It was a mug of coffee, just as the Erlking had promised. I tried to catch Ethan's gaze again, hoping I could convey to him without words that I was going to get him out of here. Somehow. But he kept his head bowed and wouldn't look at me.

"That's all," the Erlking said. "You may go."

I hated to let Ethan out of my sight, but it wasn't like I had a choice. I held on tightly to the mug of coffee he'd handed me, and that helped me resist the urge to reach out and grab him, keep him from leaving.

Still refusing to look at me, Ethan bowed to the Erlking, then left the room. I heard the Erlking fixing himself a cup of tea, but I couldn't bear to look at him, afraid of what he might see in my face.

"He is unharmed," the Erlking said softly, drawing my eyes to him against my will. "Unhappy, but unharmed." There was sympathy and sadness in those ancient blue eyes, but I didn't believe it.

"Whenever you're finished rubbing it in, can we talk about what I have to do to get Ethan back?"

He raised his eyebrows in what looked like surprise. "I'm not 'rubbing it in,' as you put it. I was pointing out to you that he is unharmed. That was meant to be comforting."

I snorted. "Yeah, right."

He leaned back in his chair and crossed his legs, holding the delicate black china teacup in his lap. "Believe me or not, as you will. As you are so impatient to begin our negotiations, please do tell me what you propose."

I took a deep breath, gathering the scattered remnants of my courage. It was vital that I phrase everything just right. Kimber and I both believed whatever agreement I made with the Erlking would be enforced by magic, so I had to be very careful to leave myself room to maneuver.

"My father told me that you and the Faerie Queens were at war once," I said, starting slowly.

The Erlking cocked his head at me. I supposed he was trying to guess where I was going with this. "We were. But that was a long, long time ago. Our relations have been peaceful for many centuries."

"Because of the agreement you reached with them. The one that keeps you from hunting the Fae unless the Queens give you permission."

Understanding dawned in his eyes, and he laughed softly. "You're planning to offer me an alternative to taking me out into the mortal world, as opposed to negotiating guidelines for my hunts there."

"Yeah, that was the idea," I said. Because no matter how bad I felt for Ethan, I still couldn't unleash the Wild Hunt on the mortal world.

The Erlking nodded and put his teacup down, sitting up straighter. "Tell me exactly what it is you propose." I couldn't read the expression on his face. Perhaps it was eagerness, but it might just as easily have been skepticism.

I spoke slowly and carefully when I answered. "One of a Faeriewalker's abilities is to carry technology into Faerie. My aunt Grace wants to kidnap me so she can use a gun to kill the Seelie Queen and take the throne."

The Erlking nodded, like that was common knowledge. "Yes. A mortal bullet can kill even a Faerie Queen."

"What about you?" I blurted, the words completely unplanned.

He smiled at me. "If I could be killed by a mortal bullet, you can hardly expect me to tell you that, can you?"

I felt the color burning in my cheeks. *Way to make yourself sound like a moron, Dana.*

"But in answer to your question," he continued, "no, I cannot be killed by a mortal bullet. Many have tried, and yet here I am."

He could be lying through his teeth, of course. Like he said, if a mortal bullet could kill him, he wouldn't run around advertising it. Then again, he'd obviously hunted in Avalon before it seceded from Faerie, and it was hard to believe his human quarry had never tried to shoot him, in self-defense if nothing else.

"Your proposal is that you'll ride with me into Faerie, allowing me to use a gun to kill the Queens and thereby remove the geis they have put upon me. Is that correct?"

I suppressed a shudder and forced myself to meet his eyes with all the sincerity I could project. "Basically."

The idea was risky in the extreme. If I did this, and the Erlking was freed from his geis, it wouldn't put anyone in the mortal world in danger, but the Fae would be sitting ducks. Which was why I had to be so careful how I worded our agreement, because I had every intention of making sure whatever gun the Erlking brought with him into Faerie wasn't in working order. Kimber had assured me that magical bindings were very literal. If I was bound to help the Erlking take a gun into Faerie, then as long as I helped him take a gun, I was in the clear. There was no requirement that it be a *working* gun.

I was practicing in my head how I was going to phrase my formal offer when the Erlking made it a moot point.

"It's a clever offer," he said with a nod of approval. "It requires me to work for my ultimate goal, in a task that would be difficult even with mortal weapons, and if I succeed, it is not your own people who will suffer for it." He grinned. "The Fae can fend for themselves, eh?"

I raised my chin and tried not to flinch. I knew the offer was going to end up making me sound pretty callous, like I couldn't care less what happened to the Fae because they weren't "my people." But I needed the Erlking to believe I was really that callous so he wouldn't suspect me of a trick.

The Erlking shook his head. "It doesn't matter. The answer is no."

"What?" Of course I'd always known he might refuse, but I thought there'd been at least a chance of success. And I certainly hadn't expected him to dismiss it without even trying to negotiate.

"I have no quarrel with either Mab or Titania," he said. "The agreement we three reached was mutually advantageous, even if onlookers cannot guess what advantage I might have gained."

I was struck speechless by the Erlking's instant refusal. My heart sank. That had been my one and only idea of what I could offer the Erlking in place of what he wanted. Tears welled in my eyes despite my best efforts to hold them back.

The Erlking reached over the tea tray to put his hand lightly on my wrist. I'd have pulled away if the despair weren't weighing me down so heavily.

"Don't cry," he said, and he brushed his thumb over the back of my hand. "All is not yet lost. I have a counteroffer for you."

His words were enough to rouse me from my stupor, and I finally pulled my hand out from under his, the motion so sudden I spilled the mug of untouched coffee in my other hand. The Erlking rose to his feet and plucked the coffee mug out of my hand, laying it on the table. Then he knelt in front of me, and there was a handkerchief in his hand—I had no idea where it had come from. He started dabbing at the wet spot on my jeans.

His touch was impersonal, his movements brisk and businesslike, nothing sexual or otherwise inappropriate. Still, the feel of his hand on my thigh was . . . disconcerting.

"I'll do that," I said, reaching for the handkerchief, half expecting him to insist on doing it himself. But he let me have the handkerchief.

"Did you burn yourself?" he asked, sitting back on his heels.

I shook my head, embarrassed at my overreaction to his touch. He wasn't being threatening, and he wasn't trying to be seductive. No big deal.

And yet somehow it *felt* like a big deal, and the hair on the back of my neck prickled. I tried to shake the feeling off.

"What is this counteroffer of yours?" I asked.

He gave me a look I can only describe as assessing, then rose to his feet and grabbed the chair he'd been sitting in, pulling it around the table so it was facing me. Then he sat down, his legs barely an inch from mine.

I fought the urge to sink back into my chair. He was so big it would have been hard not to be intimidated by him even if I didn't know who—and what—he was. I met his eyes and was surprised to see how much warmth existed in that cold blue. Maybe he couldn't help being intimidating, but he was trying hard not to be.

"I'll warn you in advance that my proposal is nothing you are expecting," he said, "and that it will both frighten and discomfit you."

Oh, great. Like I needed to be even more frightened and uncomfortable than I already was. "All right, you warned me. Now what is it?"

His eyes seemed to bore into me. "I will release Ethan from the Wild Hunt. If in turn you will pledge to give me your virginity."

chapter seventeen

My jaw dropped open, and I blinked at him in disbelief. "Excuse me, what did you just say?"

"You heard me. And I did warn you."

I shook my head, feeling like I'd somehow slipped into a dream. I replayed the Erlking's words in my head, and they still made no sense.

"You are young," the Erlking said. "Perhaps too young for the bedroom yet. At least by your modern human standards. In olden days, you might have been an old married woman with a handful of children by now. But I am nothing if not patient. I will give you the freedom to choose when you are ready to fulfill our bargain."

"And you'll keep Ethan with you until I do," I said, still too stunned to fully absorb what was happening.

"No, no," he responded. "Your pledge will be binding, and unless you plan to live a life of celibacy, you will eventually have to come to me."

"You can't be serious."

I'm not so falsely modest as to claim I'm unattractive or anything, but I'm nothing special, especially when compared to the unearthly beauty of the Fae. When I'd first met Ethan and he'd instantly started flirting with me, I'd known in my heart of hearts that there was something not quite right about it. Some girls really are so beautiful and/or sexy that they have guys falling at their feet right and left, but I'm not one of them. There was no way the Erlking was going to let Ethan go just for the pleasure of getting me into his bed.

"I assure you, I'm quite serious," he said. "If you won't ride with my Hunt into the mortal world, then there is only one way you can win Ethan's freedom."

I sat there and gaped at him. "I don't understand. What would you get out of this?"

He quirked an eyebrow at me, and I blushed hotly, right on cue. I'd been so focused on my disbelief I hadn't fully absorbed the fact that I was sitting here discussing my virginity with a man.

"My apologies," the Erlking said softly. "I shouldn't tease you under the circumstances."

He looked genuinely sorry, but that didn't make my blush go away. I'd never gotten past first base with a guy. I'm cautious by nature, and not too good at trusting people, so that made intimacy kind of difficult for me. You might even say it made me a prude. The idea of actually doing . . . *it* . . . with the Erlking made me break out in a cold sweat.

"I will not hurt you," he told me. "I can even make it pleasurable for you, despite any misgivings you might have."

That made me look up at him sharply. Had Ethan told him about having tried to cast that roofie spell on me?

"I won't do that without permission," the Erlking said, and the look in his eyes told me he knew what I was thinking. "If you'd prefer to have your mind completely clear, then I'll respect your wishes."

"Why are you doing this?" I found myself whispering, feeling younger and more lost than I could ever remember feeling. I knew beyond a shadow of a doubt that there was more to this offer than met the eye. He would be getting something other than a little fun out of it if I agreed. I just had no idea what.

"It's all a question of what Ethan's freedom is worth to you," he said instead of answering my question. "Virginity doesn't mean as much to the women of today as it did to women of old. Giving it to me would not harm your chances of finding a husband, nor would it cause you to be shunned or otherwise treated as damaged goods. Is it a fate so terrible that it is worth sacrificing the rest of Ethan's immortal life to avoid it?"

The tears were back, and this time I wasn't able to stop them from spilling over. I felt trapped, and helpless, and guilty all at the same time. There were plenty of girls my age who'd been having sex for years and thought nothing of it. And yet here I was, scared to agree to the Erlking's terms even when Ethan's entire future lay in the balance.

The Erlking reached out and took both my hands. I made a half-hearted attempt to pull away, but as I expected, he didn't let go. His thumbs stroked over the backs of my hands, his touch surprisingly gentle.

"You're frightened now because you aren't ready," he said. "That's why I'm leaving it to you to choose the time." He let go of one of my hands, reaching up to stroke a tear off of my cheek. "When you're a little older and have had time to accustom yourself to the idea, you might find the prospect of coming to my bed more appealing than you might expect."

He was smiling at me again, and despite my distress, I couldn't help noticing the beauty of his deep blue eyes with their frame of long lashes. Yeah, there were probably plenty of girls who'd fall over backward at the chance of getting into his bed. Too bad I wasn't one of them.

"And if you find I'm wrong," he continued, "if you find you cannot bear to let me take you, then that choice will always be yours."

Yeah, if I never wanted to have sex for my entire life! Maybe I wasn't ready right now, and maybe I was a bit on the prudish side, but that didn't mean I wanted to stay a virgin forever.

But how could I say no and just abandon Ethan? How could I face Kimber again, knowing I could have saved her brother but was too much of a chicken to do it? And how could I live with myself, knowing that Ethan was taken because of me, and I wouldn't lift a finger to help him?

I felt like a marionette, dangling on the Erlking's strings. I *knew* there was something more to this deal than he was telling me. And I *knew* that someday I would have to face the consequences of my decision. If the Erlking had demanded I have sex with him right now, I might not have been able to summon the necessary courage, no matter how horrible I would have felt about it. But maybe he was right. Maybe in a couple of years, it wouldn't seem like such a big deal.

"Throw in Connor, and you have a deal," I said, even as my insides cringed at what I was promising.

The Erlking looked surprised, like it had never occurred to him I might want to free my brother, too. He let go of my hand, then leaned back in his chair, brow creased in thought. Then he nodded.

"I will release Ethan immediately upon your pledge," he said. "Then when that pledge is fulfilled, I will release Connor as well."

I couldn't find my voice to agree out loud, so I just nodded instead. I was pretty sure I was going to hugely regret this one day, probably very soon.

The Erlking stood, holding out his hands to me. "Then let us seal the bargain."

I didn't know what he wanted. I stood, but I didn't give him my hands, instead watching him warily.

"We'll seal the bargain with a kiss," he told me, brushing a strand of my hair away from my face. I started to protest, but he spoke right over me. "The bargain will be enforced by magic, so that neither one of us may break it. You will feel the magic building, but don't be alarmed."

I shook my head. "I am not kissing you!" I said.

He raised one shoulder in a shrug. "We could seal the deal with blood, but a kiss will be much more pleasant. For both of us. Besides, how am I to believe you will ever fulfill the bargain if you aren't willing to part with a single kiss?"

I swallowed hard and tried to tell myself I was being a sissy. A kiss was nothing to be afraid of, even when the one delivering it was a cold-blooded killer. I didn't say anything, and the Erlking took that as agreement.

"You will feel the magic beginning to gather as soon as I speak the terms of our agreement," he said. "It will intensify when I kiss you, but it won't hurt you. It will also make the kiss . . . quite pleasurable."

I suppressed a shudder. I didn't want to enjoy it. "I don't want you screwing with my head."

"I won't. It's merely a side effect of the magic. If we sealed the deal with blood, it would intensify the pain instead, so you see why I prefer the kiss." He grinned at me, an almost boyish expression that looked all wrong for his face.

I could tell from the heat in my cheeks that I was blushing again, and I hated it. "Fine. Whatever." If the magic was only going to intensify what was already there, then I'd just have to make damn sure I didn't let myself take any pleasure from the Erlking's kiss.

He bowed his head graciously, amused by my surly answer. "Then I vow that if you will pledge to me your virginity, I will release Ethan from the Wild Hunt this very day and release Connor on the day you fulfill your pledge."

The magic prickling over my skin made me gasp. It was stronger than anything I'd felt before, and all the little hairs on my arms stood up. I wouldn't have been completely shocked if the hair on my head was standing on end, too. If it was going to get more intense than this when the Erlking kissed me, I wasn't sure how I'd live through it. It already felt like I'd stuck my finger in an electric outlet.

"Be warned," the Erlking continued, "that if you fail to preserve your virginity until you fulfill the pledge, Ethan will join the Hunt once more, and no force in Heaven or on earth will free him again. Do you agree to the terms I have spoken?"

The magic was so thick I could hardly breathe, and my skin crawled with it. I wasn't sure how I could force words from my mouth, but the Erlking was looking at me expectantly, waiting for my reply. And the faster I replied, the faster this would be over.

"Yes," I said, not sure my voice was even audible. The magic was now a roar in my ears in addition to a prickling on my skin.

The Erlking's eyes sparked with triumph, and he slid his huge hand up the back of my neck until he was cradling my head in his palm. He leaned down, and it took every ounce of my will not to break free of his grip and run for my life.

His lips were surprisingly gentle when they touched mine, and I felt a moment of relief, thinking this chaste brush of lips would do the trick. Then the magic speared through me. Suddenly, I no longer felt the prickling on my skin—it seemed to be coming from inside me instead.

I gasped, and the Erlking gasped, too. Then he crushed his lips down on mine and pulled my body against his. I went unresisting into his embrace as the magic tingled in my chest and belly. I opened my mouth, almost begging for the taste of the Erlking's tongue, and he gave it to me.

He kissed me so hard it almost hurt, and I hadn't even the faintest thought of resisting him. I wrapped my arms around his neck and pressed myself against him, feeling the hot, hard evidence that he was ready and eager to fulfill the bargain right this moment. I moaned into his mouth as pleasure zinged from my head to my toes and back again. It was the most glorious thing I'd ever felt, and I wanted more. There was no part of me, mind or body, that remembered I was kissing the bad guy and that I didn't really want to be doing what I was doing.

The magic reached a crescendo that would have made me

scream if the Erlking's tongue hadn't been in my mouth. I grabbed a double handful of his hair, holding on to it like it was a lifeline and I was drowning.

Then abruptly, it all stopped.

My knees buckled, and I would have collapsed if the Erlking hadn't held me up. His lips lingered on mine just a second more before he broke the kiss, his hands on my shoulders steadying me. I felt dizzy and weak, too dazed to remember exactly where I was and what I was doing. I had trouble untangling my fingers from the Erlking's hair, and I didn't resist when he guided me over to a chair and sat me down.

My lips felt bruised and swollen from the force of the Erlking's kiss. He squatted in front of me, looking up into my eyes as he stroked my hair away from my face.

"Are you all right?" he asked, and he sounded like he really cared. "Did I hurt you?"

His pupils were huge and dark, his breaths coming in short gasps. I suspected those tight leather pants of his were still bulging, but despite his obvious enthusiasm, he made no move to take advantage of me.

"I'm fine," I managed to say, though I wasn't at all sure it was true.

He squeezed my hand. "I'm sorry I was so rough. That was more intense than even I expected."

I'm not sure why, but I believed him. Maybe just because he looked so concerned right now.

I was still trying to pull myself together and remember which way was up when Connor entered the room, carrying an unconscious Ethan, and all thoughts of the kiss vanished from my mind.

chapter eighteen

I think that subconsciously I never expected my plan to succeed. Otherwise, maybe I would have put some thought into what to do after I got Ethan back. The Erlking had warned me he'd be incapacitated, after all. I'm stronger than a fully human girl of my size would be, but I certainly wasn't strong enough to carry Ethan anywhere.

Connor crossed the room until he came to an antique-looking sofa, then gently laid Ethan down on it. My legs still weak from the overdose of magic, I made my way to Ethan's side, hardly daring to believe I'd actually won his freedom.

"Don't fear for him," the Erlking said from right behind my shoulder, and I jumped. A guy that big had no right to move so quietly! "Being released from the Hunt has weakened him, but he will recover his strength over time."

"How much time?" I asked.

He shrugged. "He is the first man I have ever released. I cannot say exactly how long his recovery will take."

On the sofa, Ethan groaned softly and his eyelids fluttered like he was trying to open them.

"Ethan!" I said, sitting on the sofa beside him and taking one of his hands in mine. "Can you hear me?"

His lips moved a bit, but no sound came out, and he didn't open his eyes. How the hell was I going to get him home?

And how was I going to explain to everyone how I had managed to win his freedom? No way was I going around advertising that I'd agreed to give the Erlking my virginity! I also wasn't too excited about the idea of letting my dad or Finn know that I'd managed to sneak out of my safe house.

But first things first: I had to get Ethan out of here, and the Erlking wasn't volunteering to help.

"Can I use your phone?" I asked him.

He plucked a cordless phone off of its charger and handed it to me without comment. I tried to pretend my hands weren't shaking as I dialed Kimber's number and prayed she'd pick up. It was still pretty early in the morning, and she wouldn't recognize this number on her caller ID if she checked before answering.

To my relief, she picked up and said a groggy-sounding "Hello?"

"Kimber. It's Dana. Are you awake?"

She made a sleepy, puzzled sound, and I heard her moving around in bed. "Dana? Where are you? Is everything all right?"

"I'm fine." I crossed my fingers as the words left my mouth, an old, childish habit I sometimes reverted to in times of stress. "I'm, uh, at the Erlking's house."

Kimber gasped. I suspected she was now wide awake. "What?"

"He's agreed to let Ethan go, but Ethan's too weak to walk and I don't have any way to get him home."

"Wait a minute. What? Did you just say the Erlking let him go?"

"Yeah. But I need your help."

"So the Erlking actually went for the offer we came up with?" She sounded incredulous, and I couldn't blame her. I guess neither one of us had really believed it would work. It had just made us feel better to have the illusion we could make a difference.

"Er, no. We came up with something else. But I don't want to talk about it, not now. Can you help me get Ethan home?"

"I'll be there in fifteen minutes," she said, and I heard her footsteps as she got out of bed and started hurrying around.

"Hold on a sec, I'll get you the address."

"Don't bother. I know where it is."

I guessed it made sense that the people of Avalon knew where the Erlking lived. It wasn't like he and his Hunt were inconspicuous. "Okay. See you soon."

"Yeah," she said, then hung up.

I hugged myself to suppress a chill, even though the fire made the room cozily warm. For a little while, Kimber was going to be so happy to have her brother back that she wouldn't bug me too much about what kind of deal I'd made with the Erlking. But I knew that wasn't going to last, and eventually she'd start pushing me to tell. I just didn't know if I was willing to share the details, best friend or not.

I decided this was a case of "cross that bridge when you come to it" and tried to push those thoughts aside.

Ethan looked paler than usual, and there were shadows

under his eyes. The Erlking's mark was startlingly dark against his skin. I wondered if it was a normal tattoo and Ethan could get it removed, or if he was stuck with it for the rest of his life. Not that it looked bad, in its own wild and exotic way, but I imagined Ethan would prefer not to be constantly reminded of his time in the Wild Hunt.

The Erlking sat on a straight-backed chair, crossing his legs as he watched me holding Ethan's limp hand.

"I told you on the phone earlier that it's in my best interests to protect you," the Erlking said. "Even more so now that we've reached our agreement. In light of that, I should warn you that I have been given permission by Titania to hunt your aunt Grace."

"What?" The statement came from so far out in left field that at first I couldn't figure out what he was talking about.

"Word reached the Queen that Grace had ambitions to take the throne. She did not take kindly to the information." His lips curled in a wry smile.

It wasn't like I felt even remotely bad for Aunt Grace. If she got herself killed because she took it into her head to use me to kill Titania, that was just tough. I didn't know if I was mean-spirited enough to say I'd be glad if Aunt Grace died, but I wouldn't shed a tear.

"What does this have to do with my safety?" I asked.

"Grace is doomed. If she is clever, she may be able to evade me for a fair amount of time, but, powerful though she might be, I *will* catch her. This is assuming the Queen's people don't catch her first, naturally. Your aunt knows that. Even if she were to succeed in kidnapping you and forcing you into Faerie, the Queen's guards will be alert to the danger, so Grace could not get close enough to make the kill."

"Okay. I still don't get what this has to do with me."

"It has always been my experience that when a person has nothing left to lose and nothing left to gain, he or she can be expected to lash out."

He gave me a significant look, and I remembered his earlier suggestion that Grace was no longer trying to kidnap me but was trying to kill me instead. I couldn't say I knew Aunt Grace very well, but I had no trouble believing she was capable of it. My arrival in Avalon and her failed attempts to make me into her own pet Faeriewalker had driven her off the deep end. And she struck me as the kind of person who would hold *me* responsible for the mess she'd made of her life.

I sighed. "If she wants to kill me, she can line up behind all the other people who want the privilege." If I wasn't careful, having all these people wanting to kill me was going to make me bitter.

He nodded in approval. "I admire your courage, Faeriewalker. Very rare in one so young."

"Er, thanks. And I thought you were going to stop calling me that. My name is Dana."

"My apologies, Dana. And my name is Arawn. Few would dare use it, but you may do so with my blessing."

I was saved from having to answer when the doorbell rang. Kimber was here.

The Erlking—Arawn—picked Ethan up and carried him as easily as if he were a baby. Without another word to me, he headed for the door, and I hurried to catch up.

My mind kind of numbed out a bit after that. Kimber was both thrilled and panicky when Arawn handed her brother's limp body to her. As a full-blooded Fae, she was able to handle his weight, though not as easily as Arawn could. Tears streamed down her face, and there was no sign of the crankiness she usually displayed around Ethan. Probably just as well he was only sporadically conscious, or he'd never have let her live it down.

She was distracted enough by her relief over Ethan's release that she didn't ask me how I'd managed it. I felt like I'd dodged a bullet, but I fully expected her to start shooting more bullets than I could avoid when she'd recovered her composure.

We went our separate ways after that, Kimber taking Ethan to their father's house, while I returned to my safe house. I'd hesitated a long time before doing it, afraid there might be consequences Arawn had failed to mention, but eventually I pricked my finger on the brooch he'd given me. With no bodyguards, and only about half my wits available, I was a sitting duck for anyone who wished me harm, so I figured it was absolutely necessary that I hide myself from sight.

My sense of direction sucks, but I'd traveled back and forth from my safe house often enough that I was able to find my way without assistance. I didn't have the stag to light my way this time, but Arawn had thoughtfully given me a flashlight.

Finn was being very bodyguard-like when I stepped into the guardroom, his head bent over a gun he was meticulously cleaning. Several other guns lay on the table, as did a couple of silver knives. I held my breath as I walked by, but he didn't see me. I hated to admit it, but the Erlking's gift made a nice get-out-of-jail-free card. As far as I could tell, Finn never even knew I was gone.

Once I was safely in my suite once more, I debated between drinking massive amounts of coffee and collapsing into bed.

Collapsing into bed won, and I was so exhausted I fell instantly asleep.

Unfortunately, it was not a dreamless sleep. The moment I drifted off, I found myself held tightly in Arawn's arms as he kissed me. It was a kiss as deep and passionate as the real one we'd shared, only this time it wasn't influenced by magic. I pressed myself against him, letting myself feel the intensity of his arousal against my belly. It should have alarmed me, but it didn't.

I opened myself to him with abandon, letting his tongue explore my mouth, not protesting when his hands slid down to my rear and pulled me even harder against him. I was mindless with pleasure and need.

Arawn broke the kiss, and I let out a mewl of protest. He smiled down at me, his eyes dark and glittering, then picked me up and laid me down on my bed. A small part of me registered the fact that this couldn't be real. The rest of me didn't care.

Arawn positioned himself on top of me, careful not to crush me under the weight of his huge body. Somehow, my legs ended up spread, one of his thighs pressed between them. I arched my back and let out a moan. I could hardly breathe through my need, and my hands lifted of their own volition to the buttons on his shirt.

I don't know how far the dream would have gone if I hadn't been awakened by Finn pounding on my door.

"Dana!" he shouted, like it wasn't the first time he'd called my name. "Answer me now, or I'm coming in."

Groggy and disoriented, I sat up. "Be out in a minute," I managed to answer.

"Your father wants to see you," Finn said. *"Now."*

Ugh. That didn't sound good. "I'll be out in just a sec."

I rubbed at my crusty eyes and made my way to the bathroom. I wanted to at least brush my hair and throw some cold water on my face before facing my dad, who must have heard that Ethan was free and known I was somehow responsible.

I froze when I saw my reflection in the mirror. My face was flushed, and I belatedly noticed my cheeks were blazing hot. My pupils were dilated so much it looked like I'd been doing drugs, and my hair was a snarled, tangled mess.

The flush deepened when I remembered just what I'd been dreaming about. I did *not* want to think about the Erlking that way. Yes, he was gorgeous, and he had that special bad-boy appeal—*real* bad boy, unlike Keane—but he was dangerous, and cruel, and about a zillion years too old for me. Absently, I rubbed my fingers over my lips, remembering the bruising force of his real-life kiss. I had enjoyed it at the time, but remembering now made me squirm. I'd been kissed a total of twice in my whole life, and both times I'd been under the influence of mind-altering magic. I wondered what a genuine kiss would feel like, and worried that the sensation would pale in comparison.

I shook myself out of that line of thinking and shoved the memories—both of the real kiss and the dream one—to the back of my mind to be dealt with later.

It was time to face the proverbial music.

chapter nineteen

There was exactly zero chance I was going to tell my dad what I'd had to do to win Ethan's freedom, and by the time I'd gotten myself pulled together enough to leave my bedroom, I'd concocted a cover story that would get me out of having to tell *anyone* the embarrassing truth.

Dad was waiting for me in the living room, pacing restlessly in front of the couch. In the second or so I had before he noticed me, I saw that his face was tight with strain, his cheeks unusually pale even for him. I'd expected him to be furious with me, but he didn't look angry. He looked . . . scared.

I didn't have a chance to examine that revelation for very long, because he looked up and saw me. He wiped much of the expression off his face, although whatever was wrong bothered him enough that he couldn't manage his usual blandness. His eyes met mine, and he shook his head.

"Dana, what did you do?" he asked. His voice sounded bleak, and I wondered for half a second if he suspected the truth.

204 • jenna black

Then I dismissed the idea. I was pretty sure he'd be pissed, not scared, if he'd known I'd pledged my virginity to the Erlking.

I raised my chin and hoped I wasn't blushing. "What I had to do to rescue Ethan from the Wild Hunt."

"And what was that, exactly?"

Covering up for my mom had given me plenty of practice both in making up good lies and delivering them convincingly. I'd learned that it was always best to keep the lie simple, and to mix in as much truth as possible. Oh, and not to avoid eye contact, which made you look like you were lying even if you weren't.

So I looked right into my dad's eyes as I lied to him. "I didn't do anything. I just had to promise to do something in the future. And before you ask, he put a geis on me to keep me from telling anyone what it is."

The starch seemed to go out of Dad's spine, and he dropped onto the couch. He looked like I'd just told him someone had died. Since I hadn't told him much of anything, I wasn't sure what I'd said that bothered him so much.

I ventured a little farther into the room, but didn't sit down. I was too agitated for that. "What's wrong, Dad?"

"What's wrong?" He laughed bitterly. "What could possibly be wrong when my daughter has promised the Erlking something he wants so badly he's willing to release one of his Huntsmen to get it?" He let out a heavy sigh. "You don't know enough about him or about Faerie in general to make fully informed decisions. Whatever you promised him, you don't dare give him. Even if it means he takes Ethan back." He sounded resigned, like he didn't expect me to listen to him.

I thought about the promise I'd made, and knew I wouldn't be fulfilling it any time soon. No sexy dream was going to make me want to have sex with the bogeyman. Besides, Dad was right. I *hadn't* made an informed decision. I had no idea what the ramifications of fulfilling our bargain would be, and until I found out, there was no chance in hell I was going to do it.

Too bad pretending a geis prevented me from revealing the promise also kept me from asking anyone who knew more about Faerie just what might be hidden in this deal.

"I don't have to do it anytime soon, if that makes you feel any better," I told my dad.

"It doesn't!" he snapped, and I finally saw a hint of the anger I'd been expecting. "Listen to me, Dana: you mustn't give him what he's asking for. Period."

I bit back my immediate response to being ordered around. "Do you *know* what he's asking for?" I asked, wondering if that would explain the intensity of his reaction.

"I don't have to," he said. "There was nothing Titania, the Seelie Queen, could offer the Erlking that would tempt him to let Connor go. Can you really imagine he would hand Ethan over to you for something that wouldn't have devastating consequences?"

No. I might not know what those consequences were, but I knew they had to exist.

"I couldn't let him keep Ethan," I said. "Not when I could save him. I'll just have to find some way around the consequences. Like I said, it's not something I have to do anytime soon. I'll figure something out." I hoped.

Dad was far from appeased, but he backed off for the time being. I had no illusions that we wouldn't be talking about this more in the days to come.

He frowned suddenly and looked up at me. "Wait a minute.

206 • jenna black

You said the Erlking put a geis on you?" His eyes widened in what looked like horror. "How did you manage to meet him without Finn knowing?"

"I didn't," I said, not losing a beat even though I hadn't anticipated this question. "He called me." Again, a little bit of truth, mixed in with the lies to create a believable cover story. No way did I want my dad knowing about the brooch. He'd take it away from me for sure, and I had a feeling it might come in handy again someday.

"He placed a geis on you over the *phone*?"

Oops. I guessed that did sound a little unlikely. Then again, I had the distinct impression that no one was sure what the limitations of the Erlking's power were, so I stuck to my story. "Yeah. Don't ask me how he did it. I don't get this magic stuff at all." Unfortunately, that was nothing but the truth.

I wasn't sure Dad was convinced, but he didn't ask me any more questions. Perhaps the Erlking's alleged ability to place a geis on me over the phone wasn't any harder to believe than the truth of how he'd managed to get me out of the safe house without Finn knowing.

I wasn't in the least bit surprised that my mom called me not too long after my dad left. Although Dad had her under his version of house arrest, he didn't have her completely cut off. She had no idea what I'd promised the Erlking in exchange for Ethan's freedom, but like my dad, she assumed it was something terrible. *Unlike* my dad, she wasn't any good at staying calm during a crisis. I'd always thought it was the booze that caused her sudden bouts of hysteria, but apparently not.

I did my best to talk her down off the ledge, but she was still in tears by the time I hung up. I was glad Dad had removed all the booze from his house, or she'd no doubt have gone on the bender to end all benders.

I was much more surprised to receive a phone call from Alistair, Ethan and Kimber's father. Despite his rivalry with my father, the two of them were working in something that resembled a partnership to make sure I survived to full adulthood. The partnership was close enough that my dad had let Alistair have my phone number, but not so close that Alistair had any clue where my safe house was located.

Alistair was a relatively young Fae, and he'd been born in Avalon. He was more reserved than your average American, but much less so than my dad. While he, too, told me that I mustn't give the Erlking whatever I'd promised him, he thanked me so much for what I'd done that it was almost embarrassing. I think Ethan believes his father loves him primarily because of his magical abilities and what they could do for Alistair's ambition, but that sure wasn't what it sounded like to me.

I kept hoping that Ethan would call me, but he didn't. I told myself that was because he was too weak and ill after his time with the Hunt to manage it, but my insecurities weren't convinced. Kimber had miraculously failed to put any blame on my shoulders, but maybe the same wasn't true of Ethan.

What had the Erlking done to him during the days he'd been trapped in the Hunt? I was pretty sure there'd been more to it than just riding around the city on motorcycles. The Erlking had promised me Ethan had been "unharmed," but I didn't think that meant the same as "unhurt."

I fell asleep that night to visions of Ethan being tortured by the Erlking and his Huntsmen. Gruesome as those mental images were, they didn't stop me from dreaming about the Erlking. I awoke in the morning with only confused memories of those dreams, but I knew they'd involved a lot of bare skin, and I was sure they'd gone way past first base.

It's not like I'd never had an erotic dream before, but never anything like this. Never so intense, and never so tangled up with my real world. My body still remembered what it had felt like to be plastered up against the Erlking's chest while his tongue stroked the inside of my mouth. And even though I didn't want it to be, that memory was hot.

I was still feeling pretty out of it when nine o'clock rolled around and it was time for my lesson with Keane. I wondered if he knew about Ethan, but the moment I got a look at his face, I knew the answer. The look he gave me was dark and angry. I would have tried to smooth things over, but he was in no mood to talk.

It was the most brutal, intense sparring session I'd ever had. No doubt he was still holding back to avoid the risk of hurting me or I'd have been in pieces by the time he was through, but it wasn't even close to fun. As if that wasn't bad enough, he dialed up the intensity on the insults and sarcasm. According to him, I didn't do a single thing right the entire time. Usually his drill-sergeant tactics pissed me off, but today they were cutting way deeper, to the point where I was way more hurt than angry.

I doubt we'd been at it more than about ten minutes when I decided I'd had enough. Keane, of course, didn't give a damn what I'd decided and ignored me when I said I wanted to stop. He swung his fist at my face, but I was determined to put an end to our session right this second. So I fought my instinct to protect myself, forcing myself to hold still instead of blocking, or ducking, or dodging.

Keane realized at the last second that I wasn't defending, and his eyes widened in a way that might have been comical if I weren't wincing and gritting my teeth in anticipation of his punch. If he'd been human, there was no way he could have stopped the momentum of his blow, so it was a damn good thing he wasn't human.

He cut it so close that his knuckles grazed my chin by the time he'd fully put the brakes on. Not hard enough to hurt, though, and I let out a silent breath of relief. I'd been prepared to take the hit if that was what it took to make Keane stop, but I hadn't exactly been looking forward to it.

"What the fuck?" he shouted, his closed fist still hanging in the air.

"I said I had enough," I told him, and was pleased by how calm and steady my voice sounded. Maybe I had a future as an actress, because I was anything but calm and steady.

Keane let out an incoherent sound of frustration, but dropped his fist.

"Get up on the wrong side of the bed?" I asked with a fair imitation of one of his sneers.

His eyes went cold. It wasn't a look I'd ever seen on his face before. His anger had always been hot, the kind that flared up and then faded away with equal suddenness. This looked different, and a part of me wanted to take a giant step backward.

"You're making jokes," he said, and his voice was as cold as his eyes. "Guess this is all just some big game to you, and you take your sparring about as seriously as you take P.E. at school."

"What? Where did *that* come from?"

He shook his head. "You know what? You're not worth my time."

Without another word, he stomped off the mat, then practically pulled it out from under my feet so he could roll it up.

"Geez," I said, throwing up my hands. "I knew you didn't like Ethan, but I didn't expect you to throw a temper tantrum like a big baby."

He shot to his feet, then gave the rolled-up mat a savage kick. "You think this is about *Ethan*?" He wasn't looking quite so cold anymore, but I couldn't say it was much of an improvement.

I blinked at him in confusion. "If this isn't about Ethan, then what is it about?"

"You're completely mental." He ran his hand through his hair, and I think he pulled out a few strands in the process. Then he took a deep breath and spoke to me slowly and deliberately, like I was an idiot who had to have things explained to me in small words. "It isn't about Ethan, it's about *you*. What the fuck is the point of teaching you to defend yourself if you're just going to run out and deliver yourself to your enemies?"

I saw a lot of things in his eyes just then, many of which I'm pretty sure I wasn't supposed to see.

He was my friend as well as my teacher, and as a friend he certainly had a right to worry about me—even if he didn't know just how much he had to worry about. But the intensity of his reaction, the anguish in his expression . . . This was more than one friend worrying about another.

Damn it! I so didn't need another complication in my life.

What do you do when someone you think of as a friend lets you see that he wants more? I did the only thing I could at the time: I ignored it.

"I didn't 'deliver myself to my enemies,'" I said. "I know I took a calculated risk when I bargained with the Erlking, but it was just something I had to do. I couldn't let him keep Ethan when I knew I could save him. I'd have done the same for you."

Maybe I should have kept that last part to myself, but it was true. It didn't mean I had any interest in dating Keane, though. I'd have been just as willing to make a deal if it had been Kimber's life on the line.

I liked Keane, but only on the infrequent occasions he wasn't being an asshole. He was gorgeous, and, I had to admit, extremely sexy. And yeah, Kimber's obvious interest in him had sparked an unexpected jealousy in me. But I already had one really complicated boy in my life, and now I had an even more complicated man in it, too. Adding Keane to the mix would be more than I could handle. Besides, Kimber was my best friend. What kind of friend would I be if I got involved with a guy I knew she was interested in?

"Don't do me any favors," Keane growled, but he'd lost a lot of the intensity.

"I'm not the type to just sit back and let other people take care of my problems for me," I said. "I never will be. If you think that makes it a waste of your time to teach me self-defense, then I'm sure I can find someone else to teach me."

He winced as if I'd said something cruel. I didn't think I had.

"No, it's not a waste of my time," he admitted, hanging his head. "The more stupid crap you get yourself into, the more you're going to need to defend yourself."

I made a sound between a laugh and a snort. "Way to be tactful and supportive. With friends like you, my enemies can just sit back and enjoy the show."

"You're going to give me gray hair before I'm twenty."

I shrugged. "You dye it anyway, so you'll never notice."

He cracked a smile at that.

"So, are we friends again?" I asked, holding out my hand for him to shake.

He gave me an unfathomable look, then took my hand and gave it a squeeze instead of a shake. "Yeah. Friends."

He managed to say it without sounding sarcastic, and I managed to accept the words even though I knew he didn't really believe them.

chapter twenty

Each day, I woke up expecting to hear from Ethan, but he didn't call. I'd have told myself he was still flat on his back, except when I asked Kimber how he was doing, she told me he was much better. I was highly tempted to ask her if she knew why he wasn't calling me, but she'd sounded both exhausted and distracted, so I decided to stick to less emotionally charged topics. She didn't even question me about my deal with the Erlking. I didn't know if that meant she'd already heard about the "geis," or if she didn't care, or what.

Almost a week passed with no word from Ethan. I saw or at least heard from my mom and dad every day, which might have been nice if everything weren't so strained. Dad was clearly still worried, and Mom was . . . Well, Mom was a wreck. Sobriety wasn't agreeing with her, not during times of stress. She even took me aside for a private chat one day when I was visiting Dad's house and he ended up stuck on some important phone call.

Her fidgeting was worse than it had been even in her first

days after the d.t.'s had passed, and I noticed with a start that she had lost weight. Her clothes hung loosely on her frame, and I saw she was no longer wearing the gold claddagh ring that I'd never before seen her take off. I could still see the impression of the band around her finger. She noticed me staring and rubbed the spot self-consciously.

"It keeps slipping off," she said. "I'll have to see if I can get it resized."

"Are you on a diet?" I asked, though I already knew the answer. She'd always been just a hair on the heavy side, but she'd never cared, and I didn't think she cared now, either.

"Not intentionally," she said with a rueful smile. "I just haven't been all that hungry lately." She touched her stomach. "I always seem to lose my appetite when I'm stressed out."

I nodded. Now I understood. In the past when she'd been stressed out, she might have lost her appetite for food, but not for alcohol. It might not be what you'd call nourishing, but it did have calories. And, come to think of it, it probably reduced her stress, too, though at a terrible cost.

I reached over and patted her shoulder awkwardly. "Please don't be stressed about me. I'll be fine."

"Of course you will," she agreed with false cheer, then fell silent and went back to her fidgeting.

I waited to see if she was going to say anything else, but she didn't. "Is there something you wanted to talk to me about?" I finally prompted, not sure I wanted to know.

She took a deep breath, then turned to face me with a grim but determined expression. Now I felt sure I didn't want to know.

"You understand that your father is keeping me here against my will, don't you?" she asked.

I winced. Yeah, I knew that. She and I were both his prisoners in a way.

"Do you know why?"

That question surprised me. Of *course* I knew why. Dad forcing Mom to stay sober was one of the few really good things that had happened since I'd come to Avalon. Naturally, Mom didn't see it that way, especially since she wouldn't admit she had a drinking problem in the first place.

"He's keeping you here so you'll stay sober," I said, bracing myself for yet another round of denial on her part.

Mom shook her head. "No. He's keeping me here because he thinks it's what you want."

"Huh?"

"He's keeping me here because you think I'm an alcoholic, and he thinks keeping me locked up without alcohol will make you happy."

I'd never thought of it that way, but I supposed it was true. Damned if I was going to feel guilty about it, though. "Your point being?" A hint of frost entered my voice, but Mom ignored it.

"My point being that if you asked your father to release me, he probably would. I'm as much *your* prisoner as your father's."

I laughed, but it was a bitter, angry sound. "You want me to convince Dad to let you go so you can go back to business as usual. That's great, Mom. Just great. You want to go back to being a pathetic drunken loser."

She jerked back as if I'd slapped her. "Dana!"

Back when she'd been drunk all the time, I'd worked very hard to keep my rage locked tightly inside. Yelling at her or even reasoning with her when she was drunk was an exercise in futility. But she wasn't drunk now, so I let it all out. Maybe now that she was sober—however unwillingly—she'd be able to understand just how badly her alcoholism hurt me.

"You want me to pretend it's all right with me that you'd rather get drunk and pass out than spend time with me?"

"That's not—"

"Or that it's all right for you to be so drunk all the time you can't be bothered to keep your bills paid? You think I didn't mind having to lie for you year after year after year?"

"Enough!"

"No, it's *not* enough!" The anger was taking on a life of its own. My fists were clenched so tight my fingers were falling asleep, and I felt like I was going to explode. "You've been a sorry excuse for a mother my whole life, but for the last few weeks, I thought maybe you were capable of better. And now you're asking me to make it easy for you to go back to being—"

My mom slapped me, and it shocked me silent. She'd never hit me before in my life. She was so angry she was shaking. But the sheen of tears in her eyes said there was pain behind the anger.

"I said that's enough," she said hoarsely. Then she stood up, turned her back on me, and walked stiffly away.

I should have felt happy that I'd managed to save Ethan from the Wild Hunt, regardless of the promise I'd had to make to do it. Instead, I felt lousy. Dad was worried about me. Mom was furious with me. Keane seemed to want something from me I wasn't able to give him. And Ethan, apparently, wasn't speaking to me.

I finally got sick of waiting for him to call me and nerved myself up to call him instead. He didn't answer, and though I left him a message, he didn't call back. It kinda reminded me of the cold shoulder I'd given him after I'd seen him with Ashley at the party, but I hadn't done anything to deserve it. Not that I knew of, at least.

When calling Ethan didn't work, I called Kimber instead. I'd only spoken to her once since the day I'd gone to the Erlking's house, and that conversation had been brief. I was determined this one, however, would let me get to the bottom of whatever was going on with Ethan.

It had somehow slipped my mind that Kimber hadn't had a chance to interrogate me about just how I'd managed to free Ethan. She reminded me of the fact almost immediately.

"So, you said you had to work something out with the Erlking other than the deal we'd come up with together," she said, and I made a chagrined face I was glad she couldn't see. "What was it? No one seems to know."

Yeah, and that was just the way I wanted it. So even though I felt a bit guilty about it, I gave Kimber the same lie I'd given my dad. "The Erlking put a geis on me, so I can't tell anyone what I did."

There was a long silence. "Uh-huh," she finally said, and I heard the skepticism in her voice loud and clear.

I squirmed. I hadn't felt bad about lying to my dad. I mean come on, he might be my dad, but I barely knew him. There was no way I was talking sex with him. Period.

But Kimber was my best friend, and if I was going to open up to anyone about this, it should be her. I'd told Kimber the shameful secret about my mom, and at the time I'd known her

218 • jenna black

for like twenty-four hours. We were closer now, so I should be able to trust her with my new embarrassing secret.

But letting anyone know my mom was an alcoholic wasn't half as bad as admitting what I'd promised the Erlking. Honestly, what do you call someone who promises sex in return for a favor? I knew only too well, and my face was burning just thinking about it.

"You can tell me, you know," Kimber said quietly, and I heard the hurt in her voice. "Whatever it is, I'm not going to think less of you. You rescued Ethan when no one else was even willing to try."

I swallowed the lump that was forming in my throat. Kimber probably thought I'd promised to help the Erlking kill someone. Someone other than the Faerie Queens, that is. As far as anyone could tell, that was all he was really interested in. In the grand scheme of things, killing someone was a lot worse than bartering my body, but I think I'd have had an easier time admitting that than the truth.

"I can't talk about it, Kimber," I said. "I'm sorry. I just can't."

"Fine," she said in a tone that meant it was far from fine. "Whatever."

"Kimber . . ."

"I said fine! You don't want to talk about it, we won't talk about it. I'm still grateful you helped Ethan." The words were right, but the tone stayed frosty and distant.

I wished I could think of something to say to make it all better, but nothing leapt to mind. The best I could do was change the subject and hope that over time, Kimber would come to forgive me. Or that I'd eventually dig up the courage to tell her the truth, but I wasn't holding my breath.

"How's Ethan doing?" I asked. "I haven't heard from him at all."

There was a long silence during which I had no idea what Kimber was thinking. Then she answered, and she didn't sound cold anymore, just worried. "Physically, he's just about back to normal. But . . . he's not the same. He won't talk about what happened, and he keeps saying he's fine, but he's not."

My conscience twinged a bit more. It must really suck for Kimber to be shut out from both sides. Did that mean I was going to have a change of heart and confide in her? Uh, no.

"What do you mean?"

"I mean aside from the stupid tattoo, he looks like Ethan, but he isn't *Ethan*. He hasn't cracked a smile since he came back, and he's been all quiet and broody. I never thought I'd say it, but I miss the arrogant prick."

That almost made me laugh, but not quite. "He doesn't seem to want to talk to me," I said. "I called a couple of times, but he doesn't answer and doesn't return the calls. Does he . . . does he blame me for what happened?"

Kimber might be pissed at me and hurt that I wouldn't confide in her, but I guess she was still my friend, because she came right to my defense. "Of course not! How many times do I have to tell you it's not your fault?"

"Yeah, well, even if it's not, that doesn't mean he can't blame me for it."

"I swear I will beat the crap out of him if he does."

This time I couldn't help the little laugh that escaped me. "I'd pay money to see that."

"I'll bet. But seriously, Dana. I don't know why he's not returning your calls, but I'd be shocked if it was because he blames you. He's just not himself these days, and whatever's wrong, I don't know how to fix it, and neither does our father."

"I'm sorry," I said, though I wasn't quite sure for what. Maybe everything.

After I hung up with Kimber, I decided that I would do to Ethan what he had done to me. He wasn't willing to return my calls? Fine. I'd just have to go see him in person. And, thanks to the Erlking's thoughtful gift, I'd actually be able to go see Ethan without an entourage at my back. It wasn't the kind of risk I'd ordinarily take, but I'd already seen how well the Erlking's brooch worked. When I invoked its powers, I was completely invisible. Therefore, I could leave my safe house all by myself and be in absolutely no danger. That was the theory, at least, and it was time to put it to the test.

chapter twenty-one

My best chance of getting to Ethan without anyone knowing I'd left my safe house was to go at night, after I was supposed to be in bed. Finn rarely set foot in my suite, always keeping to himself unless I initiated contact, but I didn't trust my luck. If I decided to go during the middle of the day, that would be the one day Finn decided to come check on me for some reason.

I felt like a total dork for doing it, but I spent a good half hour figuring out what to wear for my forbidden excursion. I doubted Ethan would have cared about my outfit under normal circumstances, and he was even less likely to care now. But that didn't stop me from changing three times. I finally decided on jeans, paired with a simple white button-down and a gorgeous, sinfully soft gray cashmere sweater my mom had bought me.

The outfit didn't look terribly special—which was kinda the point. The last thing I wanted was for Ethan to think I'd dressed up for him, even if I had. On the plus side, if Ethan decided to give me a hug, he couldn't help but like the delicious texture of the cashmere.

I rolled my eyes at myself as I stood in front of the bathroom mirror, braiding my hair so it wouldn't get all electric from my sweater. This wasn't a date, or even anything that vaguely resembled one. I was going to talk to Ethan to see if I could find out what was wrong, and that meant the chances of him enjoying the softness of the cashmere were slim to none.

I waited until after eleven to prick my finger with the Erlking's brooch. I was sure Ethan would still be up, but it was late enough that Finn might assume I'd gone to bed. Taking a deep breath for courage, I tiptoed through my living room and eased open the door to the guardroom.

Of course, with the magic of the Erlking's brooch, I didn't need to tiptoe. Finn was sitting in his recliner reading a magazine while the TV played soundlessly in the background. He didn't look up from the magazine when the door opened, nor did he notice me when I walked right by him and opened the door to the tunnel system. Whatever the Erlking's charm did, it made me not just invisible, but unnoticeable.

Taking a deep breath for courage, I switched on my flashlight and started down the tunnel.

There was an entrance to the tunnel system in the courtyard right outside Ethan's apartment, but I hadn't the faintest idea how to get there from my safe house. Nor, come to think of it, would I have been able to lift the hatch that concealed the entrance from view. Which meant I had to take the long way. The Erlking had said the effects of his brooch would last for a half hour, so I kept myself moving at a brisk pace. I had more than enough time, but with my sense of direction, I had to allow for a wrong turn or two along the way.

There were a couple of nightlife hot spots—like The Deep—in

Avalon, but for the most part the streets were practically deserted after dark. As I exited the tunnel system and started making my way down Avalon's main road, I saw only the occasional
car, and even fewer pedestrians. The streets had never been
lively at night, but I think they were even less so now, when
everyone knew the Wild Hunt was in town.

I made good time, and for once I didn't get lost. I had a good
ten minutes to spare by the time I rounded a corner and saw the
student housing complex in which both Ethan and Kimber
lived. There was a light on in Ethan's apartment, and a shadow
moved across the curtained front window. He was definitely
home and awake. Now that I was here, however, I struggled
against an almost unbearable urge to turn around and run
away.

What if Ethan flat-out didn't want to see me? To have him
not return my calls hurt bad enough, but if he told me to go
away, I thought I might die on the spot. And then an even worse
thought occurred to me: what if he wasn't alone? If he opened
the door and I saw another girl in there . . .

"Oh, cut it out!" I grumbled to myself. I didn't really believe
he had a girl in there, not after what Kimber had said about how
gloomy he was acting. And I hadn't dragged myself out here in
the middle of the night just to stand in the courtyard and stare at
his window like a lovesick puppy.

With worries and doubts clamoring for attention in my head,
I forced my feet forward, then climbed the concrete stairs that
led to the second floor. I gave myself another silent pep talk as I
stood in front of Ethan's door, my stomach doing nervous flip-
flops and my heart beating double-time.

I knocked on the door quietly at first. Then, when no one

answered, I knocked a little louder. I held my breath, sure Ethan would have heard me this time, but he didn't come to the door. I was about to knock a third time, but I noticed the little doorbell button and rang it instead. The bell rang, and moments later I heard footsteps coming my way. Once again, I held my breath.

The door swung open, and Ethan stood framed in the light from his apartment. He was wearing a wrinkled, faded T-shirt over torn jeans. His hair was badly tousled, and the pallor of his skin made the blue stag tattoo look almost black in contrast. And yet he still took my breath away. I had come impossibly close to losing him forever, without ever having had a chance to sort out how I felt about him, and I wasn't planning to make the same mistake twice.

"Hi," I said with a nervous smile, my palms sweating. "Sorry to stop by so late, but . . ."

Except Ethan looked right through me, as if I weren't there. The corners of his mouth tugged down in a frown, and he shook his head. Then he swung his door shut without saying a word.

The pain that stabbed through me at his unequivocal rejection was like nothing else I'd ever felt before. I'd thought seeing him at the dance with another girl was bad, but having him shut me out without even a word was nearly unbearable. I'd get angry about it later, when I thought of what I'd done to save him from the Wild Hunt and how completely ungrateful he was, but for now I felt nothing but aching hurt.

I turned around, determined not to cry, and started heading for the stairs. I checked my watch to see how much longer I had until the magic of the Erlking's brooch wore off, and that's when reality smacked me upside the head and surprised a nearly hysterical laugh out of me.

Duh! Arawn had said his charm would hide me from people even if they happened to bump into me, that it wasn't just invisibility. Ethan had looked through me like that because he couldn't see me—or hear me.

I felt giddy with relief, and for a moment I thought my knees were going to give out on me. I leaned against the wall outside Ethan's door and breathed slowly in and out, calming myself little by little. Then I watched the second hand on my watch tick-tick-tick away the time until the Erlking's spell wore off.

When the thirty minutes were up, I waited a little longer, just in case the duration of the spell was approximate, but standing outside in full view of anyone who chanced to see made me too uneasy. The chances that one of my enemies would just happen to see me here for the couple minutes I was visible were extremely slim, but I didn't exactly have nerves of steel.

I rang the doorbell once again. This time when Ethan's footsteps approached, his tread sounded heavy, like he was stomping instead of just walking. He flung open the door, and magic prickled against my skin. His face was twisted into a fierce scowl, an expression I'd never seen him wear before, and his hands were fisted at his sides. The sensation of magic intensified, and my mouth dropped open as I realized he was about to cast some kind of spell. I didn't think it was going to be anything nice, either.

Ethan's eyes locked on my face, and there was no doubt he saw me this time. The magic fizzled and died, and the scowl faded to a more neutral, guarded expression.

"Dana?" he asked, as if he couldn't quite believe his eyes.

Nerves made me shove my hands in my pockets and hunch my shoulders. "In the flesh."

He blinked a couple of times, then glanced around the landing, taking in the fact that there were no bodyguards in sight.

"Idiot," he said under his breath, then grabbed my arm in a grip hard enough to bruise and yanked me over the threshold, banging the door shut behind him.

I was too shocked by his behavior to manage a protest. I thought sure he was going to apologize for manhandling me like that, but instead he shoved me against the wall of the foyer and shook his finger in my face.

"Stay here!" he ordered, then stomped into the living room and yanked on the curtains, trying to close the tiny gap between them.

Kimber hadn't been kidding when she said he wasn't acting like himself. I ignored his order and followed him into the living room, resisting the urge to rub the soon-to-be bruises on my arm.

"Stop messing with the curtains," I told him. "No one's going to see me through that gap."

He let go of the curtains with an irritated grunt. He turned to face me, but his eyes were focused just over my left shoulder, like he couldn't bear to look at me. "What the hell are you doing here?" he growled.

This was definitely not the reception I'd been hoping for, and I felt every shred of my self-confidence draining out through my toes. I felt like some geeky little schoolgirl who had a pathetic crush on a guy way out of her league. I tried not to let that show on my face.

"You wouldn't return my calls," I said, then hated myself for sounding so needy. He'd been giving me a not-so-subtle hint when he'd refused to call me back. Why hadn't I paid attention?

"Jesus, Dana! Half the world would like to see you dead, and you decide it's a good time to go wandering the streets of Avalon all by yourself late at night? Do you have a death wish, or are you just mental?"

Every word he said was like a knife in my heart. He must have been playing me all along, I realized. No way could he be this horribly cruel to me if he'd ever really cared about me. I'd come here expecting him to be unhappy with me, though I'd assumed it would have something to do with the Erlking. I hadn't for a moment expected him to be like this.

I could have defended myself and told him about the Erlking's charm. I didn't like letting him think I was stupid enough to ditch my bodyguard without any other form of protection. But explaining would have meant hanging around, and I didn't have the stomach for it.

"If I'd known this was how you were going to be, I'd have let the Erlking keep you," I said, and had the satisfaction of seeing Ethan wince. I didn't mean it, of course. An immortal lifetime of slavery was a bit of a harsh punishment for being an asshole. But I'd been getting into a nasty habit of lashing out lately, and right now I didn't have any inclination to break myself of it.

"Sorry I bothered you," I continued, turning toward the door. "I'll try to get back home without getting myself killed, but you know since I'm a crazy moron with a death wish, I can't make any promises."

I grabbed the doorknob, but before I had a chance to turn it, Ethan quickly crossed the distance between us and grabbed me. Once again, he shoved me up against the wall, only this time he stayed right there in my personal space, one hand planted on the wall on each side of my head. He opened his mouth like he was going to say something—from the look on his face, it wasn't going to be anything I wanted to hear—but no words came out.

My heart was still aching from his less-than-welcoming reception, but even so, I couldn't help noticing the faint, woodsy scent that clung to him. Nor could I help noticing the warmth of his body so close to mine, or the intense teal blue of his eyes. He leaned closer to me, and at first I thought he was about to kiss me, and my pulse started hammering for reasons other than anger.

But instead of kissing me, he merely touched his forehead to mine and closed his eyes. I didn't quite know what to make of the gesture. I told myself I was relieved that I'd been wrong about his intentions, but my body wasn't buying it. My skin felt tight and tingly, and my pulse kept rocketing. Without conscious thought, my hands somehow made their way up to Ethan's waist, the touch tentative in case I was misinterpreting his signals.

He moved even closer to me, making it easier for my arms to slide all the way around him. He raised his head, and our gazes locked. There was a whole lot of desire in his expression, but there was something else, too. Something I didn't understand, but that I instinctively didn't like.

I was going to ask him what was wrong, but before I had a chance, he was bending his head toward mine again, his slightly parted lips telegraphing his intentions and leaving no doubts in my mind. No doubts, and no thoughts, period. I forgot why I'd come here in the first place, forgot all my mixed feelings about him, forgot how harshly he'd spoken to me.

When his lips touched mine, I couldn't help the little gasp that escaped me. His lips were so soft and warm, his touch delicate without being tentative. It was the lightest of kisses, a bare brushing of lips, and yet it tingled through every nerve in my body.

"More," I whispered against his mouth, and he obliged me by deepening the kiss. My arms tightened around him, fingers kneading his back as I opened my mouth and invited him in.

The little moan that escaped him when he took his first taste sent a thrill through me from head to toe. His hands were no longer on the wall. One cupped the side of my face, holding my head at just the right angle to receive his kiss. The other rested on my waist, right above the waistband of my jeans. As his tongue began exploring the inside of my mouth, the hand on my waist began stroking up and down my side. His thumb brushed against the side of my breast with each stroke, and it didn't even occur to me to mind.

Feeling uncommonly bold, I skimmed my hands down his back until I found the edge of his T-shirt, then slipped them underneath until I found bare skin. His body was deliciously warm, his skin soft as silk. His breath hitched at the touch, but it was nothing that even vaguely resembled a protest.

I guess Ethan was feeling pretty bold, too, because his hand moved from my side to my front. He was still stroking up and down, moving slowly, making sure I had plenty of time to realize where that hand was headed and put a stop to things. But I didn't.

My back arched almost against my will when his hand cupped my breast. The touch was muffled by the sweater, shirt, and bra, but that didn't stop my nipples from tightening into hard little buds, nor did it stop the heat that gathered in my center.

Ethan's movements were less controlled now. His lips pressed against mine almost too hard, and he was no longer satisfied to feel me with so many layers between us. His hands bunched in the sweater and the shirt, shoving both up practically to my chin and exposing my bra.

He moved a little too fast for me, fast enough to let my mind clear for half a second while I tried to decide whether this was going too far. That half a second was all I needed to bring my common sense back on line.

Something was wrong with Ethan, I remembered suddenly. Kimber had noticed it, and I'd seen it, too, when he'd first yanked me in the door. Now was not the time for us to be exploring our mutual attraction, no matter what our bodies wanted. Ethan had tried to take advantage of me once before, and I worried that in his current state, he might not do too well at controlling himself if I let things get out of hand.

His hands had slipped around to my back as he tried to unhook my bra, but though a part of me was more than willing to take another step into the wild side, the wiser part of me stayed in control. I couldn't talk with his tongue in my mouth, so I settled for putting my hands on his chest and giving him a push.

Ethan made a sound deep in his throat, half growl, half groan, and though he stopped fumbling with my bra clasp, he didn't take his hands away, nor did he stop kissing me. There was no denying the arousal that lingered in my blood, but now that I'd started thinking again, I couldn't shut that part of my brain back down.

I had a lot of reasons not to fully trust Ethan, but even so I didn't believe he'd force me to do anything I didn't want to do. My fear was that his powers of persuasion and my own desires would once again sweep my common sense away and I would forget why I had to stop. And I *did* have to stop. After all, my agreement with the Erlking meant I couldn't go all the way without losing Ethan forever.

It was only at that moment that I really understood just how insidious the agreement was. If somehow all the problems between us melted away and I wanted to sleep with Ethan, I'd have to go to Arawn's bed first. Call me crazy, but I didn't think Ethan—or any other boy, for that matter—was going to like that idea. I was so screwed. In a manner of speaking.

I pushed harder on Ethan's chest, the mood now completely spoiled by my train of thought. The gesture would probably have been more convincing if I could have stopped myself kissing back, but it felt so damn good . . . *This,* I decided, was my first real kiss, a kiss untainted by magic.

I made a murmur of protest as I kept trying to push Ethan away. If he'd persisted even a moment longer, I was sure I'd find the willpower to turn my head, but he finally decided my "stop" signal took precedence over my "go" signal. He tore his mouth from mine, and I had a moment to register the look of frustrated anger on his face as he took a step backward and turned away from me.

I was being a total tease, even though I didn't mean to be. I opened my mouth to say something to smooth things over, but no words came to me. I didn't think explaining the sacrifice I'd had to make to win Ethan's freedom would improve the situation.

"I'm sorry," I finally said, feeling wretched as I pulled my shirt and sweater back down.

Ethan turned back to me abruptly, his eyes wide with surprise. "What on earth for?"

I blinked stupidly. He looked like he meant it, but I hadn't imagined the anger I'd seen on his face before he'd turned away. "I didn't mean to lead you on," I said in a tiny voice that hardly sounded like my own. It wasn't like me to be this tentative, but nothing in my life up till now had prepared me for dealing with Ethan.

He reached out and put both hands on my shoulders, giving them a firm squeeze. "You didn't do anything wrong." Again, he radiated sincerity.

"Then why were you so angry?"

He let go of my shoulders and leaned against the wall opposite me. "I wasn't angry at *you*," he assured me. "Look, I know you're not . . . experienced. I know better than to go so fast."

My cheeks flamed, and I found myself unable to meet his eyes. I kept letting myself forget how out of my league Ethan was. He was used to mature, experienced women, and right now I felt like a little girl, way more than two years younger than him.

Ethan wasn't looking at me at that moment, so he didn't see the shame that flooded me, and he kept on talking. "I shouldn't even have kissed you, not in the state I'm in right now."

The idea that he thought kissing me was a mistake sliced painfully through my chest, but I forced myself to focus on the more important part of what he'd said. "What state are you in right now?" This was, after all, the reason I'd come to see him despite the virtual DO NOT DISTURB sign he'd put out.

"I'm just . . . not myself," he said evasively, his eyes not quite meeting mine.

"What do you mean?"

He stood up straight, pushing away from the wall. "Hey, would you like something to drink? There's no reason for us to stand around in the hallway like this. Come in and sit down."

"Subtle," I said, but when I saw the look of near panic in his eyes, I backed off. "I'll take a Coke if you have it."

"Yeah. Sure. Have a seat. I'll be right back."

He ducked into the kitchen before I could answer. I was tempted to follow him, but I sensed it would be wiser to give him a little space. He might have just slammed the conversational door in my face, but the fact that he wanted me to stick around gave me hope. Maybe he wasn't yet ready to tell me what was wrong, but it wasn't impossible he'd nerve himself up to it before the night was through.

Smoothing my sweater down to make sure my clothing was all back to rights, I slipped into the living room and plopped down on the very masculine leather sofa.

chapter twenty-two

Ethan took far longer to get the drinks than I was expecting, and I considered going into the kitchen after him. I decided against it because I figured I needed the time to pull myself together as much as he did.

Apparently, it didn't matter what my logical, practical side told me about Ethan and all my reasons for doubting him. When he was near me, when he touched me, logic was useless. I'd pulled back tonight, but it was embarrassing to think how hard it had been. And if I ever ended up going on a real date with him, who knew what I'd end up doing. The guy turned my brain to mush, and that was ridiculously dangerous, for both of us. Of course, Ethan didn't know it was dangerous for him—I doubted the Erlking had let him in on our bargain.

Ethan looked a little better when he finally returned to the living room, bringing me a Coke in one of those old-fashioned glass bottles and a bottle of something called Old Peculier for himself. It was some kind of dark beer, and I suspected it wasn't anything cheap. His bottle was almost half empty already, which I didn't think was a good sign. He handed me the Coke, then sat beside me on the sofa and took a long pull on his beer. The silence between us felt awkward.

I tried to think of a subtle way to ask Ethan again what was wrong, but subtlety wasn't my strong suit. Ethan was rolling his bottle between his hands, staring at it sightlessly. Kimber was obviously right, and something was wrong. Maybe he and I weren't close enough for me to have the right to pry, but that didn't stop me.

"What did the Erlking do to you?" I asked softly.

Ethan blinked and snapped out of his brooding. He raised the bottle to his lips again, chugging the remains. I'm not a connoisseur of beer by any stretch of the imagination, but I suspected Old Peculier was meant to be sipped rather than chugged.

"I don't want to talk about it," Ethan said, setting the empty bottle on the coffee table in front of him, and then staring at it some more.

"I kinda got that hint," I replied. "But if you don't talk about it, how are you ever going to get over it? Whatever 'it' is?" Even at the time, I knew I should apply those words to my own situation, but I still wasn't ready to talk to anyone about my devil's bargain.

He shook his head. "It's just one of those things I'm going to have to deal with on my own."

"This is one of those guy things, right? You figure if you don't talk about your problems, they'll go away?"

He finally looked at me, and the expression on his face was forbidding. "When I said I don't want to talk about it, I meant it."

Maybe I should have backed down. If our positions were reversed and he were grilling me about how I'd gotten the Erl-king to let him go, I'd have been getting pretty pissed off about his questions. But some instinct inside me urged me to keep pushing, insisting that Ethan secretly *did* want to talk.

"You know, I practically sold my soul to the devil to get you back," I told him, and saw from his flinch that I was hitting a nerve. "Arawn kept telling me you were 'unharmed,' and I think I have a right to know if he was lying to me or not, because if he's lying about that, he could be lying about other things, too."

My whole argument was a pretty big stretch, but from the way Ethan's fists clenched in his lap, I guessed I was getting through to him in a tough love kind of way. He brooded another minute or two, then unclenched his fists and shook out his hands. Then he reached up and touched the tattoo that framed his eye.

"I've been released from the Wild Hunt," he said, still fingering the tattoo, "but it's not the same thing as being free." He dropped his hand and finally turned to look at me, his expression haunted. "I'm still tied to him, Dana. I don't have to ride with the Hunt, but I'm his creature now and always will be."

"I don't understand," I said, though I had a sneaking suspicion I actually did.

"When he bound me to the Hunt, when he put his mark on me . . ." Ethan touched the tattoo again. "I can't ever disobey him. His magic won't let me."

With a cry of mingled despair and frustration, Ethan collapsed into his seat, letting his head come to rest on the back of the sofa. The pain in his eyes was so intense I had to look away.

"I've been a goddamn puppet all my life," he said, his voice laced with a bitterness I'd never heard from him before. "I've always been the good son, done what my father wanted me to

238 • jenna black

do. He asked me to try to win you over, even if I had to be a lying bastard to do it, and it never even occurred to me to say no.

"Then, when I actually got to know you . . ." He shook his head without lifting it from the back of the couch. "You're your own person, Dana. I know your father wants to control you just like mine wants to control me, but you won't let it happen. You make your own decisions, and you don't let anyone push you around. I thought maybe . . . Maybe I could try to be like that, too. Maybe if my father asked me to do something I thought was wrong, I'd say no next time.

"You can bet he wasn't happy with me for trying to help you leave Avalon. It's the first time I've ever openly defied him like that, and it felt good. But now . . ." He laughed, but it wasn't a happy sound. "Now that I finally found the guts to stand up to my father, I end up with the Erlking's claws sunk into me so deep I'll never get free."

I gritted my teeth, thinking what an idiot I had been. I knew that my bargain with the Erlking had to be worded very carefully, that he would abide by it only to the letter of the law. I'd thought that freeing Ethan from the Hunt would mean freeing him from the Erlking, but now looking back I saw it for the stupid assumption it had been.

"I'm so sorry, Ethan," I said as guilt settled heavily on my shoulders.

He sat up straight, then leaned over and put his arm around my shoulders, drawing me close to his side. "You have nothing to be sorry for. I'd have been the Erlking's slave for life if you hadn't saved me."

He put his other arm around me and pulled me into a hug. I

went easily, resting my head against his chest and hearing the steady thump of his heart.

"I can't help wondering how you managed to do that," Ethan said as I cuddled against him. His arms tightened around me. "What did you have to give him, Dana?" His voice choked on the question.

I wanted to say something soothing, something to ease the guilt I heard in his voice. The truth certainly wasn't going to do that, and if I'd been able to think of a really good lie, I'd have used it already to calm everyone down.

I guess I was quiet long enough that Ethan figured I wasn't going to answer his question, because he let out a heavy sigh and asked another.

"Is it true, what you told Kimber? Did the Erlking put a geis on you?"

My first instinct was to lie. I'd lied about it so much already it was almost beginning to feel like the truth. But I just couldn't do it, not when Ethan had just poured out his heart to me. I wasn't ready to tell him the truth, but that didn't mean I had to lie.

"There is no geis," I confided. "Please don't tell anyone. It's not something I can talk about. I told everyone there was a geis so they would stop asking me."

His chin settled on the top of my head, rubbing back and forth absently. I was still aware of the warmth of him, and of my attraction, but this contact felt more peaceful.

"Maybe what's good for the gander is good for the goose?" he suggested gently.

I sighed. "Maybe it is, but I just can't talk about it. Not now." Maybe not ever, but I didn't feel a need to share that.

"All right," he said. "I won't push. But if you ever want to talk, I'm here for you."

My heart squeezed gratefully, and I knew that all my doubts and worries about Ethan were pointless. I was in too deep already, and as long as he wanted me, I would be his.

I stayed at Ethan's for about an hour. We didn't talk much, but we didn't make out again, either. I'd have been disappointed, if snuggling up in his arms on the couch hadn't felt so good all by itself. I could have stayed like that all night, but eventually I started yawning.

"We should get you home," Ethan said, and I knew he was right. He stood, drawing me to my feet right along with him. "I still can't believe you went traipsing around in the city all by yourself," he said, voice tight with disapproval. "How did you get past Finn, anyway? I thought he was stationed between your suite and the door."

Frowning, I looked up into Ethan's face. As far as I could remember, I hadn't ever described the setup of my safe house to him. I supposed he could be making an assumption, but it didn't sound like it.

He read the confusion on my face and explained without me having to question him. "The Erlking knows where you live."

Yes, I'd figured that out when I found his little charm on my bedside table. "And he told you?" I couldn't imagine why, and I didn't much like the idea of Ethan knowing. I might be halfway in love with him, but I *still* didn't fully trust him. Not that I thought he'd hurt me or anything, but I couldn't help fearing he'd tell someone he shouldn't.

Ethan stared at his toes. "Yeah, he told me. Said it wasn't inconceivable that he'd need to send me down there sometime. He's determined to make sure you don't get killed, at least not until you've given him what he wants."

I shook my head. "I don't suppose telling him I don't want his protection will do any good."

Ethan snorted. "No, I don't suppose it would. And don't think I'm letting you off that easy. How did you get past Finn?"

I opened my mouth to tell Ethan about the brooch, then thought better of it before any words came out. There were any number of reasons he might decide to take the brooch away from me, not least of which being the very fact that it came from the Erlking. He also might take it into his head to protect me from myself by making sure I couldn't get out of my safe house unnoticed again. He was a lot bigger and stronger than me, and even with my self-defense training, I doubted I'd be able to stop him from taking the brooch if he really wanted to.

"I snuck out while he was in the bathroom," I said, hoping Ethan didn't notice my hesitation. "Everyone thinks I'm really sensible, so it's not like they keep me locked up or anything. As far as Finn knows, I'm in my room fast asleep."

Ethan didn't look completely convinced, but he didn't challenge the story, either. "I'm going to walk you home," he informed me, and his tone said there would be no arguing with him.

I bit my lip. I'd actually be a lot safer if Ethan *didn't* walk me home, because then I could use the brooch. But I knew I wouldn't be able to talk him out of it without more explanation than I was willing to give. Yes, it would be a bit dangerous to

walk around Avalon with only Ethan for protection, but I decided it was an acceptable risk.

I felt more certain of my decision when Ethan took me directly
into the tunnel system through the hidden access point in the
courtyard. Traveling through the streets of Avalon, even at this
time of night, it was possible—if unlikely—that one of the bad
guys might spot me. But as vast as the tunnel system was, there
were only a few populated areas, which would be easy to avoid
now that I had my "native guide" with me.

The entrance we used led directly into one of the completely
unpopulated sections of the tunnel system, where there was no
electricity. I had my flashlight, but Ethan was using an actual
torch, which he lit by magic. It created a lot more light than my
flashlight, but I couldn't help finding its flickering flame—and
the moving shadows that flame created—creepy.

Ethan led the way, holding the torch out to his side because
the ceiling was too low for him to hold it up. Our footsteps
echoed eerily against the stone walls, and the occasional snap
and crackle of the flame set my nerves on edge. Then again, just
being in these tunnels tended to have that effect on me. As far as
I knew, I hadn't been claustrophobic before I'd come to Avalon,
but I was now.

Neither one of us talked much. The silence of the tunnels
was too oppressive, the echoes of even our whispers too un-
nerving. I'd always found the tunnels kinda scary, but the effect was worse than ever tonight. The tightness of Ethan's
shoulders and the cautious way he proceeded told me he felt it,
too. I told myself it was just our imaginations, that we couldn't

help being at least a little freaked out traveling these dark, deserted, confusing tunnels in the dead of night. That didn't stop the little hairs on the back of my neck from standing at attention.

Ethan reached back and took my hand, fingers intertwining with mine. His palm was sweaty, and that didn't do much to ease my fears. I swallowed hard, trying to convince myself I was being ridiculous, but it didn't work, and a few moments later, Ethan came to a stop.

"Something just doesn't feel right," he muttered under his breath.

I couldn't help agreeing with him. "What should we do?" I asked in the quietest whisper I could manage. But I couldn't imagine what we *could* do, other than keep moving.

Ethan's eyes were narrowed as he peered into the darkness ahead of us. The Fae have better eyesight than humans, but it seemed clear he didn't see any cause for alarm. Looking grimly determined, he took another step forward, his hand squeezing mine a little more firmly. He was going to cut off circulation to my fingers if he didn't ease up, but I was feeling anxious enough not to protest.

Something in the tunnel ahead of us made a coughing sound, and there was a little flash of light. Ethan cried out, and the torch fell from his hand.

I turned to him in alarm. "Ethan! What's wrong?" It was hard to see in the erratic light of the fallen torch, but there was a patch of wetness staining his right shoulder, just above his collarbone.

He collapsed to his knees, his fingers going limp in my hand. "Run, Dana," he said, and tried to give me a weak shove back the way we'd come. The stain on his shirt continued to spread, and he swayed. "Run!" he said again.

"Hell, no," I replied, grabbing hold of his good arm and trying to drag him to his feet. I wasn't entirely sure what was going on yet, but I did know I wasn't going to just run away and leave Ethan. When pulling on him didn't work, I draped his arm over my shoulder. "Come on!"

Footsteps echoed in the tunnel in front of us, and a ball of light slowly formed and expanded near the ceiling. I managed to get Ethan to his feet, but most of his weight was leaning on me, and he was barely conscious, too hurt even to use his healing magic. We weren't going to get far like this, but that didn't mean I wasn't going to try.

I got us turned around and took a couple of steps, but I was bracing myself for the sound of another gunshot—because what else could that coughing sound have been?—and for the pain of a bullet slamming into my back. It didn't happen, but something worse did. The light spell reached its full intensity, illuminating the tunnel for yards in both directions.

Standing in the middle of the tunnel, blocking my retreat and holding a gun big enough to qualify as a cannon, stood my aunt Grace.

chapter twenty-three

When I'd first met Aunt Grace, she'd reinforced every stereotype I'd ever had of the Fae. Way too beautiful to be human, reserved to the point of coldness, and arrogant as all hell. She was still all of those things, but with a heaping dose of crazy to top it off. Her smile was bright and triumphant as she pointed that damn cannon at my head. The scraggly, half-Fae guy who'd posed as Lachlan stood by her side. I guessed she'd bailed him out, or he'd still have been in jail. He, too, had a gun.

I glanced over my shoulder, even though I knew there was another armed enemy back there. Sure enough, an extremely large, nasty-looking human man was blocking the way. He was built like a football player—one of those fat but powerful lineman types—and made all the more intimidating by his buzz-cut hair and the jagged scar that slashed across his face. His gun was a lot smaller than Grace's, but its barrel was extended by a silencer.

We were trapped.

Heart beating in my throat, I carefully lowered Ethan to the floor. His breathing was ragged, his face squinched with pain, but at least he was conscious. And the bleeding seemed to have slowed, so maybe if I could miraculously get us out of this, he wasn't going to die. But he wasn't going to be much help, either.

I stood up slowly, putting my back against the tunnel wall so I could keep an eye on Grace and her super-sized henchman.

"And so we meet again, my dear niece," Grace said with a toothy, sharklike smile.

"Oh, joy," I responded, though I knew I should keep my mouth shut. From the first time I'd laid eyes on her, Grace had inspired me to take whatever verbal digs I could get in, and it seemed she still had that effect on me.

Her smile thinned, and her eyes pierced me, sending a shiver down my spine. "Still haven't learned to respect your betters, I see."

I raised my chin and met her stare, trying to project confidence as my mind cast about for any possibility of escape. "That one's just too easy," I said. Maybe if I could make her completely lose her temper, she'd give me some kind of opening I could take advantage of. Yeah, that was a pathetically thin hope, but I wasn't coming up with anything better.

"I'll have you singing a very different tune by the time I'm through with you," she said, her good humor restored by whatever she had in mind. "If I'd had any idea what you would do to my life, I'd have killed you when I first met you. It would have been so easy." She shook her head at herself.

Arawn had told me that she didn't want to use me against Titania anymore, that she was likely out to kill me. The fact that I was still alive now suggested either that Arawn was wrong, or that she had something worse than a quick death in mind. Dread pooled in my gut, because I didn't think Arawn was wrong.

"Why?" I asked her, stalling for time. "I've never done anything to you. Why are you so hot to kill me? I'm just a kid. Your *brother's* kid." Not that Grace had shown any sign she was attached to my father, although I thought he'd been at least somewhat attached to her.

Grace laughed. "Before you came to Avalon, I was one of the leading candidates for Consul. I was wealthy, and respected, and powerful. Now I am exiled from my home, I have a price on my head throughout Faerie, and the Wild Hunt is on my trail. All. Because. Of. You."

Yep. She was certifiable. And obviously determined to blame me for all the stupid crap she'd done. "No one forced you to kidnap me in the first place. If you'd just kept on living your life like normal, none of this would have happened." Of course, I knew I wasn't going to talk Grace out of her vendetta. In the battle between logic and crazy, crazy always wins. And however sweet Grace may have thought her life was before I came to Avalon, she hadn't gone from perfectly well-adjusted useful member of society to psycho killer bitch overnight. Whatever was wrong with her, it had been festering a long time. My arrival was just the trigger that set her off.

Aunt Grace couldn't refute my accusation, so she ignored it instead. "I'd have been shocked if you'd have lived out this year, even if I weren't after you myself. Seamus was a fool to bring a stupid mortal child here when he knew what trouble you would bring with you."

I fought back my urge to argue that I wasn't stupid, seeing as she had me trapped here. If only I'd been willing to tell Ethan about the Erlking's brooch, I'd be perfectly safe right now, and Ethan wouldn't have gotten shot.

Trying to look completely casual, I slipped my hand into the pocket of my jeans. The brooch was right there, and it was very likely that if I pricked my finger, neither Aunt Grace nor her henchmen would be able to see me, even though they knew I was here. It was tempting, but I wasn't sure how Aunt Grace would react if I suddenly disappeared.

Surreptitiously, I glanced down at Ethan. He was leaning against the wall of the tunnel, his eyes closed, his face pale. I didn't think he was unconscious, but he definitely wasn't in good shape. If I disappeared, I knew without a doubt Grace would use him as a hostage, and since I couldn't make the charm stop working until time was up, that meant Ethan would die.

"That boy is your Achilles heel," Grace said. "I knew if I kept a close watch on him, you'd show up on his doorstep eventually, but I never dreamed you'd be so accommodating as to show up alone." She cocked her gun and pointed it at Ethan.

I didn't even think about it; I just stepped between them, blocking Grace's shot. She smirked.

"You can't protect him from both myself and Fred at the same time. But I'm not planning to kill him. Not unless you make me, that is. And no, I'm not planning to let my friends kill him, either. I want him alive."

"Why?" I asked, because I couldn't imagine what she'd have to gain by letting Ethan go.

Her smile broadened. "I will explain in just a moment."

Ethan tried to call out a warning, but it was too late. I started to turn around, but before I could dodge or block or even duck, lineman Fred's fist connected with my chin and sent me flying into the opposite wall. The whole world seemed to tilt sideways, and the walls of the tunnel closed in on me.

I woke up to find my situation had not improved. My head throbbed viciously, and my stomach lurched. I blinked and pushed myself up into a sitting position.

I was still on the floor of the tunnel, approximately where I'd landed when Fred had hit me. He stood towering over me, his arms crossed over his barrel chest. He was so big he practically filled the tunnel, and even if my head hadn't been swimming, I wouldn't have been able to dart around him.

I turned to look in the other direction, and my stomach gave another lurch. While I'd been out, Grace and her other friend had dragged Ethan about ten yards down the tunnel. Her friend held Ethan's sagging body up, with his arms pinned behind his back, while Grace held her gun to his head. She smiled at me again. She was having a grand ol' time.

"As I said, your Achilles heel." She licked her lips. "You were willing to risk a great deal when the Erlking took him, now weren't you?"

I didn't really think that question required an answer, so I just stared at her. How the hell was I going to get out of this? And get Ethan out of it, too? I hadn't gone through everything I'd gone through just to let Aunt Grace kill him.

"Do you know how old I am?" she asked, and I was totally startled by the question that seemed to come out of nowhere. I shook my head. I might have mentioned that I didn't care, either, except I was still kind of dopey after that blow to my head.

"I am almost two thousand," she said.

My mind couldn't encompass that. I'd known she was old, but I'd somehow thought her age numbered in centuries, not freakin' millennia.

"When I was a young woman, all of Faerie was practically under siege."

"By the Erlking," I said, because I couldn't imagine any other reason she'd be telling me this.

"Indeed," she confirmed with a nod. "He and his Wild Hunt were the creatures of nightmare, even to the Unseelie Court, who are nightmares themselves. No one liked to admit it, but he was a match even for the Queens, and his power kept growing greater and greater. Until one of Mab's spies discovered his secret power, the power that was helping him grow stronger, and Mab spread the word throughout all of Faerie."

Her eyes shone in the artificial glow of her light spell, and I could tell she was really, really enjoying herself. Which meant that whatever the point of this story was, I was going to hate it.

"It was around this time that Titania launched her great campaign against the Erlking and learned the hard way that he had grown too powerful for her to defeat. He stole my nephew, forced him to become part of the Wild Hunt. It was a bold and brilliant move, proving to both the Queens that he had the power to take from them even those who were closest to them. However, the Courts now knew his secret power and could guard against him using it. And so the Erlking proposed a truce with the Queens. He would never again kill any member of their Courts without their permission. And they would bind their Courts to secrecy, to hide his secret power from future generations."

This was way more than my dad had ever told me about the Erlking's bargain with the Queens. He'd given me the impression that the geis wouldn't allow him to speak about it at all, but apparently that wasn't the case, at least not for Aunt Grace.

"Shall I tell you the Erlking's secret?" Grace asked, chortling.

I blinked at her. My heart was beating like a frightened rabbit's, and my mouth was completely dry. Anything that made her that happy was not a good thing for me. Not at all.

"You can't," I said, my voice barely above a whisper as dread tried to steal my breath. "The geis . . ."

She laughed, the sound echoing hollowly against the stone. "Oh, but I can, my dear. You see, the geis only applies to those who are affiliated with the Courts. Those of us who were born in Faerie were dedicated to our Courts while still infants, and unless we perform a ritual to formally sever our ties, we are still subject to them. Avalon may have treaties with Faerie, but if the Queens wanted to call their subjects back, most of the Fae would obey their call.

"But thanks to you, my own beloved Queen ordered my execution and sent the Wild Hunt after me." Her face twisted in a snarl, and the hate in her eyes was so intense I felt it almost like a physical blow. "With my life forfeit anyway, it meant nothing to me to sever my ties to the Seelie Court. And when I severed the ties, the geis lost its power to silence me."

My mind reeled as I tried to take this all in. Things were starting to click into place in the back of my head. I could feel it happening, but I couldn't seem to wrap my brain around it, and I was pretty sure I didn't want to.

"Let me take a wild guess as to what you promised the Erlking in return for your boyfriend's freedom," she continued, her eyes aglow. "Did you by any chance pledge to give him your virginity?"

I really, really wanted to deny it, but I was too shocked to say anything. Even as hurt as Ethan was, he managed to raise his head and look at me with widened eyes. I hated my own cowardice as I dropped my gaze.

"Of course you did, because there is nothing he could want from you more than that. Because, you see, therein lies his secret power. When a virgin gives herself to him of her own free will, he can take from her everything she has, everything she is. All her power becomes his, all her life force becomes his, and when it is over she is nothing but an empty shell that once was a person but will never be again."

chapter twenty-four

Everything that had happened since the Erlking came to Avalon now suddenly made a sickening kind of sense. I had assumed that what the Erlking wanted was for me to ride out into the mortal world with his Hunt so he could get his jollies killing mortals. But I realized now he'd been playing me from the very beginning. He guessed correctly that I wouldn't be willing to take him into the mortal world, so he made a big production about how he wanted it, and wanted it bad. Made me think that my riding with the Hunt was his ultimate goal, the Big Bad. When all along, he'd wanted more. Much more.

"So what you're telling me is that if I, er, fulfilled my bargain with the Erlking, he'd become a Faeriewalker himself?" I asked, just to make sure I fully understood what Grace was telling me. I knew there was at least a slim possibility she was lying to me, but her words had the devastating ring of truth.

"Exactly," Grace said, sounding incredibly self-satisfied. "And so would begin a reign of terror the likes of which the mortal world has never seen. Mab and Titania were similarly able to guess the Erlking's intent, of course. He'd have a dramatic effect on the mortal world, but the Queens must be horrified at the idea of him absorbing a Faeriewalker's ability to bring dangerous technology into Faerie. They'll be even more eager to kill you now." She made a mock pouty face. "Too bad they won't get the chance."

Yeah, that was a real shame. But I still wasn't dead, and every word Grace spoke made me more and more certain that wasn't a good thing. She touched her tongue to her upper lip, like she was literally savoring the taste of victory.

"I could kill you now, of course," she said casually, moving the gun away from Ethan's head and pointing it at me. I had the vague thought that I should take advantage of the fact that Ethan was no longer an inch from death, but I couldn't imagine how. "But where would be the fun in that?" Grace continued, and Fred the Mountain Man laughed.

The gun moved back to Ethan's head. Out of the corner of my eye, I saw Fred rubbing his hands together in anticipation.

"Naturally, I don't know the exact terms of your agreement with the Erlking," Grace said. "But I can make some educated guesses. He released your boyfriend from the Wild Hunt, so he must have felt he'd completely ensured your cooperation. Which means he has to have put in place a stipulation that there will be unpleasant consequences if you were not to preserve your virginity for him."

My stomach heaved as it dawned on me just what Grace was leading up to.

"He can't kill anyone unless given permission by one of the Queens, so he can't have controlled you with threats of killing your loved ones. I suppose he could have threatened to kill your brother, since he doesn't belong to the Courts, but you don't even know Connor, so I hardly think that threat would be potent enough."

She turned and looked at Ethan. "But this one is a different story. This one still bears the Huntsman's Mark. And I'll wager if you were to lose your virginity to someone other than the Erlking, that would void your agreement and lover-boy here would be bound to the Hunt once again."

I tried to shut off my emotions, my fear and my horror. I didn't want to give Grace any evidence that she was right, plus I didn't want to give her the satisfaction. I failed miserably. My stomach heaved again, and this time I couldn't get it under control. I puked up everything I had in my stomach, then followed that up with a few dry heaves.

"Disgusting creature," Grace said, wrinkling her nose delicately. "Are you sure you want her, Fred?"

Fred laughed, the sound nasty and spiteful. "She's not really my type, but for what you're paying, I'm happy to make the supreme sacrifice." I could hear just how much of a sacrifice he thought it would be.

I spit a few times, trying to get the foul taste out of my mouth, but it didn't work. I sent Grace my most pathetic, pleading look, even though I knew it didn't have a chance in hell of working.

"You don't have to do this," I said weakly. "It's me you're mad at, not Ethan. Just let him go. Please."

I was giving Grace just what she wanted, and her cheeks flushed with pleasure. I clamped my jaws shut and resisted the urge to beg some more.

Heedless of the gun pointed at his head, Ethan struggled

against the other man's hold. I think at that point he'd have found it a mercy if Grace shot him, which was probably why she didn't. He was too badly injured to have much hope of escaping, and his face was etched with pain.

Grace frowned at Ethan. "I don't want you distracting me. I want to savor every moment of this."

Instead of shooting him, she slammed the butt of the gun against Ethan's wound. He screamed, then went limp. Grace's half-Fae friend let Ethan's body collapse to the floor, then planted a foot in Ethan's back and pointed his gun at his head.

"I'll keep him under control," he told Grace. There was no emotion in his voice, like he didn't care what was going to happen one way or another.

Grace turned her full attention to me, and if I'd had anything left in my stomach, I'd have hurled again. Fred grabbed me by one arm and yanked me to my feet with so much force I would have fallen down again if he hadn't kept his hold on me. Then he slammed me into the wall, knocking all the breath out of my lungs. While I was still struggling to breathe, he grabbed my wrists and pulled them up above my head, pinning them to the wall with one big hand, his grip so hard I could feel my bones grinding together. Ethan yelled a protest, but injured and pinned to the floor as he was, he couldn't help me.

No one could help me. Or Ethan. No one but the bad guys even knew we were here, and we weren't anywhere near the more populated regions of the tunnel system. Fred was going to rape me, and in doing so bind Ethan to the Hunt once more. And then Grace was going to kill me.

Despite all my lessons with Keane, I knew my self-defense moves weren't going to be enough against Fred. He was just too much bigger than me. The best I could hope to do was slow him down.

My terror was like a living creature writhing in my chest and belly. Tears streaked my cheeks, but I didn't care about that, didn't care about appearances, or how much satisfaction my pain and horror were giving Grace.

I knew now what hatred felt like. It was an ice-cold burning sensation in my gut. It was an enraged scream that clawed its way up my throat. It was a narrowing of my world until there was nothing that existed except me, the hatred, and its object. Fred put his hand on my breast and squeezed brutally hard. I felt it, and the human part of me cringed, but the hatred had taken charge, and Fred was barely worthy of its interest.

I turned my head to stare at Grace. Grace, who blamed me for every mistake she had made. Grace, who wasn't satisfied to get her revenge by simply killing me, but who had to torture me and condemn Ethan.

I was in what could only be described as an altered state, and everything I did, I did from pure instinct.

I began to hum under my breath, just tuneless noise at first, but my fury searched out the angriest song I knew, and the hum turned into "O Fortuna" from *Carmina Burana*. Fred was dragging the bottom of my sweater up, but I ignored him, my entire being focused on the song I was humming so quietly no one could hear.

I felt the first prickle of magic almost immediately. I had no idea what I was going to do with it, seeing as I'd still never actually accomplished anything remotely like a spell before, but I had nothing better to try.

My utter lack of response to his groping had made Fred

complacent, sure that I was completely beaten down and help-less. I could tell by the hard lump that swelled behind his zipper just how much he liked helpless.

Maybe I really was helpless. Maybe I *still* couldn't get the magic to do anything useful. But I wasn't going to lose every-thing without putting up one hell of a fight. The magic was still gathering, but I knew I could call more, and the more I called, the more powerful the hypothetical spell I could cast. Which meant I had to find a way to stall before Fred got around to the main event.

It was hard to hum and fight at the same time, but all those lessons with Keane had created a lot of muscle memory, the kind that worked with a minimum of conscious thought. Since Fred had gotten careless enough to leave me a little room to move, I managed to stomp down on his instep.

He had me pinned firmly enough that I couldn't get a whole lot of leverage on the stomp. I think it surprised him more than hurt him, but it accomplished its purpose, interrupting his groping and slowing him down. The magic was still building, and I hoped like hell Grace was far enough away that she couldn't sense it, or she'd be sure to destroy my last chance.

I might not have hurt Fred very much, but apparently he didn't appreciate me stomping on his foot. He retaliated with a backhand that made my head spin, even though he hadn't been able to get a whole lot of leverage, either, not while keeping me pinned.

Blood filled my mouth, and my humming screeched to a halt. The magic started to recede, and I desperately reached out for it, the song rising once again in my throat. Fred was giving me a funny look, which probably meant I was now humming loud enough for him to hear. He must have thought my elevator wasn't going to the top floor anymore, but that didn't lessen his eagerness to rape me. His hand dropped to my jeans, and he began fumbling with the button.

Panic tried to seize hold of me, but I fought it off with all my might. If I allowed the panic to take hold, I was doomed, and so was Ethan. We probably were anyway, but I was determined to take that one, desperate last shot.

The magic was everywhere now, so thick in the air I could hardly breathe. Fred was so eager to get down to business he was being clumsy about opening my jeans. As long as the intensity of the magic kept growing, I kept humming, determined not to unleash it until the last possible moment, until I'd drawn every scrap of it I could to me.

The zipper on my jeans rasped down, and I realized I was almost out of time. The magic was so strong now I didn't think I could breathe well enough to keep humming, and I was starting to feel lightheaded with it.

Fred was my most immediate threat, but he wasn't the one I needed to take out, at least not first. I was probably only going to have one shot—assuming I had anything like a shot at all—and there was only one person whom I wanted to absorb that blast of fury.

Fred was trying to tug my jeans down when I unleashed all the magic I'd gathered to me, sending it at Grace with an incoherent cry of fury, a screaming high note that would have shattered glasses if there were any around.

My scream made everyone pause for a moment. Even Fred forgot his efforts to get my jeans down, gaping at me.

The blast of magic slammed into Grace, the force of it making her take a step back. Her eyes widened in alarm and shock. The light spell she'd cast fizzled out, leaving the tunnel lit only by Ethan's dropped torch.

I wanted Grace to poof out of existence, to melt into a puddle of goo, or to go up in flames. Some sign that my magic had hurt her, would destroy her even if in the end I couldn't save myself or Ethan. But other than that one step backward and the death of the light spell, nothing happened.

Grace shook her head and took a step forward so that she was standing beside her henchman and Ethan once more. There was a hint of worry in her eyes, but there seemed to be nothing wrong with her, and she smiled her evil smile again.

I closed my eyes in despair. I'd failed.

chapter twenty-five

Fred turned his attention back to me, and I was so shattered by the failure of my spell that I barely had the will to struggle. What was the point anymore? Struggling would only prolong the inevitable. However, I'm one of the most stubborn people I know, and even though my heart wasn't in it, I still put up a fight, enough to get Fred cursing. I opened my eyes just in time to see him draw back his fist to hit me.

"Now!" a deep, familiar voice shouted, the sound echoing so much it was hard to tell where it was coming from.

Everyone was startled by the sound and started looking around wildly, trying to find the source of the voice. Grace immediately started chanting something, which I figured was the start of one of her nasty offensive spells.

But one person apparently *wasn't* startled by the voice. Ethan took advantage of his captor's momentary distraction to surge to his feet and throw the bastard off. In a moment of déjà vu, I saw the glint of silver in his hand, and realized that knife of his had appeared out of nowhere again.

Grace turned to him, and I screamed out a warning. I'd seen what Grace's magic could do, seen it completely crush a car. But although Grace was now shouting the words of her spell, nothing seemed to be happening, and Ethan plowed into her. His knife found a space between her ribs, and he shoved it in all the way to the hilt.

That was the last of Ethan's strength, and he let go of the knife, falling limply to the floor. Grace stood there in shock, staring at the knife that now protruded from her chest. Her hand shook as she reached out to grasp the hilt and pull it out. She cried out in pain as she pulled, and when the knife was all the way out, blood poured from the wound.

A cloaked and hooded figure materialized out of the darkness only a few feet from me and Fred. Fred decided that the new arrival was more of a threat than I was, so he let me go and charged forward with a battle cry that might have been intimidating, if his target were capable of being intimidated. Fred's hand reached for the gun tucked into the back of his pants.

"No!" Grace yelled, but even if Fred heard her, he ignored her, firing off a muffled shot that hit Arawn in the head and momentarily rocked him back. But the Erlking had survived having his head chopped off, and the bullet didn't seem to bother him much. He let his hood slide down so Fred could see his unmarred face.

Either Fred wasn't very bright, or he was just completely desperate, because even once he saw that his bullet had failed to hurt the Erlking, much less kill him, he still kept firing. Until the Erlking's sword skewered him right through the chest, that is. The light went out in Fred's eyes, and the gun fell from his limp fingers. The Erlking calmly put his hand on the dead man's shoulder and yanked his bloody blade free.

Grace's other accomplice had much more sense than Fred, and started running like hell, quickly disappearing into the darkness. I was betting he had a flashlight on him, but he didn't turn it on. Better to run blindly than to light a beacon, I supposed.

"He won't get far," Arawn said as Fred's body fell in a heap at his feet. "The Hunt is waiting for him."

Grace had sunk to her knees, her face ashen as blood continued to flow from the knife wound. She was pressing on the wound with both hands, but it seemed to have little effect. Ethan dragged himself away from her. He was obviously still weak and in pain, but he was also obviously in better shape than Grace. Even the exertion of fighting his way to his feet and stabbing Grace hadn't started his wound bleeding again.

Either Ethan had hit a more vital spot, or my spell had had more effect on Grace than I'd thought. I remembered her light spell going out, and remembered her failed attempt to cast something at Ethan before he'd stabbed her.

Arawn kicked Fred's body out of his way and advanced on Grace, who forgot about trying to stanch the blood and held her hands out in a warding gesture.

"No!" she begged, but Arawn kept coming.

I wondered what was going on. Arawn had been able to kill Fred because Fred attacked him, but Grace was just sitting there, helpless and bleeding. I thought maybe he was trying to trick her into attacking him in self-defense—like he'd tricked Ethan—but frankly, she didn't seem to be in any shape to attack even if she fell for it.

"Please," Grace tried again, but this time, to my shock, blood dripped from her mouth, and she began to make a noise somewhere between a cough and a choke. It should have taken more than a small stab wound, no matter how well placed, to kill one of the Sidhe, even if my spell had taken her healing magic offline. So why did it look like she'd taken a mortal wound?

The Erlking's sword whistled through the air, moving blindingly fast. It sliced clean through Grace's neck without even slowing down.

I caught only the briefest glimpse of what happened, because the Erlking quickly stepped between me and her, his cloak completely blocking my view. But that brief glimpse was more than enough to haunt my nightmares for years to come. It might have been a quick death, but it sure as hell wasn't a pretty one. Even Ethan's face turned green at the sight.

Blood still dripping from his blade, the Erlking turned to face me. "Are you all right?" he asked, and the question was so absurd it startled a nearly hysterical laugh out of me.

"Oh, sure, just peachy," I said between giggles. "I was just almost raped, and I watched you stab one guy and behead my aunt, oh, and I got knocked around a bit, but other than that, I'm having a blast." I was still laughing, but there were tears on my face, and I was having trouble getting a full breath into my lungs. Okay, so maybe that sound coming out of me was more like sobs than laughter.

It was hard to read the Erlking's face in the flickering, erratic light of the downed torch. His eyes were hidden in shadow, but I felt the pressure of their gaze on me even as he pulled a rag from somewhere under his cloak and started wiping the blood from the blade.

"I am sorry I could not get here sooner to spare you some of what you've been through," he said, sounding like he meant it.

The calmness of his voice and his manner took a bit of the edge off my hysteria, though now that it was over, I started to shake all over.

"How did you get here at all?" I asked.

It was too dark to tell for sure, but I think he smiled. "As Ethan has told you by now, he is still bound to me even if he is no longer bound to my Hunt. When he was hurt, I sensed it. Then I used our bond to find him."

"And communicate with him," I said, because I remembered the Erlking shouting "Now," which had obviously been a signal to Ethan—one Ethan was expecting.

Arawn nodded. "And communicate."

"But how could you kill Grace? She's a citizen of Avalon, and you're not allowed to kill anyone in Avalon unless they attack you."

"There is one other condition that will allow me to kill in Avalon," he said.

Of course there was. Both he and Grace had mentioned that he was hunting her, and my dad had said he was allowed to pursue his quarry into Avalon. I'd assumed the Erlking had come to Avalon in pursuit of the Fae I'd seen him kill the first day he'd come, but now I figured the Fae had been a bonus and Grace his main quarry.

Ethan forced himself up into a sitting position with a grunt of pain. Arawn dismissed me for the moment and went to kneel beside his former Huntsman. I don't know for certain if it was on purpose, but he managed to position himself in such a way that his shadow hid Grace's decapitated body from my vision.

"Lie down," the Erlking ordered Ethan, and though I saw the spark of rebellion in Ethan's eyes, he obeyed. I guessed he didn't have any choice.

The Erlking put his hand over Ethan's wound, then pressed down hard. Ethan screamed in pain, and I tried to scramble to my feet. What I could possibly do to help Ethan against the Erlking was anyone's guess. But after that scream, Ethan's body went completely limp.

For one terrible minute, I thought he was dead. Then the Erlking lifted the hand he'd laid on Ethan's chest, holding something between his thumb and index finger. It was the bullet.

"It had to come out before he could heal properly," he said.

I steadied myself with a hand against the wall. "You could have just taken him to a healer. A healer could have fixed him up without hurting him."

He nodded. "Even so. And in the intervening time, he'd have been in constant pain. Better to have it over with quickly, don't you think?"

I wanted to disagree with him, but that would make me a hypocrite. After all, I'd decided to let Keane heal my hand when I'd hurt it for just that reason.

Dropping the bullet, Arawn stood up, the shadows and his black cloak making him seem even larger than he really was. "I take it you fully understand the terms of our bargain now."

"Yeah," I said weakly. I could have lied, but Ethan had heard Grace's big revelation, and it was pretty obvious now that anything Ethan knew, the Erlking knew.

I closed my eyes to stop the tears that wanted to spill out. I had known from the moment he'd made the offer that Arawn was angling for more than sex, that giving him my virginity would have some kind of unpleasant consequences. So why the hell did it hurt my feelings to discover those consequences would have included my death? He was the bad guy, a cold-blooded, cold-hearted killer. Yeah, he'd just saved my life, but he'd done it entirely for his own purposes. I couldn't put out if I was dead. So it should have come as no surprise that he was planning to use and kill me, just like Grace had planned to.

"I would not have taken your life," the Erlking said, and I jumped because he was much closer to me than I'd been expecting.

I opened my eyes and looked up at him. "Yeah, right."

"Dana, I have no need of your life. It is only your Faeriewalker magic that I crave."

"Well, you're not getting either." It seemed I was taking a life-long vow of chastity. That reality would hit me harder a little later, I knew, but with everything I now knew, there was no way I could ever have sex. Doing it with the Erlking would literally be the death of me—and of who knows how many innocent people—and doing it with anyone else meant Ethan would be sucked up into the Hunt again.

He smiled at me. "You never know what the future will bring."

"In this case, yes, you do."

His look was all confidence and conceit. "You speak with the certainty of the very young. We'll see if over time I can find the proper inducement to change your mind. I will vow to you right now that if you fulfill our bargain, I will not take your life. I would even agree to a geis to that effect."

"Which we'd need to seal with a kiss or with blood, right?"

He nodded. "No thanks." No more blood, no more pain, no more kisses.

He shrugged. "Then I suppose you will just have to trust my word." The look on his face hardened. "Trust my word on this, too. If you reveal my secret to anyone who doesn't already know, I will make your brother suffer for it every day of his immortal life."

I swallowed the lump of fear that formed in my throat. There wasn't a doubt in my mind that the Erlking would keep that promise. I didn't even know Connor, but I couldn't let him take the punishment for it if I opened my big mouth.

"I won't tell," I whispered.

His face softened into a smile again. "I know you won't," he said, his tone strangely gentle. "That is why I can make the threat in good conscience. You are very protective of those who matter to you, and it takes very little to make someone matter."

I had no answer to that, so I just kept quiet.

chapter twenty-six

It took Ethan only about five minutes to regain consciousness. The Erlking's healing spell was impressive, and Ethan showed no signs of being in pain. Well, not physical pain, at least. He seemed to be having trouble making eye contact with me. I wondered if he'd labeled me a slut now that he knew what I'd promised, but I wasn't about to ask him. If he had, I didn't want to know.

Five other members of the Wild Hunt showed up shortly after Ethan woke up. For the first time, none of them wore a mask or a helmet, so I could see their faces. They all had the typical beauty of the Fae, but there was a haunted look in all of their eyes that told me they were not happy to be the Erlking's slaves.

One of them was carrying Grace's other accomplice over his shoulder. Blood covered the accomplice's face, and the gaping wound that cut across his entire throat told me he wouldn't be doing any more time in jail. Despite knowing better, he must have been tricked by the Huntsmen into striking the first blow. The Erlking nodded in approval.

"Well done," he said, giving his Huntsman a pat on the shoulder. "I will escort Dana home." He made a sweeping gesture that encompassed both Fred and Grace. "Dispose of these and then return to the house." He looked at Ethan. "You should go home. Dana will be safe with me."

Ethan looked scared and angry at the same time. "Will she really?"

The Erlking laughed. "Safer than she was with *you,* my boy," he said, once again gesturing at our dead enemies.

Ethan's face flushed all the way to the roots of his hair, and he dropped his gaze. I guess I was too stunned in the aftermath of what had happened to feel any particular sense of self-preservation, because I kicked Arawn in the shin as if he weren't the most dangerous person in all of Avalon.

"Don't talk to Ethan like that!" I snapped. "It's not his fault he got shot and couldn't help me."

Arawn grinned at me. "Did you just attack me, Faeriewalker?"

That whole self-preservation thing came rushing back, and my stomach dropped like I was in a fast-moving elevator. But Arawn was still grinning, and there was a teasing twinkle in his eyes. He wouldn't be looking at me like that if I'd just given him an excuse to draw me into the Hunt and capture my powers for himself. I wondered if it was the harmlessness of my kick that saved me, or whether it was being female. After all, there were no female Huntsmen, at least not as far as I could tell.

Arawn surprised me by explaining.

"It's in the intent," he said. "You did not truly intend me

harm—your kick was nothing more than a reprimand. There-fore it doesn't count as an attack. It's the same thing that al-lowed me to feign striking you to trick this one." He nodded his head sideways at Ethan. "If I'd had intent to hurt you, I would not have been able to swing the sword."

I nodded, wondering if I would ever be able to absorb all the intricacies of Fae magic. And wondering about that made me remember my own spell, the desperation attack I'd launched on Grace. My first thought had been that it had failed utterly. But now I wasn't so sure.

My eyes drifted toward Grace's body, though I had no wish to see. Luckily, her upper body—and her severed head—were lost somewhere in the shadows. My gorge rose anyway, and I quickly averted my gaze.

It was frightening how well Arawn could read me. He an-swered the question I wasn't willing to put into words.

"I have never encountered magic like yours before," he told me. "I am far older than your aunt Grace, and yet never have I even heard of such a power."

"Umm, what power would that be, exactly?"

"At a guess, I'd say that you somehow made her mortal."

"What?" I cried. Even Ethan and the Huntsmen looked star-tled by that.

"Her connection to magic was completely severed when you cast your spell," the Erlking explained. "Her active spell died, and she seemed incapable of casting another, despite her considerable power. The wound Ethan dealt her was serious, but not fatal, not to one of the Sidhe. And evidence suggests she might have died even had I not struck her a fatal blow myself."

If that's really what I'd done, then I was even more of a

threat to the Queens of Faerie than they knew. Like they needed one more reason to kill me! To have the power to make an immortal Fae mortal . . .

I tried not to let my thoughts show on my face, but the Erlking hadn't lived as long as he had without learning a thing or two about reading people. Or maybe it was just that he was thinking the same thing himself. He looked down at me with an expression that was both grave and slightly sinister.

"There are a few things you should keep in mind, should you find yourself tempted to use that spell on me. You cast it this time in a moment of extreme stress. How sure are you that you'd be able to replicate it at will? It's not exactly something you can practice, unless you're much more ruthless than you let on. And, of course, just because it worked on your aunt Grace is no guarantee it would work on me. I am not Sidhe."

"If you're not Sidhe, what are you?" I asked, although that was hardly the most important question to ask at the moment.

One corner of his mouth curled upward. "I am the Erlking. I am one of a kind." From someone else, that might have sounded arrogant, but Arawn presented it as a simple statement of fact, no hint of pride in his voice.

"I'm sure both your world and mine are thankful," I said, and he laughed again. He seemed to find me pretty funny, considering we were in the process of discussing how I could be his Kryptonite, the one person in the universe who might actually be able to kill him.

Again, he seemed to read my thoughts. "I don't fear you, Faeriewalker. You would not attempt to destroy me out of malice, and I will not put myself in such a situation as to give you good cause to unleash your powers on me. Besides, if you try, and you fail, then you *will* join my Hunt, for that would constitute an attack."

I did actually believe he wasn't worried, and unfortunately, I thought his reasoning was spot on. Could I have unleashed that spell on Grace if we hadn't been in the heat of battle? Much as I hated her, could I have killed her in cold blood? I doubted it.

"Come now," he said. "Let's get you home."

I was more than ready to get out of there, to get away from the blood and the bodies. I thought for sure Ethan was going to come with us—after all, the Erlking hadn't technically ordered him to go home—but he murmured some excuse and slipped away, taking his torch with him, before I had a chance to protest.

Arawn retrieved a flashlight from Fred's body, handing it to me before casting a light spell that made the flashlight unnecessary. Then he put a hand on my shoulder blade to guide me forward while his Huntsmen converged on the bodies. He turned the first corner he came to, and I suspected that was more to distance me from the carnage than because it was the direction we needed to go.

"If you can just get me to someplace I recognize, I can use your charm," I told him. How I wished I'd done that in the first place.

"Not necessary," he said. "I'll take you all the way."

I came to a stop. "No, you won't. No one knows I've left my safe house, and it's going to stay that way."

Arawn turned to face me, one eyebrow lifted. "So you plan not to tell anyone about Grace's demise and your part in it?"

I felt my eyes widening. "Oh, hell no! People are already

lined up around the block wanting to kill me. The last thing I need is to give them yet another reason. Not to mention my dad would go completely ballistic if he knew I snuck out." And considering what had almost happened to me because of it, he'd be perfectly justified.

"You underestimate your own strengths," Arawn said, and I could have sworn I heard admiration in his voice. "You are not so easy to kill."

"I'd have been dead meat if you hadn't showed up tonight."

"But I did. And I've already told you I won't let anyone hurt you. Your power lies not only in what you can do yourself, but in what others can do for you. I am not a bad person to have on your side when both Queens of Faerie wish you dead."

"Yeah, well, I'm not so good at counting on others." I don't know what moved me to be so frank with him. A smart person would be extra super careful about every word out of her mouth when talking to someone like the Erlking, but I was chatting with him like we were best buds.

He nodded his agreement. "You must always count on yourself first. But don't discount your friends and allies."

I met his blue, blue eyes. "Even allies who've played me for a fool and planned to kill me once they got what they wanted?"

He didn't flinch from my gaze. "I never planned to kill you. Just because I'm capable of doing a thing doesn't mean I'm going to do it. As for playing you . . ." He shrugged. "You made a deal with the one and only King of Faerie. You can't possibly have expected to come out of that unscathed. In fact, I know you *didn't* expect to. I played my part, and you played yours. And for all that you feel that I've deceived you, I did release Ethan from the Hunt."

"But you didn't release him from yourself."

"Which is a good thing," he countered, "else tonight would have ended very differently."

I let my shoulders sag, tired of arguing. "The bottom line is you're not going to let me sneak back home and keep everything under wraps, right?"

Arawn leaned his back against the wall, crossing his arms over his chest. His eyes looked far away, like he was thinking hard about something. He stood like that for a good minute, long enough for the silence to start getting on my nerves.

"You are not of the Wild Hunt," he finally said. "It is not for me to declare whether you should or should not share your . . . adventures with your guardians. But as your ally, I can advise you, and it's my advice that you not keep so many secrets from those who have the power to help you. Your father and your bodyguard are substantial assets, and you would do well not to keep secret things that could destroy their trust in you when the truth inevitably comes to light."

Unfortunately, I feared it was a little too late for that. Finn had forgiven me for sneaking out with Keane, and he'd done me the huge favor of not telling my father. But if he were to find out I'd snuck out two more times after that, he'd be massively disappointed in me. Most likely he would never trust me again. Also, he would probably tell my dad about the first incident, and that would cause all kinds of problems. Dad would be mad at me, of course, but I bet he'd also be mad at Finn, for not telling him in the first place, and at Keane for being my accomplice. And let's not even talk about what they would think if they found out about my magic!

I could totally see Arawn's point that keeping such massive

secrets from them could come back and bite me in the butt. But I'd crossed the point of no return long ago, and if I was to have even a modicum of freedom, I would have to keep those secrets hidden.

"I can't let them know I snuck out," I told Arawn. "Please just point me in the right direction and let me use the charm to sneak back in."

He frowned at me, like he was displeased with my decision. Then he shrugged. "Very well. If that's what you wish."

"It is," I said.

At the very last moment, I could have sworn I caught a glint of satisfaction in Arawn's eyes, and it occurred to me that he might have played me yet again. But I was too exhausted and wrung out to care, so I just let it slide.

chapter twenty-seven

We didn't talk anymore as the Erlking guided me through the twisting labyrinth of the tunnels. He never showed a moment's hesitation, though I was hard-pressed to tell the difference between one tunnel and another.

Eventually, the tunnel we were traveling along led to a lighted section, and soon we arrived on familiar ground, the entrance I habitually used to go into the city proper. From there, I could find my way back to the safe house with ease.

I dug the Erlking's charm out of my pocket. I desperately wanted to get home to the safety and security of my bed, but to tell you the truth, I wasn't looking forward to plunging into the darkness on my own.

"I don't have to leave you here," Arawn said, once again reading my thoughts. "I can accompany you farther without announcing myself to your bodyguard."

I took a deep breath for courage. "I appreciate the thought, but I can take it from here. I'll be home in just a few minutes."

He smiled and shook his head. "Such a stickler for independence."

Yeah, that was me all right. But I had a feeling that if I let myself chicken out of navigating the tunnels by myself now, I might have trouble letting go of my fears later.

"Thank you," I said, though the words seemed awkward in relation to the Erlking. "You saved my life tonight. I won't forget that."

He waved my gratitude away. "You needn't thank me for acting in my own best interests," he said, and the reminder that he hadn't saved me for my own sake helped me put the situation back into perspective.

I opened up the brooch, exposing the needle-sharp point. This was only the third time I'd used the charm, but I was already getting sick of jabbing myself. I did it anyway.

When I'd used the charm before, there had been no outward sign that anything had happened, no tingle of magic to let me know it was working. This time, however, I felt a tingle just above my left shoulder blade, a tingle that quickly turned to a sting. I looked up at Arawn in alarm. He reached out and took my hand, giving it a firm squeeze.

"It will pass in a moment," he said soothingly as the sting intensified until it brought tears to my eyes.

"What have you done?" I asked through gritted teeth. There was plenty of accusation in my voice, but even so I was gripping his hand like it was a lifeline.

"Nothing to be frightened of," he answered, and the pain faded as quickly as it had come.

I finally woke up to the fact that I was holding his hand, and I let go with a jerk, taking a step backward. "What have you done to me?" I asked again, and this time it was almost a yell. After everything I'd been through that night, I'd begun to think my body had used up all the available adrenaline, but my suddenly speeding pulse proved to the contrary.

He patted the air in a calming gesture. "Nothing dire, I assure you. Some of the most intricate magic can be triggered by blood and by the power of three. You have now activated the charm for the third time with the use of your blood, and that has triggered the secondary spell I put on the brooch."

Shit, shit, shit! The bastard had played me yet again! Fear and anger warred within me as I waited for the Erlking to explain what he'd done to me.

"You'll find you now bear my mark on your shoulder. It doesn't have the power of the mark my Huntsmen wear, but it will allow me to locate you wherever you are. Not in the mortal world, of course, but at least in Avalon or in Faerie."

I opened my mouth, ready to call him every filthy name I could think of and then some, but he shocked me to silence by putting his finger to my lips.

"It is not a malicious spell, Dana. Should you ever find yourself in need of my aid, simply feed some magic into the mark, and I will come to you as quickly as I am able. I cannot always count on you having Ethan by your side to alert me should danger befall you."

I jerked my head to the side, and he let his finger fall. "So it's for my own good? Is that what you're telling me?"

"In a manner of speaking."

I snorted and shook my head, disgusted with myself for being so gullible. I'd felt vulnerable enough as it was when I learned he knew where I lived and could get to me there despite all my protections, but this was far, far worse. I could never escape him, never hide from him, and instinct told me I would one day need to. "You were so convinced it was for my benefit that you decided to do it without telling me what would happen if I used the brooch a third time."

"I am not a fool, and neither are you."

Debatable at that point, as far as I was concerned.

"The spell is not malicious, and you can use it to your advantage. Your aunt Grace was only a minor threat compared to your true enemies. I can help you against them if you need it. But I won't pretend the spell isn't equally useful to me, and I know you would not have used the brooch a third time had you known what would happen."

He was right on the second count, that was for sure. I felt like a dog who'd just had a microchip implanted. Maybe in the future, I would remember to be wary of Faerie Kings bearing gifts. I held the brooch out to him, and I thought for a moment he was going to take it back as I intended. Instead, he folded my fingers around it once more.

"It will still work as always," he said, "and there are no other spells to be triggered."

"Yeah, and I'm supposed to believe you?"

"When you catch me in a lie, you have my leave to doubt my word. But I have not once lied to you except by omission, nor will I ever."

"Okay, if the brooch still works like always, then why can you even see me?"

He looked amused. "Because it is my own magic you're using. It doesn't work against me, though it will work against my Huntsmen and against Ethan."

Wow. Volunteering information. He was obviously very anxious for me to keep his stupid gift.

I wanted to stand firm, to tell him I would never make the mistake of believing anything he said again. I wanted to drop the brooch on the floor by his feet, then walk away with my head held high.

The problem was I couldn't bear to part with it. It was my ticket to independence, or at least a semblance of it. Without it, I would never be able to leave my safe house again without at least one bodyguard by my side, and that was no way to live my life.

I glared at him, just to let him know how unhappy I was about the whole situation, then stuffed the brooch back into my pocket. He gave a slight nod but didn't say anything as I turned my back to him and hurried into the tunnel that would lead me toward home.

I made it home without any further adventures, thank God. It was after two in the morning by the time I got there, and Finn had made up the sofa bed and turned in. He slept facing the entryway, and I was sure he would spring awake at the slightest disturbance, but the Erlking's brooch allowed me to sneak in without alerting him.

Once I was back in my own suite, I wanted to collapse into bed and sleep for a week, but I couldn't resist the urge to check out the Erlking's mark on my shoulder. I stripped off my shirt and sweater, then stood in the bathroom with my back to the mirror, craning my head to see.

The mark was smaller than the ones the Huntsmen wore,

but it was otherwise identical, a stylized blue stag in mid leap. If I didn't know what it was and what it signified, I might almost have said it was pretty.

I was never going to activate it, I decided. I couldn't make it go away, and I couldn't keep it from being a homing beacon for the Erlking, but that didn't mean I had to *use* it. In fact, if I could avoid ever having to see or speak to him again, that would be best all around. I had no defenses against his cunning, no matter how wary and cautious I thought I was. If I couldn't defend against him, then the best I could do was avoid him.

But was avoiding him really such a good idea? He was by far my most powerful ally, even if his motives were far from pure. Even the Faerie Queens were afraid of him, and as long as he wanted something from me and harbored some hope of getting it, he would defend me to the best of his considerable abilities. Of course, eventually he was bound to realize that I would *never* give him what he wanted, and his mask of pseudo-friendliness would come off and I would be faced with the Nightmare of Faerie.

I didn't come up with any satisfactory answers. The lack of answers didn't stop my mind from whirling, and when I climbed into bed and tried to sleep, the whirling increased.

It was while I was tossing and turning and generally feeling miserable that I really started to understand everything Grace had told me in her attempt to torture me before killing me.

Grace was old enough to remember the time before the Erlking made his agreement with the Queens. So was my dad. Aunt Grace was able to extrapolate from what she knew that the Erlking would be looking for a way to trick me into giving him my virginity. So did my dad. Aunt Grace had known when the

Erlking freed Ethan exactly what I'd had to promise in return. So had my dad.

Aunt Grace had been so hell-bent on revenge that just killing me wasn't enough. To make me as miserable as possible, to make me feel like a total fool, she'd broken her ties to the Seelie Court so she could tell me the Erlking's secret power. And that was where she and my dad differed.

Knowing what was at stake, knowing the kind of danger I was in, he still hadn't been willing to break with his precious Seelie Court in order to warn me. Instead, he'd stuck with his vague, useless warnings about how I mustn't do what the Erlking wanted; warnings that were so vague they were easy to ignore.

Granted, even without any warnings from my dad, I'd known from the beginning that there was something more to my bargain with the Erlking than met the eye, and I'd had no intention of going through with it until I figured out the ramifications. Also granted, my dad didn't know that having me under twenty-four-hour guard wasn't enough to stop me from seeing the Erlking. Maybe Dad would eventually have decided he had no other choice but to sever his ties to the Court so he could tell me what I needed to know. But I wouldn't, *couldn't* forget that for the time being, at least, he'd chosen to leave me in ignorance.

I clung to the belief that my dad loved me, and that he loved me for reasons other than what I could do for his political career. But not only was he Fae, he was *old* Fae, and the old Fae in particular had a very different value system than us mere mortals. I vowed that I would never again allow myself to forget that.

chapter twenty-eight

Considering how momentous and life-altering that night in the tunnels had seemed, my life pretty much returned to normal—at least, what passed for normal these days—almost immediately.

There were a few ripple effects, of course, one small one being my need to keep the Erlking's mark hidden at all times. No more wearing tank tops to spar with Keane. At least Avalon never got hot enough for me to want to wear tanks outdoors. If Keane noticed my wardrobe change, he made no mention of it. He was as surly and unpleasant as ever, and when I made an attempt to smooth over our last argument, he cut me off at the knees. Typical guy, not wanting to talk about it. Which, to tell you the truth, was fine with me.

There was a much more significant ripple when the Erlking paid my dad a personal visit. I wasn't there to see it, but my mom told me about it afterward. She was pretending our fight had never happened, and I was happy to let her. There were a lot of things I'd done since I'd come to Avalon that I felt guilty about, but forcing my mom to stay sober wasn't one of them.

Arawn informed my father about Aunt Grace's death. According to Mom, Dad took the news with typical Fae stoicism, although he was no doubt both relieved and saddened. Grace had been his sister, after all.

Mom didn't hear the whole conversation, but it seems that somehow, Arawn managed to convince my dad that I was in no danger from the Wild Hunt. I suppose it wasn't that hard. After all, my dad knew what the Erlking wanted, and he knew I had to be alive to give it to him, so he, too, would realize keeping me alive was in the Erlking's best interests.

The upshot of all this is that I don't have to make as big a production about leaving my safe house anymore. I still have to take Finn with me wherever I go, but I don't have to ask Dad's permission, and I don't have to scrape up a second bodyguard. I felt positively liberated. Amazing how my standards had changed since I'd come to Avalon.

Even with my new "freedom," it was a bit awkward trying to find a way to be alone with Ethan for a while, but he and I needed to talk. I tried calling him a couple of times, but he always seemed to be in the middle of something and couldn't stay on the phone long. I was sure he was lying, but I didn't want to start our heart-to-heart with accusations. There were a lot of reasons he might want nothing to do with me now that he knew about my deal with Arawn, but I needed to clear the air between us anyway. Even though he wasn't—and now never could be—my boyfriend, there was no denying his importance in my life.

In the end, I decided the best way to trap him into talking

was to show up on his doorstep again. I briefly considered using the Erlking's brooch, but I still had the uncomfortable feeling that I didn't want Ethan to know about it. Which meant I was stuck taking Finn along. I hadn't really gotten a good look at Ethan's apartment when I was there last, but I assumed it was just like Kimber's, which meant the only place we could go for a private conversation was his bedroom. I wasn't entirely sure Finn would go for that—I remembered how he'd played chaperone when Ethan and I went to the movies—but I didn't see another choice.

I called Kimber before I set out and asked her to confirm that Ethan was home. She was happy to oblige me, and as far as I could tell, Ethan hadn't told her what he'd learned about my pact with the Erlking. She still thought I was under a geis not to talk about it. Yet another secret I was keeping that could come back to bite me. Kimber would be very unhappy with me if she ever learned the truth.

I arrived on Ethan's doorstep on a typical Avalon summer afternoon. Meaning it was gray, and chilly, and gloomy. Finn gave me a disapproving look as soon as he figured out I was there to visit Ethan, not Kimber, but he didn't go all paternal on me and start issuing orders.

Kimber must have been watching for me, because her door cracked open when I rang Ethan's bell. She didn't say anything, just gave me an encouraging smile and mouthed "good luck." I appreciated her encouragement, even as I felt another pang of guilt. No doubt she thought I was here to try to cheer Ethan up after his ordeal with the Wild Hunt. He surely wasn't acting any more normal now than he had before we'd encountered Aunt Grace.

The look he gave me when he opened the door was so neutral it hurt. I held my chin up and forced myself to face him.

"Hi," I said, then wanted to slap myself for being so lame. I sounded tentative, almost scared. Okay, so maybe I *was,* but that didn't mean I had to show it. "Can I come in?"

Ethan darted a quick look at Finn, but he had to know we were a package deal. "Sure," he said, sounding less than thrilled.

I had to remind myself that I'd done nothing wrong. Nothing to earn his cold shoulder, at least. It was hard to face him now that he knew the terms of my bargain with the Erlking, and I couldn't help feeling kind of slutty, but I'd done it for Ethan. He didn't have to like it, but he should be at least a little grateful.

Finn and I walked into the apartment. Ethan gestured me into the living room, and Finn remained by the door, once again doing his best to give me a little privacy. But a little privacy wasn't enough, not for this conversation. I faced Finn, wondering how difficult he was going to be about this.

"Ethan and I have a couple of things we need to discuss in private," I told him. "Is there any chance you could stand guard outside?"

I was trying to take a page from the Erlking's book, asking for something I wasn't expecting to get so that my second request—that he let me go into Ethan's bedroom—would sound more reasonable. Finn surprised me by nodding.

"I'll wait outside." He fixed Ethan with a penetrating stare. "I'm sure you'll behave like a gentleman."

Ethan's eyes widened, and he held up his hands in a gesture of innocence. "Don't worry. I won't get any funny ideas."

Finn seemed satisfied with that, slipping out the door and leaving me alone with Ethan. I took a seat on his sofa, trying to figure out how to start this conversation.

"Would you like something to drink?" he asked, not quite looking at me.

"No," I said, more sharply than I'd intended. "I'd like you to sit down and talk to me."

"Fine."

Instead of sitting next to me on the sofa, he sat on the far end, his posture stiff and formal. Was this really the same boy who'd kissed me so passionately just a few days ago? He looked like he could hardly wait to get away from me. I couldn't decide if I was more hurt, or angry. I was certainly some of both.

"So, are you going to treat me like some kind of leper from now on?" I asked, hoping my voice was relatively level.

"I'm not treating you like a leper."

Wow. That was a convincing argument, and it just gave me tons of warm fuzzies.

"You won't look at me, you won't talk to me, and you're sitting as far away from me as you can possibly get," I pointed out.

With a grunt of frustration, he turned to face me, although he didn't move any closer. His eyes, usually so warm and lively, were ice-cold. "Forgive me for being unhappy to learn my girlfriend has promised to sleep with another man."

I gaped at him. "I'm not your girlfriend," I said, though the protest sounded kind of thin even to me. Considering our last make-out session had included some partial nudity, it certainly made sense that he would think of me that way, even if I wasn't wholly convinced that it was true.

290 • jenna black

Ethan rolled his eyes. "If you found out I'd promised to sleep with another girl, it wouldn't bother you at all?"

I felt the color flooding my cheeks. I could hardly argue his point, not after I'd been so mad at him just for *dancing* with another girl.

This time it was me who had trouble holding eye contact. "You know why I did it," I whispered, staring at my hands, which were clenched on my lap. "Would you be happier if I'd just let the Erlking keep you?"

"I don't know," he said, and that startled me enough to make me look up at him in surprise.

"You don't know?" My heart clenched in my chest. "You're telling me I did what I did for nothing?" My voice rose, well on its way to shrill. "I've made it so I have to stay a virgin for the rest of my life, and not only are you not grateful, you're angry with me and can barely stand to look at me." The hurt and the anger combined to hollow me out. It was all too much to absorb, which was actually a good thing, because it made it possible for me not to cry. I'd cry my eyes out later, but I didn't want to do it in front of Ethan.

"I'm not angry with you!" he protested angrily.

"The hell you aren't. And I was a total moron to come here." I started to get up, but in a manner eerily similar to our last encounter in his apartment, Ethan grabbed my arm to keep me from going anywhere.

"If we're going to talk about this, then we might as well talk," he said, still sounding angry.

I wanted to get out of there, wanted to pretend I'd never come. Ethan had always been too much for me to deal with, and I should have known recent events would make it even worse.

"What is there to talk about?" I asked bitterly. "You think I'm some kind of slut because I cared enough to do just about anything to make Arawn let you go. I'm not sorry I did it, but if that's the way you think of me, then I want nothing to do with you."

I tried again to jump to my feet, but Ethan didn't let go.

"Will you just stop?" he asked, his voice a little calmer, though it looked like it took a lot of effort. "You're putting words in my mouth."

"You don't need to say the words for me to get the message. If you could see your face right now, you'd know I'm getting it loud and clear."

"Loud, maybe," he said with a snort, "but obviously not clear. Let me explain this again: I'm not mad at you." I opened my mouth for an outraged protest, but he spoke over me. "Stop being an idiot! I'm mad at *myself,* not at you."

That surprised me enough to shut me up.

Ethan let go of my arm, then jammed his hand through his hair, probably pulling a few strands out along the way.

"Don't you see, Dana? I fell for the Erlking's stupid trick. I was so full of myself and so eager to impress you that I had to jump in and play hero when I should have known better. And because of that one stupid mistake, I'm now bound to him forever, and you're stuck in your devil's bargain. Way to save the day, huh?"

He was so upset he turned away from me to punch the arm of the sofa. Good thing it was heavily padded, or he might have broken his hand.

My rage and hurt eased as I considered what he'd said. I suspected he wasn't telling the whole truth when he said he wasn't mad at me, but I believed he was a whole lot madder at himself. I swallowed back some of the fiery emotions and took a deep breath in search of more calm.

"If it hadn't been for you," I pointed out, "I'd have been dead weeks ago, when Aunt Grace threw me into the moat."

He shrugged. "So I did one thing right. I've done too much else wrong to feel good about that."

Tentatively, I put my hand on his shoulder and gave it a squeeze. "You know that so far, you, me, and Kimber have all blamed ourselves for the Erlking capturing you?"

Ethan blinked at me in surprise. "What?"

"I felt bad because if I'd never come to Avalon in the first place, you'd never have been put in that position. Kimber felt bad because it was her idea to be sitting out on that patio, and she left us alone. I wouldn't be surprised if my dad and Finn blame themselves, too. After all, if they had stayed closer instead of being nice and giving me a little space, the Wild Hunt wouldn't have been able to cut us off like they did. Maybe we all need to lighten up on the blame game."

Ethan thought about that a long time, then let out a long sigh.

"All very reasonable," he agreed. "But easier said than done."

I tried a feeble laugh. "Tell me about it."

He finally slid over next to me on the sofa, then put his arms around me and held me close. I closed my eyes and breathed in the scent of him. For a few minutes, I was able to lose myself in the sensual pleasure of being held. The hurt and anger that had flared in me died down, leaving something vaguely resembling

peace. I knew it would be short-lived, but I reveled in it anyway.

Ethan's cheek rubbed against the top of my head. "Are you
sure you're not my girlfriend?" he asked softly.

The question made my belly flutter pleasantly, but it also dis-
pelled the peace that had settled on me. I pushed myself out of
his arms so I could see his face.

"I'm not such good girlfriend material these days," I said.

Ethan smiled at me. There was warmth in that smile, but
not the same warmth there had been before the Erlking got
hold of him. His smile was older, and somehow sadder now.

He brushed a strand of hair out of my face. "I'll be the judge
of that. And I say you'll do quite nicely."

My throat tightened with longing. "You say that now, but let's
be realistic. I can't ever . . . go all the way with you. Not unless
I'm willing to hop in the sack with Arawn first, and that's just
not happening."

"No, it isn't," Ethan agreed through gritted teeth.

"How long can you really imagine being with a girl who
can't sleep with you?"

He put on his most stubborn expression. "Sex isn't everything."

I truly believed he meant it. I also believed he would eventually get frustrated and change his mind. He'd already proven
that he wasn't willing to wait for me, even when I didn't
have the Erlking's bargain hanging over my head. No matter
how many times Ethan told me Tiffany didn't matter to him,
I would always remember the blatantly sexual way they'd
danced together at Kimber's party. Ethan had been with me
only a few days before, and had acted as if I was the love of

his life, but that hadn't stopped him from dirty dancing with her. That wasn't the behavior of a guy who'd be satisfied in a relationship doomed to remain without sex. If I let myself fall for him any harder than I already had, he was going to break my heart.

Ethan cupped his hand around my cheek. "Don't give up on me. Please."

"I'm not giving up on you. I'm just—"

"Then say you'll give me a chance. Give me a chance to prove you're way more important to me than sex. I'd rather have you without the sex than any of the girls I've been with before *with* the sex."

His words were perfect, and yet . . . I'm a realist at heart. I wasn't going to fool myself into believing Ethan and I had a shot in the long run. No matter what he said, I knew he wouldn't be satisfied with me forever under the circumstances. I would save myself a world of future pain if I could just find the courage to end this now. All I had to do was ignore the longing Ethan stirred in me. Ignore the way looking at him made my heart flutter and my skin heat. Ignore the intoxicating reality of being wanted by a guy who I'd thought was out of my league.

I couldn't do it. No amount of common sense or willpower could convince me to say no to Ethan. Maybe I couldn't have him forever. But I could have him for now, and that would have to be enough.

Without answering him in words, I settled myself back into Ethan's embrace and turned my face up toward his. His shoulders sagged in relief, and his eyes shone with emotion. He lowered his head to mine, and when our lips touched, all my worries and cares faded into the background where I could pretend to ignore them. I vowed I would make the most of whatever time we had together, and I told myself that the inevitable heartbreak wouldn't hurt so badly because I was prepared for it.

Maybe I'm not as much of a realist as I'd like to think.

Dana Hathaway's adventures in Avalon continue in this thrilling third installment

sirensong

A Faeriewalker novel

After an attempted murder of the Seelie Queen rocks Avalon, Dana is suddenly a fugitive. Will she be able to prove her innocence before the Erlking and the Wild Hunt catch up with her?

Available July 201

"A delightful tale of faerie intrigue and adventure."
—*New York Times* bestselling author Rachel Vincent on *Glimmerglass*

 St. Martin's Griffin
www.stmartins.com